Acknowledgments

I would like to give thanks to Jesus, who did speak those words to me in a strawberry field when I was eighteen years old. The scripture verse from Joshua changed the trajectory of my life. It took a young girl who was ready to end her life and allowed her to find hope.

My husband, Ian Hassam. My biggest cheerleader. The man who always dares me to dream even bigger than I know is possible. I hope I have done justice to you in this book. You definitely inspired Rose's first boyfriend. From the kindness you showed me on our first date, to our present day romance. I couldn't do any of this without you.

To my mom and Claude. I am forever grateful to both of you for coming more into my life in my twenties. During my growing up years, my dad was never really free to love me. Claude stepped in and showed me the love of a father. His kindness to me will never be forgotten. He loved me as his own daughter, and I always felt safe in his arms. My mom, who continues to be steadfast in my life. From being strangers in my teens, to being one of my best friends in my fifties. I don't know what I would do without you.

To my dad. Who decided to show up for me in my present life. I didn't know that I had a hole in my heart until you filled it. Thank you for not giving up on me returning to you.

My sister, Joy. The relationship that I wrote about holds so much truth. Looking back, it was my privilege to help raise you. You have always been one of the most precious people in my life. I am so proud of the woman you have become. Thank you for allowing me to use our past, in order to write Rose's story.

My brother, Tony. I couldn't have survived all that I did without you. I am so glad that you are in my life. I love that you and me have a special relationship. I value you so much. I will always be your greatest fan. I am so proud of the man you have become.

To Tanis. Although I was never one of the kids that lived in your trailer, or was a runaway, I could have been. I know you have rescued so many other kids and saved them out of terrible circumstances. The kindness that I wrote about, is the kindness I see daily. I have been touched by the foundation that you built A&T equestrian on.

To Kat. From being my coach, my friend, and currently my boss. I want to thank you for your encouragement and belief in me. You always think I am much more capable than I think I am. I am forever grateful for you introducing Mia Rose into my life. You saw what was possible way before I did. You showed me that I had to give up the grape juice in order to taste the Cabernet. Bless you!

To the many friends that are in the fabric of this novel, I thank you. There are too many to list by name. Writers take inspiration from their surroundings, and I am no different. The names in the barn have changed over the past ten years and it has been lovely to remember all of you. I hope you enjoy seeing your names in my story.

My high school group of friends. You probably never thought that your names would end up in a book one day. But I thank you for encouraging me not to stay in a bad home life situation. Thank you for having my back and for cheering me on.

Fulton Books Publishing. I have appreciated working with you to make this book a reality. The whole team was so helpful in making this come to life.

To my readers. I am so grateful to each of you who read my books. I love creating and using my imagination to paint a story. To write truly is to breathe. As long as there are readers there will be writers. And for those who desire to write, but haven't found the way yet, just start. The only difference between you and I—is I have started—now it's your turn.

Introduction

This has been a book that has taken me many years to complete. However, I am a big believer that God's timing is much greater than my own. In this novel, I take real moments from my life and weave them together with my own fiction. As I say—it is truth, disguised in fiction.

This isn't an autobiography; however, those who know me will recognize aspects from Rose's life and my own. My desire is that you prepare your heart to be touched by Rose's journey. Many of her pain points are my own. As well as what brings her peace and happiness are also my own.

Much healing has taken place in my life from the start of writing this book to the present day. Which is why I feel I was delayed in releasing this novel.

My own relationship with my father, has been restored in a way I could not have imagined. However, the picture of anguish that I paint was also true. I tried not to write from a place of bitternes—but hope. As long as both parties have breath in their lungs there is hope.

Whether you picked up this book because you are a horse enthusiast or you know me, I hope you enjoy the world that I have created on these pages.

Sincerely,
Rebeckah Hassam
April 18, 2022

Chapter 1

My life was in shambles. It was better than when I had endured daily beatings. However, the amount of emotional abuse I had to face daily was enough. So I had left home, or the only home that I had known.

I lived a Cinderella-type life. I, being Cinderella. I grew up with six other siblings—a mix of stepsiblings, a full brother, and a half sister. The girls, my stepsisters—Jackie, Nancy, Maggie, and Jenna—weren't evil but ill informed. They weren't where my mistreatment came from. Rather, it was at the hands of their mother.

For the most part, I got on well with them. I was always one to try to keep the peace. My circumstances had placed me as a middle child, so I tried to stay out of everyone's way. Sure, we had our squabbles, but I think even in families that aren't governed by Cruella de Vil, siblings argue.

My stepbrother, Robert, was clueless. He adored his mother, so I didn't share a lot with him. We were friends at one point, and we also respected each other's space.

My full bother, Ivan, was my hero. We had been through a lot of ups and downs—the two of us being the brunt of my stepmother Martha's wrath which made for an interesting allegiance. We were both fiercely protective of each other, yet at the same time, we were constantly at war. At school, I always made sure he didn't get picked on too much, but at home, I had become the bully. It got better as we grew up, but I wasn't proud of my earlier actions.

Then there was Jenna, my youngest half sister. She was the hardest to leave. In order to survive, I made a decision to protect myself. It was one of the least selfish things I had ever done. I left with so much guilt. I also left with a huge amount of determination.

I remembered Jenna coming home from the hospital. I was so excited to get a baby sister. There were almost seven years between us. By the time I was eight, I was staying home to help raise her. Because of not going to school, I failed both grades 4 and 8. It wasn't until grade 10 that I entered high school as a full-time student. It wasn't a normal way to live, but I loved my time with Jenna. I was proud to raise such a beautiful girl. All that made me a fighter. I fought my way to the honor roll by grade 12. It was something I was fiercely proud of.

My dad was blinded by love, or lust. I wasn't sure. Martha had a control over him that none of us could break. At one point, I told him about all the awfulness of Martha. He listened with compassion and empathy. Then after living with her for over a decade, he married her. During those years, they had pretended that they were not together. All of us kids knew the truth. Even Jenna, in truth being my half sister, was nothing that was ever acknowledged. However, her blond hair and blue eyes meant she looked a lot more like me and Ivan. She was always treated differently from the rest. We traced it back to her lineage.

There were a few people who knew what was going on in our home. I did have a couple of close friends whom I let into the truth. The problem was, they always asked me why I didn't just go live with my real mother in Nova Scotia. That would mean not only leaving Ontario but also telling my mom the truth. I wasn't ready to tell her. Seeing as I was no longer presently at home, I was sure she would be worried sick. The problem was, I had already decided to leave before I had thought about calling her. If only my life had turned out differently…if only. I just couldn't handle one more beating or to be berated once more. To be told you're fat, ugly, and stupid on a daily basis does something to one's spirit.

When I left, all I had taken with me were the clothes I was wearing, a small bag of essentials, and the courage to leave. Thankfully, it was August, so I hadn't had to worry about being cold. I had been wearing an old pair of blue jeans, my used paddock boots, a blue T-shirt, and a gray hoodie. I figured I could pull the hood over my long blond hair so that I wouldn't get some idiot guys trying to pick me up. I was sure that I looked a mess when I came across the farm that had agreed to hire me. I couldn't be sure why they took me on. I gave them a false name to avert any suspicion. My real name was Rose, Rose Maureen Stevens. I decided on the fly to tell them my name was Rain. I had always wanted a cool name, and Rain fit the bill.

I was only a few hours from home and with my sister Jenna still riding, I really hoped that my stepmother didn't know the owners of the barn I'd found. I had been on the run for a couple of days when I saw the horses at the front of the farm. The horses seemed to draw me in. I had been lost in my thoughts when Tanis, the owner of the barn, found me.

The nicest thing my stepmother did during my short life was to let me ride horses with Jenna. However, it wasn't enough to continue living with her. I had given up my dream of riding when I left the house, but at least for now, I was still around horses. As I had recently turned eighteen, the owners of the barn hadn't asked many questions. Seeing as I looked fifteen, I was a bit surprised that they hadn't.

What I hadn't told Tanis was that since arriving, I had been living in the smaller barn's hayloft. I'd only been there a couple of days, and she was bound to notice I hadn't changed my clothes, and I must have stunk. I tried to stealthily hose myself down, but there were just no substitutes for a good shower. My bones were aching from the hard work, but at least my bruises were healing. There was another girl I had met and thought was friendly named Lindsey. She was tall and had long brown hair with matching brown eyes. She was also away from home, but not for the same reasons I was. I almost told her the truth, but I figured I'd better wait to see if my instincts about her were correct.

Lindsey had a rare day off, so it was up to me and some volunteers to get things cleaned up. I thought it must be about 6:30 a.m. as I was already up to my arms in horse manure when I heard Tanis calling me. She sure never missed a beat. Only two days in and I had that figured out.

"Rain, Rain, are you in here?" Tanis had a voice full of authority, but she was also kind, especially since she was giving me a chance to earn my way.

"Yes, I'm over here." I came out of one of the stalls with a pitchfork full of horse manure and dumped it in the wheelbarrow.

"Have you had anything to eat?" She looked at me with her blue eyes full of concern.

"Uh, I'm okay," I lied. I had no money till my first check, so carrots and apples were all I had eaten in days. I wasn't that small, but with all the work I had been doing, I was sure I was down a few pounds.

"Here, I brought you a sandwich and some coffee as you're looking a bit too faint for my liking."

"Thanks so much." I was sure the way my blue eyes lit up had given away my nonchalant attitude. I pushed my hair out of my face, shoved the pitchfork to the side, shed my gloves, and took the sandwich from her. "Peanut butter, my favorite."

"You can bring the plate in later. How far along are you with the stalls?"

"I'm about halfway through the small barn. Is that okay?" I really wanted to please her, or it would be back to my old hell-on-earth life.

"That's great. I just have some people coming to see Eye Spy, so I want to make sure the stables are clean." I smiled, relieved for a minute, until she asked another much-scarier question. "Rain, are you sure that no one is looking for you? I mean, I need the help right now, but I would hate to think what it would be like if my daughter was away without my knowing where she was."

I nearly choked on the sandwich. What could I tell her? I had to lie; my life was a lie anyway. Wasn't that what I was taught growing up, that truth didn't matter?

"Rain, have I lost you?"

"No, no, no one is looking for me, and trust me, no one misses me." I couldn't hold her gaze, so I hastily gave her back the plate. "Thank you for breakfast, but I need to get back to work, or I won't have the place ready," I finished cheerily.

"Okay, if you say so. I'll see you in a little while then." She turned to go. I hoped that I could own a barn when I got older, but for now, it was back to the stalls. I took a sip of coffee, thankful that she had put cream and sugar in it, as I could never drink black coffee.

As I shoveled dirt and sawdust back and forth, I knew that I couldn't stay here forever. My dad would eventually have to tell my mom that I'd run away. I never knew my real mom well, but in my heart, I knew that she loved me. My mom had married a lovely man named John. He was probably the loveliest man I'd ever met, besides my grandpa on her side. As I rarely saw either of them, both of them became sort of heroes in my mind. I was sure that wasn't necessarily a healthy outlook, but it was mine.

My real dad was no villain, just too weak for me. I had decided that at eighteen, whomever I would marry would need to be strong, or there would be no point in dating me. So far, I had had boyfriends for a few weeks here and there. I always knew that I would leave Dundas, so there was never any point in getting serious. Plus, girls who found the man of their dreams in high school were selling themselves short, or so I thought.

I moved easily around the horses. Most of the horses were happily munching on their hay, which made it easy to get my job done. I then came to Mia's stall. Lindsey had cleaned her stall while I had been there, and I was quickly finding out why. I had foolishly decided to enter her stall without introducing myself, which apparently was a mistake. Mia had the entrance to her stall almost barricaded by her hind end. This was not a good sign. I didn't have long to finish, and I was on my last two stalls, but this could take me forever. I was currently without anything to bribe her with.

I slowly closed her stall door back up, and she moved away from the entrance toward her mound of hay. I looked at her. She was a beautiful bay with an obvious attitude. Hmmm, I'd muck out Ellie's stall and then come back and tackle Mia's.

"Mia, don't think you are going to win this battle, because I'll be back." She turned and looked at me; her eyes seemed kind even after our altercation. Who knew, maybe she hadn't eaten in a long time.

I walked, pitchfork in hand, to Ellie's stall, and just like the last fifteen horses, she let me in with no problem and even neighed contentedly as I stroked her. Ellie was a cute dark-colored pony with a large white stripe on her head. I could tell she was loved by her owner.

It was time to tackle Mia's stall again. This time, I decided not to go empty-handed. I grabbed a couple of carrots from the staff room and walked back to her stall. Before going in, I decided I'd try introducing myself to see if it would help. I looked at her from behind the black bars on her stall and quickly got her attention.

"Hi, Mia. I'm Rose. However, for now, you may know me as Rain. I know what you're thinking. It's a silly name, but you're the only one here who knows my real name." She looked at me curiously, and so far, her hind end was away from the entrance. I showed her the carrots and decided to make my move. I opened the latch, and her brown eyes were still facing in my direction.

"That's a good girl. Can I come in?" She sniffed my hands, and I gave her the first carrot. "There you go. Now I am going to have to clean your stall whether you like it or not." She started to turn away from me again. "Come on, girl. It doesn't have to be this way." She saw the other carrot and decided I was okay. I broke it in half and kept one-half in my pocket for insurance.

I grabbed the pitchfork again and quickly moved around her. I was almost done when I saw her pin her ears back at me. "Mia, here you go. There's no need to get nasty." I gave her the last of the carrots and quickly got out of there. Note to self: maybe put Mia outside before I clean her stall next time.

I moved my wheelbarrow away from Mia's stall, and the funny thing was, she was now looking at me as if she wouldn't mind some love. I suppose one minute wouldn't hurt. I opened up the grate so that she could stick her head out of her stall, and she sniffed my hands for more treats.

"I see it has to be on your terms, does it?" I cooed as I gently petted her lovely dark-brown head. I noticed that under her forelock, she had a tiny star marking. "Hmm, Mia Star?" She seemed to like that. I gave her a kiss on her muzzle. It was so soft. "There's nothing like kissing a horse on the nose. I don't care who the guy is, right, Mia?"

I turned from her quickly as I was sure I wasn't alone. How embarrassing. I hoped no one heard me. "Sorry, girl, I've got to go, but I'll see you soon." I closed the grate behind me.

I went back to the task of dumping the wheelbarrow out on the heap outside. I still had to sweep before Tanis came back with her potential clients. Maybe this wasn't the best day for Lindsey to have taken off. I really hoped I wouldn't let her down today and that the guests wouldn't get there too early. I also hoped that the people coming up were not from my circle of riding peers. I wasn't sure what I would do if I got recognized out here.

I swept the barn in record time, and I was just putting the brooms away when Tanis came back.

"Rain, it looks great in here. Good job." Tanis was now wearing a pair of light breeches and a pair of tall riding boots. She had a red T-shirt on that looked great with her sun-kissed skin. I was so pale in comparison to her; I really hoped that I would be able to get a little color the longer I stayed. I wasn't used to getting praise, but I managed to stutter out a thank you to her.

"So who taught you how to be such a hard worker, your mom?"

"Uh, no, not really. I just figured that working hard would help me keep this job."

"Well, you thought correctly. Rain, you are a bit of a mystery to me. How old did you say you were?"

"Twenty," I lied.

"Twenty, are you sure? You sure don't look twenty."

"Good genes must run in my family." I walked away from the storage area and moved toward Domino, one of the ponies there. I could tell that Tanis wasn't quite finished questioning me.

"So do you have a favorite horse here yet?"

"Um, well, I'm not sure. That Mia seems interesting, and well, who can resist Domino?" It was true Domino was adorable. He was a gray-and-white Appaloosa with a black mane. Tanis joined me by his stall and stroked his eager face.

"Yes, he is special. Do you know he's only four?"

"Really? How long have you had him?"

"Only a month. So you find Mia interesting?"

"Yeah, I'm not sure why, but I like a challenge. And well, cleaning her stall this morning was a challenge. Plus, she's beautiful. My sis, uh, never mind." Crap, I couldn't tell her about Jenna, not yet.

"Yes, she's beautiful. Maybe after I've seen you ride, I could see whether you'd be ready for her. Actually, my daughter Kat will be home soon, and I'll get her to teach you for a lesson on me if you keep up the great work."

"Really, you'd do that?" She hadn't even mentioned my slip, but I was sure she'd heard it.

"Yes, yes, I can see you would love that." I was sure my eyes were brimming with excitement. I had to keep this job! "Well, I will see you in a bit. Have you put the horses out yet?"

"No. I'll do it now. Who needs to go out?"

"There's a list on the whiteboard, but make sure Eye Spy, or Spy, as we call him, stays in."

"Okay, will do. Do you need me to walk him out before your clients get here?"

"Actually, I'm going to get him ready now, but thanks, and I'll let you know if I need help."

"Well, I'll be off to get the ponies out. I hope your meeting goes well." I left her by Eye Spy's stall and walked toward the halters and lead ropes.

"Thanks, Rain."

As I got the horses out, I marveled at what I had found. Kat must be the luckiest girl in the world to have such a nice mom. Then again, maybe I had one too. Maybe I would just call my dad tonight and let him know I was safe. There was no way I wanted the police to show up here and take me in or, worse yet, think that Tanis had anything to do with my disappearance.

I wondered how Jenna was getting along without me. I had hidden a letter for her to find when I left, but I wasn't sure when she would find it. I tried talking to her before, but how could she believe the mother she loved so much was actually cruel? I wouldn't want to believe that about my mother either. I sighed. So much to give up for my safety, but was it worth it? I guess only time would tell.

Chapter 2

When I came back from taking out the ponies, I noticed that Tanis was already warming up Eye Spy. I mentally went over the list that Lindsey had left for me, *Feed and water the horses, done; clean stalls, done; put out the ponies, done; refresh sawdust; and then feed again.* All right, so my list wasn't done, but I felt like I was. I came out of the barn and just allowed the hot sun to bathe my face. I took my hair out of my long ponytail and realized just how badly it needed washing. I eyed the hose suspiciously. Was there time? I could use the horse shampoo as I wasn't picky. I took a couple of steps closer to the hose when I heard a car pull in the driveway. Shoot, too late. I pulled my hair on top of my head and created some sort of messy bun. I hoped that Tanis wouldn't be embarrassed with my greeting her guests.

I noticed that they drove a sleek gunstock gray Impala. I thought that the car looked too nice for the barn. I walked slowly toward it and noticed that it was a couple of younger people, a guy and a girl. They must be related as they looked too much like each other not to be. They both had beautiful slightly darkened skin. The guy had dark jet-black hair with just the hint of silver streaks coming through. His face looked too young for the silver. Before I could analyze any further, he spoke.

"Hi there. You aren't Tanis, are you?" He spoke in such a warm way that it was like the sun had just spoken to me.

"Hi. No, no, I'm Ro—uh, Rain. I'm Rain, and Tanis is in the arena waiting for you. That is, if you're here to look at Eye Spy." I was such an idiot. Why couldn't I remember my fake name for more than a day?

"Rain, that's an interesting name. Well, Rain, it's nice to meet you. I'm Ian." He stuck out his hand for me to shake. My hands were so dirty. Would he mind? I figured that I'd better risk it so I wouldn't come across as rude. I took his hand, and he shook mine.

"Ian, uh, it's nice to meet you too." I smiled in spite of myself. What he must think of me, this young smelly barn girl.

"Come on, Ian. Quit flirting with the barn staff," the girl rudely interrupted us.

"Yes, yes, sis, I'm coming. Rain, I shall see you again." He smiled at me, and his smile seemed to reach even his chocolate-colored eyes. The whole time we spoke, he held onto my hand without even flinching at my grime.

"See you again." I watched the two of them walk to the arena, literally dumbstruck. Now that was a guy who could tempt me to date.

I walked back into the barn and began feeding the horses their hay for the second time that day. One by one, I was greeted with enthusiastic neighs. The only downside was, the horses down the end of the barn got impatient and started banging their stalls with their hooves.

"I'm coming, all of you. Don't worry. Hold on to your hooves."

I was almost at Mia's stall when I noticed that she had already popped her head out of her stall when she heard my voice. "Yes, Mia, I'm almost there." When I got to her stall, I hesitated for only a moment before walking into where she was. "Hi, pretty girl, I've got some lunch for you. Can I come in?" She moved over for me, and I placed the hay in the corner for her. She quickly started eating contentedly and let me move around her.

I loved the smell of hay and the sound of the horses eating. It was balm to my soul. Even with all the problems at home, whenever I went up to the barn with Jenna, the scent of the barn would make me forget my troubles.

I closed Mia's door and continued on with the last horses, happy that I was almost done. I was thinking of what was next when I was not so rudely interrupted.

"Rain, are you in here?" It was Ian.

Be still, my beating heart. I hoped I could keep my thoughts straight. I moved out from the stalls. I was sure I was covered in hay, but I wiped my hands on my jeans and tried to smooth out my hair. "Hi, Ian, what can I do to help you?"

We walked closer to each other and met in the middle of the barn.

"Rain, I was wondering if you ever get a chance to get out of here and go for lunch, or does Tanis work you too hard?"

"Uh, no, she's great. I haven't asked for time off, but I'm sure I could have time for a lunch," I stuttered out.

"Great." Ian's eyes seemed to sparkle at me. "So can I take you out tomorrow?"

"Well, it's kind of complicated. It's a long story, but I really can't. I appreciate the invite." I really wanted to go with him, but I didn't even have clean clothes with me, and I would definitely need a shower.

"You can't, but you want to?" He smiled at me.

I looked down at the barn floor. "Yes, I'd like to, but really I don't have, well, like I said, it's complicated. I haven't been here long, and I'm not sure if I could get away. I also didn't really bring any going-out clothes with me when I came here."

"Hmm, well, can I call you sometime?" He was so persistent. No guy had ever seemed that interested in me.

"Well, if I had a phone, then I would definitely say yes." I brushed my hands nervously on my jeans, really hoping that I hadn't said too much.

"Rain, you're a bit of a mystery, but I will see you later, and I'll bring you a little surprise."

"Thanks, but there's no need. I'm fine."

"Sure you are. I have to get back to the arena, but I'll see you soon." He put out his hand to shake mine again. I took it even though I was sure he'd really regret shaking it this time.

"Have fun with Eye Spy," I said, feeling a little stupid.

"Yes, and have fun when you get my surprise." He let go and walked back toward the arena. He was wearing blue jeans with black boots. I noticed that he chose a burgundy top that worked well with his skin color.

Yup, trouble, I thought. Well, that date would never happen. It was a nice idea all the same. I hadn't even thought about dating when I left, and I couldn't think of it now, not when I had more pressing things on my mind.

I thought that I should make myself scarce when Tanis came back with Ian and his sister. Then again, maybe she would want me to walk Spy out. Should I check? What could it hurt?

I decided to give the barn another quick sweep, then headed to the arena.

I intercepted the three of them coming from the arena all looking happy. Ian grinned as I walked toward them.

"Tanis, do you want me to walk out Eye Spy?"

"Thanks, Rain. That would be great. We need to go over some things before Ian and Yasmin leave."

I took hold of the reins and stroked Spy's beautiful face. "There's a good boy."

"Rain, why don't you come in for lunch in half an hour?"

"Okay, thanks." I was so hungry. Little did she know that at that point, I'd rather have food right then than almost anything.

I walked away with Spy and decided to take him to the outdoor arena to cool him off. He was such a character. He must have been over seventeen hands, but he had such a gentle way about him. He was such a social horse, probably the first horse to pop his head out of his stall before any other horse.

I opened the gate and let us both in, then closed the large gate awkwardly behind me.

"Easy, boy. We're almost there." Spy nudged me as I put the chain back up. "One second, buddy." He nudged me again. At five foot four, I was no match for a nudging horse. I led him away from the gate, loosened his girth, and started to walk him around the arena.

My thoughts quickly raced ahead to my flawed plan. As long as I was moving, I could keep my thoughts at bay. Now under the bright sun of the day and with a horse beside me, I became reflective. Why had I chosen to leave? I had been living under my stepmother

Martha's heavy hand for almost thirteen years. What was it that caused me to bolt? I had been bruised beyond what I could endure. I had been cut with a knife by her own hand. I had been through more than any eighteen-year-old I knew.

Our home looked like any other home on the street, but unbeknownst to anyone living on our block, things were not as they seemed. I didn't know much about good and evil, but after reading some books, I was sure that it was evil that was lurking through our doors. Jenna was always my reason for staying, but she was now eleven and becoming a young woman. It was not that I didn't think that she needed me any more, but more like I needed to finally protect myself.

I wished there was a way I could contact my mother without my dad knowing, but that would involve more lies. Now that I had started lying, I wasn't sure how to stop. I also didn't know if I was ready to leave Ontario and move to Nova Scotia.

I was so deep in my thoughts that I didn't realize that someone was calling my name. Of course, the fact that I wasn't used to be called Rain didn't help. I was almost at the gate again when I saw Ian leaning over it, waving at me. What a wreck I was. "Stay away!" was what I wanted to yell out.

"Hi again," I said nervously.

"Hi, Rain, I just wanted to say bye before we left."

"Oh, bye then." I wiped my hair out of my face with my dirty hand.

"Rain, that is your real name, right?"

"Of course it is. Why would you ask that?"

"Well, call me crazy, but you don't seem to answer to it."

"Sorry, I was deep in thought, you know, horse stuff." I was going to say teen stuff, but then I remembered I wasn't supposed to be a teen.

"They are incredible animals." He petted Spy's majestic face, and Spy looked as though he thought Ian might have some treats for him. "Can I come up and feed the horses later?"

"Of course you can. Just make sure that you check with one of us so you don't get bitten accidentally."

"Done. Well, I guess I'll see you later then. Are you sure you don't have a phone?"

"Yes, I'm sure." I needed to move, or Spy would get restless, and I didn't want this guy to break my resolve.

"Okay, bye for now then." He grinned at me once more.

"Bye." I moved Spy away from the gate and watched Ian leave out of the corner of my eye. Too good-looking and charming for any good to come of this.

One more lap and Spy should be good to go in. I'd give him a quick brush, and then it was food time. Thank you, Tanis! I really should have planned my escape better, but so far, so good.

Chapter 3

The lunch that Tanis had prepared was fantastic. Trying to keep her at arm's length was proving almost impossible. I knew that she knew I was lying, but she didn't press the issue. This made me want to confide in her even more. It was then that I saw an article in the paper regarding missing children. I held my breath as I scanned it. Phew, nothing about me. I figured that as much as my dad would want to find me, that Martha wouldn't want to admit they had failed in any way.

My brother Ivan had conveniently been moved to a foster parent's place all without my real mother ever knowing. I could be gone a year, and they wouldn't let my mom know. I needed an alibi though, and I needed one fast! I didn't want to take the risk of Tanis turning me in.

Tanis's home was comfortable and really clean, especially seeing as she owned a barn. The home I grew up in was only clean if I had cleaned it. How children could be so messy, I never knew. Maybe it had to do with our home being evil as opposed to good. Her house wasn't very large, but it was big enough for her and her daughter. It looked like they also had an extra guest room. I felt rather self-conscious being in such a clean house seeing how dirty I was.

Tanis came back to the kitchen table, where I was still munching on my lunch. I quickly moved the newspaper away from me.

"Are you enjoying that, Rain?" She sat down across from me and smiled.

"Yes, thank you so much. This is probably the best lunch I've had in a while."

"So tell me, Rain, how far away do you live from here again?"

Crap, there it was again, another lie. "Uh, I don't live very far from here." That wasn't a lie seeing as I was living in her hayloft.

"Hmm, does it have everything you need, or do you need a place to crash?" She must have noticed that I hadn't showered since we'd met.

I looked down at the plate in front of me. "Well, it's missing a few things to be honest." I still couldn't look at her.

"Listen, Rain, I have a trailer here that is empty right now. It has a bathroom, a shower, and everything you'd need. Would you be interested in crashing there for a bit?"

I couldn't believe my ears! How could this be? I now looked up as I thought it would be rude not to. "Tanis, I don't know what to say. That would be wonderful!" I had to keep it together, or I would start to cry.

"Then it's settled. After lunch, I'll show it to you. As soon as you can, get yourself ready and move in." She got up from the table and cleared our plates.

I swallowed hard before I could talk. "Thank you so much. I promise, I won't let you down."

She smiled at me again. "I know that. I have a hunch about you, and my hunches are almost always right."

"I hope this one is too. I'll go check and see if anything else needs doing right now." I got up to leave.

"Before you go, we might as well go check out your new living quarters. I'll be right back after I get the keys."

While I was waiting, I looked around at all the pictures of Kat and Tanis with their various horses. It looked as though Kat had been riding since she could walk. There were some large ribbons over the dark wood mantle. It looked as if either Tanis or Kat was really good at dressage. I had a few ribbons at home, but I had only done schooling shows. Jenna was the showgirl in our house. I was only her groom. I didn't even mind, at least I got to be around horses and Jenna.

I didn't see any wedding photos of Tanis or any pictures of a dad. I assumed that there must have been a story there, but I wouldn't pry.

I hadn't encountered this kind of kindness since visiting my mom when I was younger.

"Ready to go, Rain." Tanis was back, but she had changed into a pair of fitted jeans. I was a little jealous of her being able to change into clothes. I would have to wait a long time before finding the local Walmart.

"I can't wait to see it." I followed her out of the house and across the parking lot to the medium-sized trailer. We walked up the three steps, and I held my breath as she unlocked the door for me.

"Ta-da! Here is your new home, Rain."

I walked inside and was amazed at how cute and modern it was. There was even a small TV in the living room. There was queen-size bed in one end, and as I walked around, I noticed that there was a really cute sitting area in the kitchen. Wow, it was miles above the hayloft!

"What do you think?"

"What do I think? This is amazing!" I gushed in spite of myself.

"Are you sure?"

"Of course I'm sure. Here are your keys. Why don't you go get your stuff and move in? Jen will be back later to help do the night feeding, and you both will need to get the lesson horses tacked up. Why don't you get settled and start back at four?"

"That sounds great. Uh, I don't actually have a lot with me. You see, I pack light." I didn't mean to say that, but it was useless to take a shower when I didn't have a towel or clean clothes.

"Well, you can go get your few things, and the rest you can get later. Is there anything else you need right now?"

I wanted to say towels, but I had a feeling there just might be some hanging in the bathroom already, or I at least hoped that there were. "No, this is beyond perfect." She gave me the keys, and I held on to them for dear life.

"I'll see you at four then. Get comfy, and welcome to your new home." She patted my shoulder and let herself out.

I slowly walked around the trailer, still amazed at my luck. I ran my hands over the kitchen counters, the small sofa, and then the bed. The bed had covers on it for which I was grateful. I unlaced my boots and put them by the side of the bed. I couldn't help it. I lay down and took a deep breath. If Martha could see me now, she wouldn't be happy. In fact, she would probably be calling me lazy for taking a nap.

I pushed the thoughts of her out of my head as I didn't want memories of her to ruin this almost perfect day. I did, however, decide that I needed to write to my mother to tell her I was safe. I was sure she would trust that I was okay, or at least I hoped that she would. My eyelids were growing heavy. Was it fair to sleep on this clean bed without taking a shower? I still had some things stowed in the hayloft. Would it look suspicious if I ran over there to get them? What to do, sleep or shower?

My heavy eyelids won the battle, and I fell into a troubled sleep. I didn't know whether I dreamed it or I was really back in Dundas. I felt a pain in my arm as if it were being badly twisted. I then heard a loud knock and found that I had fallen asleep in an awkward position. No wonder I was dreaming about being hurt by Martha. The knock was there again.

Where was I? Oh yeah, trailer, barn… *Ack, someone's at my door.* "Coming!" It was an old habit; Martha always made me say that rather than anything else. I looked at my watch, hoping that I hadn't slept past my start time. It was three thirty. Relief washed over me as I really didn't want to let Tanis down. I got up quickly and opened the door.

"Hello, Rain." It was Ian with a package in his arms.

I moved my messy hair off my face. I was sure I looked like a disaster, seeing as I was still in my dirty barn clothes and had fallen asleep with my hair in a ponytail. "Uh, hi, Ian. What brings you here?"

He gave me a wide grin. "I went in the barn to look for you, and I was told I could find you here. Can I come in?"

"Sure, sure, come on in. I have to warn you, I just moved in, so I have nothing to offer you." I moved away from the door and let Ian into the trailer.

"I didn't come to get anything from you but to give you something."

"Why did you bring me something?" I was really taken aback. This was way too much kindness in one day.

"Here, I'm hoping this will help persuade you to let me take you to lunch." He handed me the package, and I took it gingerly. It was wrapped in brown paper with a ribbon tied around it. "You can open it later, but I'll warn you that my number may be in there in case you change your mind."

"I don't know what to say." My eyes were about to give me away.

"What's wrong? I don't usually have this effect on women." He put his strong hand on my shoulder. I shuddered slightly. "Are you okay?"

"Yes, yes, it's just…never mind. Just know I appreciate it, whatever it is."

"Enjoy, and I really hope to hear from you soon."

"Thank you again. I have to get to work, but I'll try to call." I meant it too.

"Have a good shift, Rain."

I let him out of the trailer and locked the door behind him. I watched him get in his Impala and smiled to myself. What had he gotten me? I moved back into my bedroom and opened the package. Just what I needed, a new pair of dark-blue jeans and a couple of T-shirts. True to his word, he had written me a little card, and at the bottom was his number. The card said:

> Rain,
>
> It sounded like you needed a lunch outfit in order to go to lunch with me, so I hope this helps. I would love to get to know you better, so if you can get away from the horses, give me a call. Your servant awaits your call.
>
> Ian

If I had a phone, I would have called him just to say thank you, whether or not lunch would happen. How thoughtful. I touched the clothes, then laid them out on the bed. They looked like they would fit me. His sister must have helped him, as most guys weren't this good. I looked at my watch again—three forty-five. So much for doing anything. At least after work, I had a bed and a shower and even clean clothes to change into. Today was much better than the last three weeks had been, that's for sure.

Chapter 4

I cleaned up quickly and left my little home for the barn. I noticed that there were quite a few volunteers around, a lot more than I'd seen before. My heart started to race a bit as I was sure that there would be someone who might recognize me. Maybe I would need to cut and dye my hair red in order to ensure my escape to freedom. I kept my head down as I walked toward the large barn in search of Jen. Jen and Lindsey were the two main instructors I had dealt with in my short time at the barn. Both of them seemed pretty fantastic so far.

I got to the small staff area where the brooms hung and, sure enough, found Jen. Jen was a pretty girl with blues eyes and long brown hair. She was really tanned, probably from working outside all summer. As it was still hot out, she had on a red horse T-shirt and a pair of gray shorts. I was slightly envious of the shorts, but until payday, my jeans would have to do. As I entered, Jen turned and smiled at me.

"Hey, Jen, I'm here to be put to work. Would you like me to start with the feeding?"

"Hey. Sure, that would be great. Why don't you start with the hay? I'll take care of the grain. Make sure that you give Mia some extra hay as we need to fatten her up."

"No problem." I turned to leave.

"Oh, Rain, I heard that you're the newest renter of the trailer on the lot."

I was a little taken aback by this; I really hoped she didn't think I was some kind of freeloader. "Yes. Tanis has been nice enough to let me stay there."

"Hmm, Lindsey stayed there before you, so the two of you may have more in common than you realize. Can I ask where you were living before here?"

I paused before answering her. "Quite close by." Jen looked at me with prying eyes. I put my head down, not wanting to finish the conversation. I turned to leave.

"Listen, Rain, I don't know you well, but there are many who have been where I think you have been. I need to tell you to be careful. Also, Tanis is a good person, so don't take advantage of her. Just work hard, and I'm sure we'll get along fine. I may come across as bossy, but it's my job to make sure this place is clean and organized."

"I promise, I won't take advantage. And I promise, I will work hard. I have worked hard all my life, and I won't quit now." I looked up at her now. I needed to win her respect in order to stay here. I would find a way to earn it, as I didn't want to leave.

"That's good to hear, Rain. I don't mean to scare you, but it's important that we start off on the right foot."

"I understand. I'll get to feeding now." I left feeling more discouraged than I had in the last few days. I was sure I could prove my worth soon.

There were kids coming in and out of the barn, so I got busy piling up the hay in the wheelbarrow. It looked like the parents were coming to collect their kids from lessons.

"Please, may no one recognize me," I pleaded to no one in particular.

I moved from horse to horse, making sure I was feeding them the right amount. I saw Jen busying herself with feeding them their grain. When I came to Mia's stall, I waited for a minute and regarded her. I don't know why I found her so beautiful, but I did. "What would it be like to ride you?" She nuzzled my hand but then saw the hay. "Dinnertime, Mia." She hardly let me into her stall while I brought in the hay. She started eating from my hands before I could put it down. "What a hungry mare you are." I didn't stay long in her stall as I didn't want Jen to say that I was slacking.

I moved on to Elli, who was next to Mia. Elli was so cute. All the horses here seemed so well behaved, especially compared to the horse I used to ride. Rambo was one of those horses I used to ride, and boy, did he like dumping me on the ground. Between Rambo and Martha, I had bruises everywhere on my body. Good thing I rode, or I would never have been able to explain all my welts.

It wasn't long before the horses were fed, and the kids had started cleaning the stalls. I needed to give them a hand as I didn't want to relax till the barn was good to go. It looked like the kids were making good progress, so I decided to start putting down the fresh sawdust. Jen passed me as I was busy doing this.

"Good job, Rain. It does look like you know how to work hard after all. When's the last time you've been able to ride?"

"It's been a little while actually."

"Do you miss it?"

"Of course I do!" I couldn't help myself. I missed riding so much, especially while being around horses daily.

"Haha, I thought so. Well, we'll have to find some time for you to get on a horse then."

"That would be amazing!" I left the stall I had been in and closed it behind me.

"Rain, I know I may have scared you earlier, but if you need someone to talk about whatever, you can talk to me." She smiled at me. She had such a pretty face, which seemed to give me the confidence I needed for the moment.

"Thanks, Jen. I appreciate it." I went on to the next stall and spread the fresh sawdust.

We all worked hard together, so before too long, the work was completed. I was tired, smelled extremely bad, and my stomach had begun growling again. I wanted to stay on Jen's good side though, so I didn't assume I was done. I saw her talking to some of the other girls, giving them instructions, and decided to wait till she was done.

"Rain, are you all finished?" she spoke over the other girls' heads.

I walked closer to her before answering. "I think so, unless there's anything else you want me to do."

"We're all good, but do you know your schedule for the rest of the week?"

"Not really. I assumed I'd be in the barn at six in order to start the feeding."

"I'll get the schedule to you tomorrow, but yes, six is your start time. Lindsey will be back on tomorrow too."

"Thanks, Jen. I'll be in the trailer if you need anything."

She went back to chatting with the girls, and I decided to quickly retrieve my stuff from the hayloft. I could pretend I was looking for something if I got busted.

There were quite a few cars still coming in and out of the parking lot, so I put my head down and walked briskly to the small barn. I didn't realize until too late that someone was calling my name. The only problem was, they were calling my real name.

"Rose, Rose, is that you?"

I stopped dead in my tracks and looked up slightly. It wasn't my worst fear, but it wasn't going to help. "Hey, Sandra, how are you?" It was one of my old friends from high school who had graduated a year before me. It also had been probably the same length of time since I had seen her.

"What are you doing? You look awful. Sorry, but it's true. What happened to you?" Sandra always looked good, and this evening was no exception. She had thick, long dark-brown hair and the biggest brown eyes I had ever seen. Her smile was almost small in comparison to her eyes. She was just beautiful, and all the guys in school had crushes on her.

"Come here for a minute, and please don't call me Rose." I motioned her to move away from the parents and kids who were arriving, hoping to keep my secret quiet. "It's a long story, but you have to call me Rain, okay?"

Her brown eyes widened in disbelief. "What, why?"

We moved closer to the barn and away from all the hustle.

"Do you remember how you used to always try to get me to leave home?" She nodded. "Well, I finally did it! Although, I didn't have a real plan, so after a couple of days, I ended up here."

"I'm proud of you, but don't you think you're going to get caught? Especially as you're still in the horse community. I mean, I recognized you even though you don't look like yourself."

"I know. I think I need to cut and dye my hair."

"No, don't do that. I know how much you love your blond hair, but if you need someone, I've got a great girl who is easy on the pocketbook. Her name is Rena, and she owns her own salon. I came across her when I came home from school."

"Uh, thanks, but it'll have to be a home job for now. I didn't exactly bring much with me. Sandra, you never answered me. Why on earth are you here? You never ride." I looked at her fitted jeans and dressy short black boots. She could have walked out of a magazine.

She looked away and blushed slightly. "The truth is, the guy I'm interested in likes horses. I figured I'd take a few lessons so I wouldn't look like an idiot."

"Ha, oh, Sandra, you are funny. How was your lesson?"

"Good, although I'm super sore. I signed up for four lessons. I guess that means that I can make sure that you're okay. I'd offer to have you come live with me, but it would be too close to your house."

"That's okay. The owner is letting me stay in the trailer over there." I pointed to the white trailer on the lot. "Actually, I was just about to go get my bag from the hayloft. How long are you in town?"

"Just till the first week of September. Then it's back to school. How long do you plan on staying away?"

"I'm not sure. Like I said, I didn't really have a plan. I was just fed up! It was one beating too many."

Sandra put her hand on my shoulder and squeezed it. "Rose, I mean, Rain, I'm so sorry. All our group of friends never knew how you survived living with that woman for so long. For what it's worth, I hope you don't get caught."

"Thanks. Do you want to come and see my new home?" I was grateful for the support as it strengthened my resolve to stay on the run.

"I would, but my mom wanted to hang out, so she's picking me up soon. Rain check, Rain?" She smiled at me.

"Ha, yeah, rain check for sure. I have no phone, but when you are here, make sure you say hi. I'd better go as I can't see your mom. Please don't say anything to the others." The others were the group of friends I had before they had all graduated on me.

"I won't. I'll see you later." She gave me a hug, and I hugged her small frame back. "Stay strong, Rain, and I'm sorry we lost touch."

"Me too. Bye for now."

"Bye."

I watched her leave, and it saddened me to think how close we were in high school. I had failed grade 8, so I was always older than my classmates, which caused me to befriend the grade ahead of me. The drawback was, they all left me to finish grade 12 without them. This meant I had the best marks in my last year as there wasn't much else to do. Seeing as I didn't start going to school full-time until grade 10, it was a miracle that I graduated at all. Martha loved to keep me home from school to clean the house and look after the kids. At sixteen, I decided to stop being her puppet. That was probably why life took a turn for the worse.

I walked up the stairs to the hayloft with no one paying me much attention. I worked here, so I could go up there even if it was to get my small bag of goods. I looked around. There were fresh bales of hay that had been delivered today, and someone had taken out the rain sheets for the horses. It was a good thing that I had cleaned up and hidden my stuff, or I would have been found out today.

I took a few steps to the corner and found my black bag where I had hidden it in the far corner. Just as I was getting ready to leave, I heard footsteps. What now? I put my bag back where I had taken it from and walked out to see Jen. Crap, just when I was getting on her good side.

"Rain, what are you doing up there?" she said, placing her hands on her hips.

"Uh, just sorting out the hay for the morning." I couldn't think of anything else to say.

"But the hay is already in the big barn."

"I know, but I thought we might need some more after feeding tonight."

"And your plan was to carry some down now?" She wasn't buying my story.

"No, no, I was going to come a bit earlier in the morning. I just wanted to be organized."

"I see. Well, are you organized?"

"I only just got up here, but I have an idea of what I need," I stammered out.

"Good. Why don't you come back down as you're off for the night? Sounds like you might need some rest." Her hands relaxed slightly.

"Will do. Thanks. See you in the morning." I left her quickly. I walked down the stairs with my heart practically beating out of my chest. That was close. I went straight to the trailer and let myself into my safe haven.

Chapter 5

It was finally time to take the shower I had been dreaming about all day. I was so fortunate that Tanis had some travel-sized shampoos and conditioners in the shower already. My hair would be even more of a mess if I didn't have conditioner. There were some clean towels put out for me as well. I figured out how to work the shower and let it warm up. The bathroom wasn't very big, but it would do the trick.

I got changed, then hopped into the shower and let the warm water wash the filth off of me. The bruises I had received before I left home were healing. It would take longer for the deeper scars in my heart to heal. Back at home, I had been forced to take freezing cold showers in order to wake up to do more work for Martha. Other times, my showers were timed in order to make sure I didn't spend too much time "relaxing." Today, however, I did relax as I washed. It had been days since I had the opportunity to feel clean.

I hadn't really decided on my next move on the run, but writing a letter to my real mother seemed like a good start. I turned off the shower and dried off. I looked around for a blow-dryer, and as luck would have it, there was a small pink dryer I could use. This might not be the Ritz, but to me, it felt like it was a little bit of paradise. I still needed to get my bag from the loft, but I didn't want to run into Jen again. I wanted to stay on everyone's good side for as long as possible.

After drying my hair, I found a brush and did my best to brush out the knots. I had short hair for most of my life as Martha always tried to keep me looking as ugly as possible, but after my sixteenth birthday, I finally had control over my hair. I had decided to grow it as long as possible, but as it had grown almost past my waist, it was time for at least a trim. My friend Sandra always swore that her hairdresser, Rena, was the best, but I never had the privilege of going to her. I usually took care of it myself, but maybe if I saw Sandra again, I could go with her.

I eyed myself in the mirror and smiled. I was free! I did it! Sure, my heart ached for Jenna, but I was free from being a slave, and for that, I was grateful. I nearly skipped from the bathroom to the bedroom when I remembered I even had clean clothes, thanks to Ian. I pulled on the jeans and cute T-shirt, then went to work at cleaning my other clothes in the sink. As the weather was still warm, I could hang them out tonight, and they'd probably be dry by morning.

I didn't feel like watching TV, and I didn't have a book to read, so I found some paper and a pen. I decided to get the letter done before my mom learned about me from the papers. I gazed out the window and saw that there was still a lot of activity. This was a busy place. I really hoped that I didn't have too many more Sandra run-ins.

What would I say to make my mom's mind at ease? I took a deep breath, pulled my hair back off my face, and began.

Dear Mom,

This may come as a surprise to you, but I decided to leave Dundas and go on the run. Don't worry. I'm fine. In fact, I'm better off than I've been in years. There's a lot you don't know, although you may have suspected. I don't want to get into all the details in a letter, but I wasn't treated well at home. It isn't my dad's fault, so please don't blame him.

I've landed a good job at a barn not too far from home but far enough that I'm out of sight. I haven't told Dad where I am, and please don't tell him. I'll call him when I'm ready. Please give my love to John, and I'll write more soon.

Love,
Rose

It wasn't much, but my eyelids were starting to get heavy, and morning would come far too soon. I wouldn't have the horses waking me up tomorrow morning, so I hoped I'd find an alarm clock in here. I folded the letter up. I'd have to ask Tanis for an envelope and stamp tomorrow.

I closed the little drapes. It wasn't late, but I hadn't slept much in the past week, so I might as well hit the hay now. I had a quick drink of water, which only made my stomach rumble. Food. I needed to get food in order to keep up with my workload. Sleep would help curb the hunger, or so I hoped.

I made sure that I had locked the trailer and got into my new bedroom. The room was simple, and the bed was covered with a light blanket with a horse on it. I braided my hair to keep the knots at bay and fell back on what seemed like the most comfortable bed ever. I was still in my new jeans and T-shirt as I didn't have any pj's, so they would have to do.

Before I closed my eyes, I remembered the alarm. Sure enough, there was one by the bed. I set it and fell back, ready for a good night's sleep. It took longer than I expected for sleep to come as a wave of guilt threatened to engulf while I took in my surroundings. What would my dad and Martha think if they knew where I was? I was sure the house was a mess by now, seeing as I was the one who kept it clean. What would they do, hire a maid?

I was supposed to start college in the fall for nursing, but it seemed like that would have to be put on hold. As my marks were good, I had been accepted into most of the colleges I had applied to, but I just couldn't wait for school to leave home. I hadn't sent in the money yet, and seeing as though I left without any, I would have to think about a new career. Had I made the right decision? Should I go back home? Maybe I had given up too much for the freedom I was feeling right now.

Sleep. All I wanted to do was close my eyes and my mind to my thoughts. I tried counting sheep and then switched to horses. I thought about Mia and hoped that I'd get to ride her sometime. I remembered riding Rambo, my old favorite horse, and pretended that we were out jumping. Before long, sleep came...

Far too quickly I heard a beeping sound that could only be a foreign alarm. I woke up confused and a little disturbed. I found the alarm and turned it off. Was it really 5:30 a.m. already? I needed to start work by six, and so far, I had been early every day since I'd started, but that was a lot easier when you were sleeping in a hayloft. I then remembered that I really wanted to get my stuff from the loft before Jen or Lindsey started today.

I needed to get out of bed before I closed my eyes again. I sat up and threw the covers off. It was going to be another warm day today; I could tell already. I probably shouldn't have slept in my new clothes, but I didn't have many options. My stomach growled in anger at me. I pushed the thought aside and hoped that Tanis might decide to feed me again.

I got up and made the bed. Then I decided that a glass of water would help push my hunger away. I quickly washed my face and pulled my hair out of the braid. My plan had backfired as I must have had a restless night, and my hair was a mess. I brushed it as best as I could, then rebraided it for work. This was one place that I didn't have to worry about how I looked. Then again, I wondered if Ian would be up here again.

I opened up the trailer and brought the clothes in that I had hung up last night. They were a bit damp, so I left them outside. I guessed if Ian came up, he could at least see that I used his gifts. I looked at the clock. I had fifteen minutes before work, which would give me just enough time to get my bag.

I left the comfort of my new home, locked it, and headed to the small barn. It was a beautiful summer morning. The sun was up, and the sky was a pure blue. I took in the smells of the farm and slowed my step. I could get used to this. I was still lost in my thoughts when I heard my name being called.

"Hey, Rain, how are you?" It was Lindsey. She was here early. There went my plan for retrieving my goods.

"Hi, Lindsey. I'm good. How about you?" I made up the short space between us.

"So you're the newest member of the trailer home?" She said this kindly, although I was a bit taken a back at her comment.

"Uh, yeah, I guess I am." I smiled weakly at her.

"Did Jen tell you I lived there a little while ago?"

I thought she had, but I didn't want to seem too nosy. "She mentioned that you might have."

"Yup, I moved here from good old New Brunswick. Bad family situation and such. Let me guess, you were in the hayloft for a few nights, weren't you?" Lindsey tied her long brown hair up into a ponytail while she chatted with me. Should I tell her the truth?

"I may have stayed there a couple of nights. Does this happen often?"

She laughed easily and motioned me to follow her to the small barn. "Thought so. Tanis has a heart of gold. She rescues kids just as much as she rescues horses. If it wasn't for her, I don't know where I'd be. The trailer's comfortable, isn't it?"

"Yes, it is, and I'm so grateful to sleep in a bed, that's for sure." Lindsey started moving the hay into the wheelbarrow. I followed her lead. "Actually, seeing as I've admitted that to you, do you mind if I grab my bag quickly from the loft? I've got my toothbrush in there, and I'm dying to use it."

"Haha. Of course, go ahead. I'll start preparing the grain. You can feed the horses the hay."

"Thanks so much. I appreciate it." I gave Lindsey a genuine smile and quickly ran up the stairs to the loft. I was grateful it was still where I left it. I grabbed it and made my way down the stairs.

I shouted my thanks to Lindsey, then made a beeline to the trailer. I let myself in, brushed my teeth, then went back to the barn to start feeding.

As soon as I started moving the hay around, the horses started neighing, and some of them were even kicking their stalls. "I'm coming. I'm coming, kids."

Lindsey popped her head out from the grain area and laughed. "When they're hungry, they're hungry." She had the grain ready and started scooping it into their bowls.

"I understand, trust me."

"Yeah, have you had anything to eat?"

"No, not this morning." A loud rumble from my stomach almost answered the question before I could.

"Maybe you'll be lucky and have a girl like I do that brings me coffees and treats on a daily basis."

"I hope so. When is payday here? I forgot to ask Tanis."

We both moved around the horses easily as we talked. There didn't seem to be any horses like Mia in the small barn.

"We get paid tomorrow, but if you need some help with food, I can help you."

"Thanks so much. I just need to get some bread and peanut butter. Oh, and coffee."

"Those sound like my staples too. After work, I can take you out to the store if you'd like."

"Really? That would be great! I'll even muck out all the stalls for you in exchange."

"You don't need to do that, but I'll let you know if I ever need a shift covered."

"Deal." I couldn't believe how nice everyone I had met so far was. I hadn't had many friends at home, so it was odd to be treated like this.

"Watch out for Cavi. He really likes his breakfast. He may try to trample you as you walk in to his stall."

"Thanks for the warning." I was almost at Cavi's stall, so I would see for myself.

After feeding Coco, I moved to him. Sure enough, he reminded me of Mia. "Here you go, big boy. You have to let me in to feed you." He started eating the hay out of my hands, so I let go of the bale and spread it out. "There, see, it's all yours." I closed the door behind me and did up the five locks to keep him in. He must be a Houdini with all the locks on the door. He looked strong. I guessed that he was over sixteen hands as he was large. He also had beautiful chestnut coloring and looked like he was a fun horse to ride.

"Rain, I'll meet you in the big barn. You can do the hay again, and I'll do the grain."

"Okay. See you in a minute." We looked to be making good time, although I couldn't check as I didn't have my watch on me.

It wasn't long till I had caught up with Lindsey in the big barn. I was excited to see Mia today and see if we had the same kind of connection that we did yesterday. My stomach continued to growl, which made even the horse's food seem like a good idea. I pushed the thoughts away and loaded up the wheelbarrow full of hay.

Lindsey and I both worked in silence. It wasn't an awkward silence but more an efficient one. I was happy to listen to the horses eating contentedly. I could escape here anytime my thoughts turned too dark. It really was my happy place. I still needed to devise a plan of action regarding my dad. His health had been only so-so, and I didn't want to cause more worry, even if it was his choice to be with my stepmonster. I would have to get word back to him. Maybe I would send a letter to him as well, but then again, Martha was sure to get her hands on it. No, I would have to call and hope for him to pick up.

Coming to Mia's stall got my head back to the task at hand. As I came to her stall, she peeked her head out of her stall as if to say, "Good morning."

"Hi, Mia, how are you today?" I stroked her beautiful face, and she nuzzled me, wanting breakfast of course. "Here you go, pretty lady." I opened her stall door with my arms full of her breakfast. She hardly let me in. "Yes, yes, I know you're famished, aren't you?"

It almost looked as if she nodded at me with her mouth full of fresh hay.

Lindsey came by Mia's stall as I was feeding her. "You like her, don't you?" she asked while looking at us.

"Yes, I do. She seems feisty, but lots of fun."

"She is that. Maybe after Kat or Tanis see what you can do on a horse, they may let you ride her. She's used as a lesson horse, but she's kind of for sale."

"Are there any people who are interested in her?" I paused. "I know it's only a dream of mine owning a horse right now."

"I get it. Don't worry. I don't think anyone is interested. But you never know." She stroked Mia's head as she chatted. "I'm finished with the grain. I'll meet you in the small barn so we can start with mucking out the stalls."

"Okay, sounds good." I left Mia's stall after giving her some more love. "I'll be back, Mia." She neighed at me and continued eating her hay.

I wondered if Ian would be up here to look at Spy again. I moved over to Spy's stall and gave him his hay. He had his big head out of his stall. He was so friendly. It would be hard to say no to buying a horse like him. I petted him as he grabbed the hay from me. All the horses here were pretty nice; it reminded me of West-over, the place where I once rode. Horse people were good all over, that's for sure.

I proceeded to finish feeding, then grabbed my tools and headed back to the small barn. Lindsey and I moved quickly and efficiently around the horses. Except for Cavi being a bit of a brat, there wasn't too much excitement. I could tell that Lindsey had been doing this type of work for a long time, as she was so good at it. My arms were tired, and my hands were covered in calluses. I wouldn't let on how much my body ached as I still hadn't proven myself. I had learned the hard way that if you didn't work hard, the punishment would be severe.

The morning went by quickly, so I was surprised when Tanis came into the barn all dressed to ride.

"Morning, Rain. How are you doing today?" She smiled at me, her blue eyes sparkling, and I noticed she had a coffee tumbler and sandwich with her. My heart skipped a beat. "Ha, are you hungry?" She obviously noticed my eyes looking hungrily at what she was carrying. She handed me the tumbler and the sandwich. "Yes, these are for you. Enjoy, Rain."

"Thanks so much. I appreciate it. I haven't had time to stock my fridge yet." I put the shovel to the side and took the sandwich and coffee.

"How's the trailer?" She petted Sunshine's face as she spoke with me.

"The trailer is fantastic! I so appreciate it, and the bed was so comfortable." I took a bite of the sandwich as I couldn't wait.

"Rain, are you sure there's nothing you want to tell me or maybe need to tell me?"

I swallowed guiltily. "I'm not sure what you mean." She was going to wear me down with her kindness alone.

"Enjoy your breakfast, and I'll see you later on. Lindsey told me you're interested in riding Mia."

"I am, well, I'm interested in riding. It feels like it's been too long."

"I'll talk to Lindsey about it. I'll get you on someone easier first, then we can see about Mia. She needs to be ridden more often, and seeing as you are here anyways, it could be a good fit. I'm off to take Martini out. Jen will be here in a bit to get the camps organized. I'm sure she can use your help."

"Whatever you need, I can do." I smiled at her, hoping I was coming across as sincere and not a suck-up. She smiled back at me. "Tanis, if you have time later, I should maybe fill you in on some things." I didn't know what I was doing, but I didn't want to risk getting her into trouble.

"That sounds like a good idea. Why don't you come to the house for lunch? We can chat then."

"Thanks again for breakfast." I took another bite. I had never had such a fantastic peanut butter sandwich in my life. I swallowed a few mouthfuls of coffee and was instantly in a better mood. I finished off my breakfast and put down the tumbler outside the stall and went back to my cleaning.

Tanis was brushing Martini as I finished, and Lindsey had taken the gator out to dump all the horse manure out back. I saw that Jen had arrived and was catching up with Tanis. I quickened my pace as I moved. It wasn't long before the barn would be overrun with kids waiting to experience horses for the first time. Little did they know how one week could change their lives forever.

Jen came over to me and smiled. "Hey, Rain, I hear that you've been holding your own this morning." She had on a white A&T shirt and black shorts and had piled her long brown hair on top of her head.

"I try." I smiled at her. "What do you want me to do after I finish with the shavings?"

"I'll give you a list of the horses I need to get tacked up, and if you could get that done as soon as possible, that would be great. Actually, the list will be on the board, so you can look at that. Oh, and can you tack up Eye Spy first? The same people are coming by to check him out again."

"Ian is coming up here?" I almost gushed out.

"Ian? Oh, I see you've met them. I didn't realize that. Did you see Yasmin ride?"

"I don't know if she rode yesterday. I think she watched Tanis ride him."

"Well, Spy is pretty special, so Tanis wouldn't sell him to just anyone. Anyway, start with Spy and go from there. Spy's tack is in Tanis's tack room, which I've unlocked for you. I'll see you in a few."

"See you." I hoped I hadn't given my excitement away at the mention of Ian's name. He'd see me wearing the outfit he gave me, if nothing else. I put my wheelbarrow and pick to the side and moved to get Spy's tack.

Tanis's tack room was almost as large as the boarder's room. There were several saddles on saddle racks on the wall. The other side of the room had bridles of all sorts hanging on hooks. There was one wall dedicated to big ribbons. As I was gawking, Tanis came in to get her helmet.

"Uh, hi, Tanis. Can you tell me which saddle and bridle I should be using for Spy?"

"Sure, you can use this one." She pointed to a beautiful dark-brown leather saddle. It looked way too clean to be used very often. Then again, maybe they kept their tack a lot cleaner than I'd kept Jenna's. She then took down a plain dark-brown bridle and handed it to me. "Here you go."

"Thanks. Do you think they'll buy Eye Spy?" I inquired.

"I'm not sure, and to be honest, I may try to persuade them to look at Calvin. You see, I'm not sure if we're ready to sell Eye Spy. He has been off for a while, but whenever Kat rides him, he is sound, no problem. I think the two of them belong together."

"Doesn't Kat own Jackson?" I had noticed this while I was meeting all the horses.

"Yes, that's her main horse, but before him was Spy. We've both loved many horses, but some stay with us for a lot longer, and Spy is one of those horses. I'll get you to tack Calvin up as well. Must get Tini out to the ring. I'm looking forward to our chat later on though."

"Yeah, me too."

I grabbed the brush caddie and put it over by Spy's stall. He stuck his large head out, sniffing around for treats. I petted his muzzle and looked into his dark-brown eyes. He looked like a special horse, so full of character. I assumed Tanis knew what she was doing. I wondered, with Yasmin coming up again so quickly, that it might be too late to try to switch her to another horse.

I went and got all the tack I needed and put it down by Spy's stall. I really hoped that I'd have a minute to freshen up before Ian came by. There wasn't much I could do as I hadn't brought makeup with me. Maybe I could at least wash the grime off my face. I'd like him to see that I didn't usually walk around so dirty. I hadn't ever been popular at school, but I was often told I was pretty. I had been asked out at one time or another by a boy or two. I was athletic, which I was sure turned some guys off, but I figured they were half-wits if they were turned off by a strong girl. It wasn't that I worked out a lot but rather rode my one-speed bike to school daily. One speed made for some pretty muscular legs.

I still hadn't learned to drive. Seeing as I was trapped most of the time and had a bike, I hadn't seen the need to try to learn. It wasn't as if my dad would have let me get a car anytime soon. So I cycled everywhere.

I brushed Spy's coat as he tried to nuzzle me. He was so affectionate and adorable.

"Well, Spy, I don't know. I think if I got to ride you, I'd be hooked on you, too." He nuzzled my side in reply. "Exactly." I finished tacking him up but left the bridle off as I wasn't sure when Yasmin would arrive.

I figured I could quickly tack up Calvin, finish with the shavings, then make a quick trip to my new home before getting the camp ponies ready.

Lindsey was helping Jen already, so I moved quickly. I wasn't vain, but I wanted to at least brush my hair out. I also had some ChapStick I could put on. I wasn't sure what I was thinking, even considering liking someone while I was in such a mess, but Ian's kindness had touched me.

I was putting the wheelbarrow back when Jen found me.

"You've been working hard all morning, Rain. Are you ready for more?"

I rubbed my hands nervously on my new jeans, hoping that she wasn't going to give me too much more to do. I still needed to get the camp ponies tacked. "Of course I am." I smiled brightly, ignoring the pain in my hands and the need for a quick break.

She looked seemingly right through me. "Why don't you take a fifteen-minute break? Then get to the camp ponies. I know I was hard on you yesterday, but I do see the worth you bring to the team. We can always use hard workers."

I breathed a sigh of relief. "Thank you, Jen. You have no idea how appreciative I am of your kind words and for the quick break."

"My pleasure. When you get back, start with Coco in the small barn, then make your way to Nippy and get them tied up in the arena. The kids will be here in the next hour, and I want to make sure we're organized."

"Will do. I'll see you in fifteen minutes." I hung up my shovel and pitchfork in the staff room and closed it behind me. I couldn't believe my luck. My plan was working!

I entered my trailer and set my alarm for ten minutes. I wanted to get back early. I brushed my teeth again as I had actually had breakfast. I decided to unbraid my hair and pull it back into a high ponytail. I thought it looked nice, albeit a little impractical. My hair still hung long even in a ponytail, but it was wavy because of the braids. I wasn't sure how long it would be before it would become a messy bun, but I had hoped it would be after Ian had come by. I ruffled through my bag and found my ChapStick. "Yup, one thing I never leave home without." I applied it and smiled. "This is as good as I could be for now."

I grabbed one more drink of water; I hadn't realized how parched I'd become. The alarm rang just as I peered outside to see none other than that gray Impala.

Chapter 6

I moved at lightning speed after the alarm went off. I really needed to at least thank Ian for his kindness. I locked the trailer door behind me and saw that Ian and his sister were just getting out of his car. *Perfect timing,* I thought. I noticed that Ian was in light-blue jeans and a white T-shirt, which paired perfectly with his skin. Yasmin was very pretty too and was dressed in her riding gear. Her hair seemed as black as Ian's, and she had beautiful waves. My mom would love her hair. She always had hoped that mine would be wavy, but no such luck.

I walked over to them, and it was then that Ian noticed me.

"Hi, Rain, nice outfit. It looks like I have good taste, eh?" He smiled at me, his chocolate-brown eyes sparkling.

I blushed and looked away for a second. I found my courage and answered him, "Yes, you have great taste. I wanted to thank you so much for the gifts. They really came in handy."

Ian closed his door and locked the car while Yasmin made her way over to me, wearing a huge grin.

"I may have helped him pick out the jeans," Yasmin said.

"I thought you may have assisted him. I appreciate it." I smiled warmly at her. She seemed genuinely kind.

"Well, my dear sis, why don't you go see Eye Spy? Rain and I will be along in a minute."

"Actually, Ian, I have to get back to work." Yasmin started walking toward the barn, which was where I needed to be going as well.

"It'll just take a minute." He steered me away from the kids who had started to arrive.

"I guess I have a minute, but honestly, Jen will be waiting for me, and I can't let her down." He stopped, and so did I. My heart was doing little flutters as he had his hand on my arm. No, I couldn't afford to like anyone right now.

"Did you think any more about my offer? For me to take you out to lunch now that you have a proper outfit to wear, that is?" He chuckled.

"Um, I wouldn't mind, but I don't have a phone. I'm actually staying here in the trailer right now. I want to be close to work, you know." I didn't want to say too much as I didn't even know this guy, but he did seem trustworthy.

"That's convenient. When do you get a break?"

"I'm not sure, but I'm supposed to have lunch with Tanis today."

"How about dinner?" He was tough to say no to.

"It's hard for me to plan right now. I really have to go. Do you know what time it is?"

"You don't have a watch?"

"No, I do. I just didn't bring my good one with me." *Stupid, what was that supposed to mean?*

"That's tragic. Here, let's walk back, and I'll come by at seven. If you're off, I'll take you to dinner. Oh, and it's almost eleven."

My heart did another flutter. Would I really let Ian take me out? "Thanks, and if we do go out, it can't be anything too fancy, okay?"

"Whatever you say, Rain. You are interesting, that's for sure."

We had arrived at the barn doors, and I saw that Jen was already delegating the kids into their groups.

"Talk to you later, Ian." I moved away from him, not wanting to draw attention to myself and Ian walking in together. No one knew me well yet, and I didn't want them to start any rumors about me.

I realized that the ponies I needed to tack up were in the small barn, so I motioned to Jen that I was on it. I walked back across the parking lot. I hoped my diversion with Ian hadn't cost me too much time.

I got the ponies tacked up without any complications. I was starting to develop a bit of a crush on Coco, as well as Mia. She was just so cute, with her big brown eyes, her black forelock, and her white mane. I wondered what she'd be like to ride. I hadn't ridden in what seemed like a long time, and to be around horses and not ride them was hard.

I brought Nippy out to the arena and tied her up. As I walked back to the barn, I passed the outdoor ring where I saw Yasmin on Eye Spy. Ian and Tanis were watching her ride. Ian saw me and waved. I waved back but kept walking. I had planned on talking to Tanis today, but with the impending date with Ian, the truth might have to wait.

Coco was next, and she walked with me with a spring in her step. Yup, I was right. She'd be fun to ride. I went to find Jen to see what else she needed before I got distracted with my dreams of riding.

I entered the big barn and found Jen organizing the rest of the kids. I noticed that there were more people working with us than normal. I held my breath hoping that I wouldn't run into any of Jenna's friends. I really should have run farther away, or maybe I shouldn't have landed at a barn. I kept my head down while I scanned the room. It looked like I was safe for the moment. Jen saw me and motioned for me to come over to her.

"Hey, Jen, where would you like me?" I asked eagerly.

"Actually, before you do anything else for me, can you take Calvin out to Tanis? I know she's hoping Yasmin doesn't love Spy."

"I've got him tacked up already, so it'll only take me a minute. Spy's pretty special. I can see why she wouldn't want to sell him."

"He's special all right. Kat would not be happy if he got sold, and the final decision is hers, so good luck, Calvin."

"Yeah, good luck."

I walked to his stall, picking up his bridle as I entered. "Hey, Calvin. We need you to wow some people. Do you think you can do that?" I petted his dark-brown face as I put the bridle on him. He was friendly, although not as friendly as Spy. I had my own reasons for wanting Yasmin to get a horse from here.

I led him out of his stall, and Jen ushered the kids into an empty stall so they'd be out of our way. Calvin walked like a horse full of regality, which caused me to chuckle. "You know what you have to do, don't you, Mr. Calvin?"

I saw Yasmin getting off Eye Spy, looking a little concerned. That was never a good sign. I brought Calvin over to the ring, and Tanis ushered me in. Ian was standing by the fence, but I avoided his eyes.

"Hey, Rain, can you walk Spy out? He seems a bit off, so maybe take him out for some grass after you cool him out."

"Sure thing. Here's Calvin. He looks ready for a ride."

"Thanks, Rain. Yasmin, why don't you give Calvin a whirl? I think you may really like him."

"I really liked Eye Spy, but I can't buy a horse that is continually off." She sounded so disappointed but came and took Calvin from me. She eyed him warmly and petted his shiny coat. "Hi, Calvin. Let's take you for a little ride."

I led Spy out of the ring and loosened his girth before I started to walk him out. I hadn't walked far before Ian came up beside me.

"Rain, what do you think happened?"

"You mean with Spy?" I hadn't really slowed down, but Ian kept up with us.

"Yeah, what causes a horse to be off?"

"Are you a horse guy or not really?" I had to ask.

"I'm a good brother who likes to help his sister."

"Ha, that's good to hear. Well, Spy could be off for any number of reasons. I don't really know his story as I haven't been here long."

"What brought you to this barn?"

Was he really interested in me? It seemed like he was, but he must have been at least twenty-five. Too old for me, I thought. Mind you, a dinner out would be nice. I pressed on. "Um, well, I kind of stumbled upon it. I hadn't planned to come here, but it found me."

"Are you in university in September, or are you out of school?"

"I'm out of school right now." I looked away as I answered. I hadn't really lied, had I?

"What did you take?"

"Nursing." That was what I was going to take.

"You're too young to have finished your program, aren't you?"

"I'm just taking a year off." That was almost the truth.

"Hmm, I see. How old are you? I hope you don't mind me asking."

I was sure I was the same color of a beet right then. "I-I'm twenty as of April." Yup, there I was, making things up.

"You're twenty? You look pretty young for twenty, but that's good."

"Why is that good?" I had to ask.

"Well, I wanted to make sure it was okay to take you out to dinner." Ian flashed me a crooked grin.

"And how old are you?" I figured I'd better ask too.

"I guess seeing as you told me, I should tell you. I'm twenty-five as of September. So now that we have that out of the way, I'll pick you up at seven. I'd better get back to being a good brother, especially seeing as I'm helping pay for her horse." He stroked Spy's neck and winked at me.

"See you at seven." I sighed. Twenty-five years old to my eighteen. Would this really be wise? Maybe I could get his advice on what to do with my messed-up life. At his age, he must have more of a clue than me.

I brought Spy back to his stall, untacked him, and gave him a good brushing. He was so lovable. He practically cuddled with me. "Spy, I don't think you want to leave here either. When I get some carrots, I'll be sure to give you some, you handsome devil."

It looked like Jen and Lindsey had things under control, so I asked if they wanted me to get the horses fed. I thought that I was making headway here, as both Jen and Lindsey were grateful for my help.

I had fed the horses in the small barn when Tanis found me.

"Rain, why don't you come to the house for lunch once you've got the horses fed?"

"That sounds great! Hey, how did Yasmin like Calvin?"

"She liked him. She'll be back tomorrow to try him again. I think Ian may like you too."

"What, really?" I almost tripped over a bale of hay. How embarrassing.

"Yes, really. As if you didn't notice. I've seen him up here several times, but he's never gone out of his way to talk to anyone before. Rain, be careful. He seems really nice, but just be careful."

"Thanks, Tanis. I'll see you soon." There I was, red as could be again. Jeepers, I did have to be careful so I didn't get a reputation. I wondered if I could find a way to cancel tonight. Then again, I really wanted to get to know him better.

I kept my thoughts to myself as I fed the horses. There were more friendly people around me. If Jenna needed a new barn in which to ride, I would definitely tell her to come out here. There were some barns that were so stuck-up, but this wasn't one of them.

I finished with the feeding. I had some of the volunteers helping, which made it go faster. I walked over to the house. It looked like Tanis's house had sported a fresh paint job. Her home was a dark gray with darker gray trim. The dogs greeted me as I entered. I stroked their heads to their delight. I still wasn't sure what I was going to tell Tanis, but I needed to make sure she was warned. I knocked on the screen door and took a deep breath.

"Come in," Tanis called out.

I entered and removed my dirty boots. I needed to wash up again, but really, what was the point? I'd be dirty again in half an hour.

"Hi, Rain, come on in." Tanis was still in her breeches, but she made them look stylish.

I followed Tanis to the small table and sat down in front of a couple of sandwiches that were laid out. She had also put out a plate of veggies in the middle of the table. I could also hear the coffee percolating. My stomach started to rumble as I looked at the food. If Tanis said I could have food in exchange for information, I would be a lousy liar.

"Thanks again, Tanis. I really appreciate this." I breathed in the smell of coffee. It smelled so good.

"I thought getting food into you would be wise. You haven't stopped working since you came here. Someone sure taught you the meaning of hard work." She sat down across from me and picked up some veggies.

"Uh, well, it's a long story." I looked down and started fidgeting with my hands.

"It's okay, Rain. Why don't you eat a bit before you tell me more? Dig in. I'll get the coffee."

She left me, and I took a couple of bites of the tuna sandwich. This was so good. I used to be a picky eater, but not eating for a couple of days was changing that. Tanis came back to the table with the steaming coffee.

"I shouldn't really be drinking more coffee today, but it'll be a long day, so I figured why not? Are you enjoying that?"

"It's delicious. Thanks so much."

She joined me again at the table. "You must be hungry, as I'm not much of a cook. Sandwiches, are easy. So what can you tell me about the adventure that brought you here?" She paused for a minute before continuing on. "I know you may not want to tell me everything, but if there's anything I can do to help, I'd like to be able to." She took a sip of her coffee, and her blue eyes cut through my facade.

I swallowed and took a sip of coffee to ease my nerves. "As I said, it's a long story, and I don't know how much to tell you, but I do want to tell you something. You've been so kind to me, and I would hate to get you into any trouble because of me."

"Thanks, Rain. I appreciate you looking out for me." She almost chuckled.

"Well, I'm an adult, so there wouldn't be too much trouble. Let's just say my background isn't exactly white picket fences and lollipops." I took another sip of coffee, which I was sure wasn't going to help my nerves.

"I figured you had a story that's a little colorful. Go on." She smiled encouragingly at me.

I started. "I left a bad situation without any notice. I don't feel too bad about leaving except that I don't want to worry my dad. I left a note for my sister, but I don't even know if she's found it. My real mom is in Nova Scotia, so I have written her a letter to tell her that I'm okay, but I still need to mail it." I couldn't stop myself from talking. The words rushed out of me. Tanis leaned closer to me, encouraging me to keep going.

I paused. "If I tell you more, will you promise not to call the cops on me?"

"You said that you're twenty, so you're an adult and able to make your own decisions. Unless, you aren't twenty." She continued, "However, even if you aren't, I'm not going to send you back to a terrible situation, Rain." She took a sip of her coffee and leaned a bit further back. I assumed to give me room to think.

I hesitated, but I had decided to press on. "I am an adult, but not quite twenty. I do appreciate that you don't want to send me back though. I can't go back, as much as I miss my family, especially my youngest sister. I can't do it anymore. My stepmother pushed me to the brink of crazy, not to mention how she beat me. She hasn't beat me as much as she used to, but she tormented me all the time." I looked away and swallowed the lump that was growing in my throat.

"I'm so sorry to hear that. I can't imagine anyone wanting to hurt you, Rain. That's awful. I'm glad you got away, and I'm glad you came here. How did you manage to get away?"

"I waited till everyone was asleep and snuck out. I didn't really have a plan except to leave that horrible house." I shuddered involuntarily. "Martha, my stepmother, had pushed me too hard that day, and I decided that this time I wasn't going to chicken out. I had left before, but never for this long. I made sure that I didn't fall asleep. I used to sneak out all the time, so it wasn't that difficult. Then I started walking. I was lucky that it was a nice night out. Then again, maybe I would have been more prepared had it been raining. I didn't really stop until I found your farm. I didn't want to take any chances in getting caught." I stopped, desperately hoping I wasn't wrong in sharing.

Tanis leaned toward me, compassion showing in her kind eyes. Before she could comment, her cell went off. She looked at it then at me apologetically. "I have to take this, it's Kat. I'll be right back."

As I watched her leave the table, I resisted the urge to run from the kitchen and leave the barn. I took a deep breath and looked around. I wasn't able to hear the conversation, but it sounded like Tanis was concerned. I hoped that there was nothing wrong with Kat.

Finally, Tanis came back into the kitchen. "Sorry, Rain. It looks like we may have a problem." She sat back down. As she did, I sucked in a breath. "Kat was teaching at one of her friends' barns, and she overheard a lady talking to the owner about a runaway girl. She said she was looking for a girl named Rose, but other than the name being wrong, she matched your description. I'm assuming that your real name is Rose, right?"

The room felt like it was turning before I could answer. I needed to not faint. Fear washed over my whole body. If Martha found me, she would be so angry at me I would never live this down.

"Rain, am I right?"

I looked at Tanis. What could I do? I had already told her everything. In a small voice, I answered her, "Yes, that's right. I'm sorry I lied." Where had my resolve gone?

"Rain, I mean, Rose, it'll be okay."

"No, no, it won't. She'll never let me live this down. You don't know her." Why had I left? Why had I thought I could get away with this?

Tanis came around to my seat and put her arm around me. "It'll be okay. She doesn't know where you are, and I'm not going to tell her."

"But if she's going from barn to barn, she'll come up here. Then what will I do?"

"I have an idea. She's still quite far away, plus you said you're an adult. How old are you?"

"I'm eighteen," I said quietly. I had lost my nerve now.

"It's okay, Rain. How about we get hold of your dad so that he knows you're safe then? We'll tell him you're not coming home."

"It won't work. You don't know her. She won't give up."

"Listen. None of us is going to give your secret away, and I'm the only one who knows. Kat suspects, but I haven't given her all the details." She stood up and got her cell.

"Tell you what, I'll call your dad and let him know that you're safe. What do you say?"

I sat there numb, not knowing what to do or where to go. I could leave here and go farther away, or maybe I could call Ian and ask him to drive me somewhere. Tanis waited for an answer, but I had none to give.

Chapter 7

After the shock wore off, Tanis told me to leave the planning of what to do with her. She saw I was pretty shook up, so she tried to give me the rest of the day off. I decided that I'd spend a bit of time in my trailer, but I figured spending time with the horses would keep me more distracted. I looked at the clock on the microwave and saw that it was only 3:00 p.m. If I couldn't get hold of Ian, he'd be up here by seven to pick me up. Was I crazy to go to dinner with him? I wanted to just get away from my own life for a bit, so maybe that was my motivation, not to mention his charming personality.

I heard a knock at my door. Fear washed over me, but I resisted the urge to hide. I walked to open the door, and to my surprise, it was Lindsey.

"Uh, hi, Lindsey. Do you guys need some help?"

"Hi. No, I was just checking on how you're doing."

"Come on in and make yourself comfortable. I mean, it was your home before it was mine." She came in, and I closed the door behind her.

"Yes, it was a little while ago though. So tell me, Rain, how are you really doing? Are you hanging in there?" She sat down on the bench by the table in the kitchen, and I joined her.

"I'm hanging. Did Tanis talk to you?" I was starting to worry that everyone knew my business now.

"No. She just mentioned that she was giving you the afternoon off, so I figured something may have come up. I also know Tanis was the first person I told my story to."

"Well, I did come clean on some things, but I really don't want to get you involved. The fewer people who know, the better."

Lindsey smiled at me, her dark-brown eyes filled with understanding. "So I saw Ian talking to you again."

This time, a blush covered my face. "Uh, yes, he did. He's very nice." I looked down at the floor.

"Ha, yes, he is. So did he give you his number?"

"Why would you ask that?" Did everyone know everything here?

"He asked me if you were single. I told him I thought so, and then I saw him talking to you. He seems like the kind of guy who finds a way to get what he wants."

"Funny you should say that, as I think you might be right."

"Is he taking you out?"

As much as I was uncomfortable talking to Lindsey about Ian, it was better than talking about why I had run away.

"He asked me out. Actually, he's supposed to take me out tonight. Do you think it's a good idea with how little you know about me?"

"I understand how you must be craving a real dinner, so I bet the idea was tempting, to say the least."

"Yes, well, the truth is, I said yes and partly for that exact reason."

"And the other part?" She looked at me sheepishly.

"The other part is, well, he's charming and very nice and seems trustworthy."

"Just be careful, okay? Do you have a cell phone?"

"No, I don't."

"Hmm, maybe I could lend you one. I think Tanis has an old flip phone used only for emergencies that she could lend you. This way, you could at least call us if there was a problem."

"Thanks. That's a great plan."

"Make sure you tell him that you have a phone and that we're expecting a call from you, okay?"

"Okay. Thanks, Lindsey. But you're sure you'd do this, or is it safer to stay away from him?"

"Well, Tanis knows him, so I'm sure it'll be fine. I'll go get the phone for you and be right back." She got up to go. I was really touched by her concern for me.

"Thanks again. Do you need any help in the barns?"

"We've got it handled. Besides, you have to get ready for your big date. Haha."

"It won't take me four hours, especially since I don't have a lot of clothing options."

"Well, if you want to see if Jen needs anything, she's in the outdoor, or seeing as you have a crush on Mia, why don't you take her out for some grass?"

"Really? That would be okay?"

"Of course! You already put in a full shift earlier, and you're on the barns first thing in the morning, so don't stay out too late." She smiled playfully at me.

"I won't. Don't worry." I smiled back at her.

"Good. Well, have fun with Mia, and I'll get you that phone. Don't forget to clean up, as I don't think eau de horse is Ian's favorite perfume."

"Then too bad for him, as it's my favorite scent."

"Mine too, but boys don't always agree with us crazy horse girls."

"They're the crazy ones then."

Lindsey laughed and walked to the door. "See you out there."

"See you." I closed the door after her and smiled to myself. It seemed my date with Ian was less than four hours away. I didn't need to spend any more time in my little place, as there were horses to play with. I could get ready in less than an hour, but I already had a feeling that Ian would be early, so I'd make sure that I was waiting for him.

I decided I'd wear one of the other T-shirts that Ian gave me and my old jeans. I hoped it wouldn't be too fancy a place, as my only shoes were my riding boots. Maybe I could borrow some polish to spruce them up a bit. In the meantime, I left the trailer and walked over to the outdoor where Jen was teaching.

"Hey, Jen. Do you need any help?" I saw she had about six campers riding around the arena. All seemed to be laughing and having fun.

"Hey, Rain. I will in about half an hour."

"Okay, I'll go play with Mia, and I'll see you in a bit."

Jen waved and smiled at me.

As I walked over to the big barn, I kept my head down, as there were still too many parents around for my liking. Maybe I should get Ian to take me somewhere far away from here for the evening so I could spend one night not being paranoid.

I grabbed a halter and a lead line off the wall and petted the other horses on the way to Mia's stall. They neighed at me in return. They seemed to know I usually brought them their food. Finally, I saw Mia stick her head out and look at me with her large brown eyes.

"Hi, girl, how are you doing?" She allowed me to stroke her head and smelled my hands for some treats. "Sorry, girl, I come empty-handed, but hang on a sec." I remembered that I would need to bribe Mia in order for her to let me into her stall. I grabbed a couple of carrots from the communal treat area and went back to Mia. I gave her a carrot and let myself into her stall. She nuzzled up to me, and I put her halter on and gave her the rest of the carrots.

The carrots worked like a charm. Mia was all loving and snuggly. I put the lead rope on her halter and led her out of the barn. She was quick in her step as she seemed to think that her rear end was in danger of being nibbled. Although she wasn't very big, she was extremely strong. The grass seemed to call her name, and as soon as we were outside, she found the greenest area and started eating.

"Well, there. Are you happy now, Ms. Mia?" She answered me with a content neigh. "Thought so."

I stroked her bay coat, which was warm from the sun. She was so beautiful. It made me wonder why no one had bought her yet. I looked over at the other paddocks and saw the other horses looking longingly at the grass, and although they were outside, they weren't close to the grass.

Being out there reminded me of when I used to cool out Jenna's horses. I loved being her groom. I would have loved to be the one riding too. I hoped that she was okay and that she had found my letter. I wondered if Kat had been able to dissuade Martha from looking for me. I needed to mail my mom's letter so she would have her mind at ease, and then I could at least breathe easier.

Mia continued to walk me around to the places where she saw the greenest grass. I let her lead me as I didn't feel like fighting her. I didn't have much longer before Jen would need my help. I took a deep breath of the summer air and let it out, trying to numb my worries.

I heard a voice say to me, "I will never leave you or forsake you."

I looked around, but I didn't see anyone. My mom had told me stories about how God had talked to her. Was it that? "God, is that you?" I stayed quiet and closed my eyes again.

I heard that voice again, "I will never leave you or forsake you."

Something stirred within my heart, and I felt a sense of peace that I hadn't felt since leaving home.

I really needed to talk to my mom, but it just wasn't possible. Instead, I gathered up the lead rope and decided to bring Mia in. I wasn't sure what had just happened, but I was sure that it was something that had the potential to change the course of my life.

I spent the rest of the afternoon staying busy with camp and doing what I could to speed up the time before Ian would come to pick me up. I still needed to shower and change before Ian came. I tried to clean my boots so that I wouldn't look like such a barn girl, although seeing as Ian had only seen me at the barn, I figured it wouldn't be a huge deal.

I checked the time again, hoping that Ian wouldn't be early, as there was no way that I'd be ready before seven. The shower was a quick one, and I decided to dry my hair and keep it down for tonight. I put on the jeans I had been wearing earlier and another one of the shirts that Ian gave me. As I was putting on the finishing touches, I heard a knock at my trailer. My heart skipped a beat. Was that him already? I crossed over to the door and opened it. Phew. It was Tanis.

"Hey, Rain, you look pretty."

"Thanks. Come on in."

She walked into the trailer, and I peered out to see if I could see the Impala. No Ian yet.

"Is it almost time for your date with Ian?"

"Yes"—I gulped—"do you still think it's a good idea?"

"Yeah, here's the phone that you can use in case you need to." She handed me a small black flip phone, which I put into my back pocket. "My number is programmed as speed dial 1, so if you run into any problems at all, call me."

"Thanks so much." I saw a car come into the parking lot through my kitchen window, and sure enough, it looked like Ian's. "I think he just pulled in." I started to get flustered as I realized I still needed to brush my hair out and put on my boots.

"It's okay. I'll go have a word with him. You finish getting ready. And, Rain, please be careful."

"I will. Don't worry."

Tanis smiled at me and let herself out. True to her word, I saw her go and meet Ian in the parking lot. I hoped she wouldn't scare him away.

I brushed my hair, put on my ChapStick, and quickly laced up my black boots. "Well, here goes nothing."

Ian saw me come outside, and it looked like he had been having a good chat with Tanis, which helped me relax a bit. They both smiled at me.

"Hi, Rain. Are you ready for our night on the town?" Ian was dressed in jeans too, which encouraged me.

"As ready as I'll ever be." I smiled weakly at him.

"You two have fun, but don't keep her out too late as she gets up pretty early." Tanis waved at us then headed back to the house with a couple of the dogs following her.

Kat was teaching a lesson in the outside ring, and there were still people coming and going, but it seemed as though no one was paying us much attention, which suited me just fine.

Ian opened the car door for me, and I got in. It was probably the first time any guy had ever done that for me. He got in the other side and then turned his charming smile on me. "What's your favorite place around here to get a bite to eat?"

"Uh, I'm new around here, so I don't really know. Besides, I don't eat out much."

"So it's up to me to decide then?"

"Nothing too fancy as I'm not dressed for that."

"Ha, neither am I. Not to worry. So do you have a cell phone with you?"

"Yes, and they're expecting me to call in a couple of hours." I wiped my hands nervously on my jeans.

"Good. I mean, you don't know me very well. I hope you feel like you can trust me." And at that, he started his car.

"So, where to then?"

He backed out of the parking lot, and as he did, I felt as though I was leaving my safety net.

"It's a surprise. Do you feel like eating first or going for a walk?"

"Definitely eating. Sorry, but after the day I put in, food would be great." For some reason, I was comfortable with Ian, even though he made my heart flutter.

"Okay, food it is. I'm hoping you'll tell me a bit more about yourself. I sense there's some mystery with you."

"I'll tell you what I can, but I can't promise mystery. I'll try to keep you interested though."

"That I'm not worried about, Rain." Ian glanced at me and then back to the road.

I wasn't sure where he was taking me, but I recognized some of the places we were passing from when I had walked in the area. It didn't take very long before Ian pulled into a funky-looking restaurant. Ian appeared a bit more dressed up than I did, with his dark jeans and light plaid shirt. Even though I had tried to clean my boots, there was still no denying it—they were barn boots.

"Ian, you do know that I'm not in anything fancy, right?"

He smiled over at me with a twinkle in his brown eyes. "You're perfect just as you are. Don't worry." He opened his car door and came over to let me out. "Let's go have some fun, Rain."

"Sounds good." I had to smile back at him, as his smile was infectious.

Ian took my hand as he led me into the restaurant. I was sure that my palms were sweaty, but at least I knew I didn't smell like the barn.

The host led us to a nice, quiet table in the dining room. The place looked as if it had once been a tack room that was converted into a restaurant. It was perfect. The booths appeared to have been made of different trees as they didn't match, but they were cool-looking. Ian ordered for us a couple of glasses of water and Diet Cokes. I wasn't usually quiet, but I felt like letting him take charge of ordering.

"So, Rain, what do you feel like having tonight?" Ian leaned over his menu and looked expectantly at me.

I needed to find my personality and fast, or this would definitely be a one-time date. "What's good? Have you been here a lot?" Apparently, that was funny to him as he laughed to himself. "What's so funny about that?"

"Well, if truth be told, I kind of found this spot and thought of you, but I haven't tried it yet. We'll have to see if the food's as good as the atmosphere. I think I might get a burger. They look tasty."

"Yeah, that sounds like a plan, and some fries too." I then looked back down at the menu to avoid his eyes. Although I knew nothing about Ian, I got the feeling that I could trust him at his word, and I would feel better if I unburdened myself a bit.

The server came over, and we placed our orders, and I lost my menu to hide behind. Ian took a sip of his pop then looked back at me. I seemed to have nothing to say for the first time in my life.

"Rain, why don't you tell me about yourself?" He put his glass back on the table and leaned over as if to hear me better. The music wasn't too loud but loud enough so that we wouldn't be overheard.

"Uh, well, there's not too much to tell," I said nervously.

"I find that hard to believe. Here you are living at the barn, and I've been there a few times, so I know you haven't been there long. I also know you told me that you didn't have a lot of clothes with you, so I surmised you may have had to make a quick getaway. Am I close?"

I didn't wrestle with myself for long. Ian's brown eyes drew me in. I also knew that he had no contact with my former life. I swallowed hard and proceeded to tell some of my story. "Truth be told, you're pretty spot on, but what I tell you has to stay between us."

"As I mentioned earlier, you can trust me. Blabbing your story won't help me if I want to take you out again, now would it?" Ian finished that sentence with a smile.

I answered him with a laugh. "You'd actually want to take me out again, even though I've hardly spoken two words?"

"You're speaking now, aren't you? I have a good feeling about you. Now how about you tell me what you're running from and why you had to flee so quickly?"

"I can't go into all the details, but I'm sure you're familiar with the story of Cinderella." He nodded. "I practically was her. It wasn't the cleaning that bothered me, nor taking care of my sisters and brothers. It was my stepmother's anger. I couldn't handle it anymore. She had abused me from the time I was eight, both physically and verbally. Then one day she lost her temper on me one too many times, so I decided it was time to leave."

"I'm not sure what I expected you to say, but it wasn't that. You're not going back there, that's for sure."

I was surprised at how mad Ian seemed to be getting. "I'm not planning on going back, although I ache to be near my youngest sister again. The thing is, I may have to make a move before too long. My stepmother doesn't like to lose a battle, and so far, she is losing this one." I took a sip of my pop before continuing. Ian stayed quiet, so I went on. "The tides have turned though. Tanis told me that she was going around the different barns asking about me." I couldn't believe I was telling him all this information, but maybe he could help.

"Rain, you've told Tanis the truth?"

"I had to, or she might have called the authorities on me. I also couldn't get her in trouble after she's been so nice to me."

"But you're an adult, so they can't just take you without your consent."

I should have come clean about my age, but I wasn't ready. So I took another sip of pop instead. I was a terrible liar. Thankfully, our food arrived, so I didn't have to answer that last remark, or so I thought. We both looked over our burgers. My stomach rumbled. After all the work I had done, I was ready to enjoy dinner.

"Enjoy your burger," Ian said.

"You too."

We ate in silence, but then Ian circled back to the age thing.

"So why do your parents think that they can still control you?"

"It isn't because of my age, but when you've been under their control for years, then it's hard to break out of it."

"Hmm. Well, you need to break out of it, and if you need help, I can help you."

"I don't know how you can help me, but I appreciate the support."

"Are you sure the barn is the safest place for you, seeing as your stepmother is already snooping around other barns looking for you?"

"So far, it is. Tanis and Kat are willing to help protect me, and everyone is so friendly. Of course, I love being around the horses too. I'm basically doing my dream job right now, so as long as I can stay, I will."

We both finished our meals, and when the server returned, Ian asked for the dessert menu. He apparently knew me better than I thought.

"What's your choice for dessert?"

"Anything that has chocolate in it works for me. Chocolate's my weakness. Well, chocolate and peanut butter, that is."

"It looks like it's your lucky night, Rain! Look, there's a peanut butter cookie with ice cream on the menu." He showed me the menu, and sure enough, there was a large peanut butter cookie on it. "Are you in?"

"I'm in, if you'll share it with me."

"Done." Ian ordered it with coffee for the two of us. I really shouldn't have been having coffee seeing as I had to get up so early but decided to go for it. "So will you let me help you?"

"I'll let you know if you can, but for now, I think I'm all right. I do, however, need to let my dad know I'm okay, but Tanis is helping me with that."

"Be careful of that. Won't he tell your stepmother?"

"Probably, but I can't have him stressed out because of me."

"If he lets your stepmother treat you that way, then he doesn't deserve to know what you're up to."

"Yeah, I can understand that, but I still don't want him to worry. Besides, it's not all his fault. He's working a lot, so he's not there to intervene for me."

"I don't care, working or not! Your dad's job is to protect you and not allow you to get hurt by fleeing the scene of the crime. You may be an adult, but if you've been going through all this, it isn't fair on you."

The server came by with refills for us, which was probably a good thing, as Ian and my conversation was getting a bit too intense for a first date, if it was a date.

I avoided Ian's eyes and got back to my dessert. This was the best meal I had eaten in days. For that alone, I felt a little indebted to Ian. I really wanted to change the subject, but I wasn't too sure how.

"So, Rain, it looks like you're enjoying this place." I nodded in agreement. "Does that mean you'd trust me for a second date?"

At this, I flushed a bright crimson red. This was a date! I swallowed hard before answering. "Well, uh, if I stay at the barn, I'd have to say yes. I'd be happy to go out with you again." I smiled at him, and he seemed to match my happiness.

"That's good to hear, and let me know if you want to hit the local Walmart to pick up some essentials."

"That would be super helpful, although I'm not sure when I get paid. I'll keep you posted. Hey, what did Yasmin think of Calvin?"

"Oh, she liked him, but she was really set on Eye, so it's hard for her to change her mind. I heard that Mia is for sale too, so she might look at her as well."

"Mia?" My heart dropped. Oh, I so wanted to ride her. "Yeah, I heard that she might be for sale too."

"What's wrong with Mia?"

"Nothing. She's just really special, or I think she is, although I've only just met her. Would you keep her at A&T?"

"To start, we would, as we don't have enough land at home."

"Oh, good. Well, I'm sure she'll love her, and I'll give her some tips of dealing with her in her stall; she can be a bit of a princess."

"Point taken. So she's a high-maintenance pony, is she?"

I had to laugh at the way he put that. "Yes, yes, that's right."

We had finished our dessert, and our server was back to thank us for coming and dropped off the bill. I went to look at my watch to see what time it was, but it seemed in my excitement, I had forgotten to put it on. I was sure I needed to get back, but I didn't really want to finish this lovely evening of escape. Ian paid the bill, and I took a deep breath. Back to reality, which meant that I still was no closer to finding a solution to my problems.

"All ready to go, Rain?"

"Sure thing. I have to thank you again. This was pretty amazing, and dessert was divine!"

"Glad you thought so." Ian got up and came to my side to pull my chair out for me. Yes, it had been worth the wait to go out with a guy like this.

Chapter 8

As I set my alarm later that evening, I couldn't help but relive the entire evening. From start to finish, it had been the perfect date. I really hoped that Ian would be back at the barn soon. Most of the chaos from the day had died down by the time I arrived back, so I really only needed to talk to Tanis and tell her that Ian was a perfect gentleman. She was relieved, although not too surprised. If she hadn't expected that, she would have made more of a fuss about my going out with him.

Tanis didn't have any news for me, either good or bad, regarding my renegade ways. She also seemed to side with Ian on the matter of not telling my dad where I was yet. She did mail my letter to my mom and told me that if we could at least tell one parent where I was, it would lessen the trouble that I could get into. If only in my haste I had taken my mom's number with me. But it wasn't as if my mom and I were really close. My dad made a point of not making that possible. When I thought of my mom, I felt hope.

I closed my eyes and took a deep breath. The morning would be here soon enough, and I needed my sleep. Tonight I was determined to dream of all things horsey and not of fleeing the scene of my captivity.

Beep, beep, beep. There it was, my alarm. I smacked it off and stretched out on my bed. Where was I again? Oh right, with the horses in my little trailer. Before the panic started in like it usually did, I remembered…Ian and our lovely date. I woke up for the first time in days with a smile on my face instead of dread. That did it. I needed to get ready for my day of work. There it was again, the grumbling of my stomach. After being so well-fed last night, it was back to kicking up a storm. I would need to fix this problem if I was going to keep my strength up.

I got up and headed to the kitchen and opened up the fridge knowing full well it would be empty when, to my astonishment, there was food in it! What, when did this happen? I saw a note tacked onto a loaf of bread. It read:

Rain,

Here is a little something to keep you nourished as you work with us. See you soon.

Tanis

"Tanis, I love you!" I practically yelled. "God, if you are there, thank you." I couldn't help but think this all couldn't be coincidence. I looked at the clock. I didn't have much time, but I could make a quick sandwich and take it with me. I didn't wait. I made my breakfast, put my hair in a ponytail, washed up, was out the door with minutes to spare and got to work.

I made it out to the small barn in time to see both Lindsey and Jen arriving for work. Today would go fast if all three of us were on. *There must be camp today,* I thought. I walked over to them, allowing the early morning sun to bathe over my face.

"Someone's in a good mood," Lindsey said while giving me one of her sarcastic grins.

"Who, me?" I blushed.

"So spill, Rain. How was your date?" Jen chimed in.

I wasn't used to being the center of attention, but there was no way I was going to get out of this one. So I came clean. "Well, it was pretty amazing, actually." I smiled in spite of myself.

"I knew it. See, I told you, Jen. Older men, they know how to treat a woman."

"He's not that much older than me," I squeaked.

"Sure, Rain. It's all good. I'm happy to see you up with a smile on your face." Lindsey patted my arm.

"Well, ladies, let's feed the beasts. Time waits for no man or woman," Jen said in a friendly yet efficient voice.

We walked to the barn and got our stuff together. Lindsey started with the feeding of the grain, and Jen and I took care of the hay. A few of the horses started banging on the stalls as soon as we entered.

"Hey, Jen, is there camp today?" I asked as I maneuvered around Coco in her stall.

"Yeah, and it's advanced camp, so Kat is teaching it. There's been quite a bit of buzz about it, so I expect us to be busy all day. We have volunteer staff starting at eight and camp begins at nine."

"How exciting." I always wished I could actually ride in advanced camp, but I wasn't ever good enough, or I always needed to be Jenna's groom. Oh well, at least I got to be around horses. *Jenna*—I gulped—*would she come to a camp like this?* I stopped feeding as a shock wave coursed through me. Lindsey must have noticed that something was wrong with me, because when I looked up, she was in front of me with an expression of worry on her face.

"Rain, what's wrong? Are you okay?"

"Um, do you know the names of the people coming today?"

"Not offhand. Why?"

"Can you please tell me when you find out if there's a Jenna Stevenson on the list?"

"Sure, sure. I promise, I'll let you know as soon as I find out. And here I thought you were hoping that Yasmin would be on the list."

"What? Oh yeah, Ian's sister. You can tell me that too." I chuckled, and it seemed to break my shock from moments ago.

"Deal." Lindsey went on to the next horse, and I did my best to maintain my good mood.

Before I knew it, we were finished feeding and halfway through mucking out stalls. I couldn't wait to go see Mia. I wondered when I could actually get on a horse as my legs ached to ride again. I decided to be brave and ask Jen about this. *No time like the present,* I thought.

"Jen, do you know when I'd be able to do my assessment ride?"

She looked up from Ellie's stall and smiled. "Actually, we were going to surprise you and let you do it tonight, provided you were free and not out on a date with your new man."

"Really? Oh, that would be fabulous!" I would double my efforts at cleaning after this news. I had found hope again. This was the reason I couldn't give up.

"Rain, you haven't stopped since you've been here, so we thought it was about time. You definitely know your way around horses, so let's see what you can do on one." She laughed at her own humor. I joined in as I was seriously happy.

I left Jen and continued with my duties. I had a spring in my step that I hadn't had for years. Joy, that was what was bubbling up inside of me.

What a different way of life I had found in the past week. I had found people who seemed to like me for me and people who cared with no ulterior motive. It was foreign to my upbringing, but I was willing to embrace it. If only I could legally separate myself from my father and emotionally from my stepmother. I couldn't go back to my captivity. "Please, God, make this real," I pleaded, not knowing if anyone would answer my plea.

Then I heard that voice again, "I will never leave you or forsake you."

Who is that? I wondered. What were those words that seem so familiar yet distant? I needed to talk to my mom. I was sure that she could help me.

Finally, I was at my favorite bay's stall. "Hello, Ms. Mia, how are you today?" I had picked up a carrot on my way to her so I could bring a peace offering to her.

Sure enough, she came over to me, sniffed my hands, and took the carrot.

"Hi, pretty girl, I've come to clean your stall, so be good, okay?" I gave her the remaining carrot and let myself into her stall. I petted her beautiful face, amazed at her kind eyes. "You are a horse of truth, aren't you? No one gets anything over you, do they?" She looked at me once more and playfully nudged my hands, looking for more treats. "That's all I have, Ms. Mia, but I'll be back with more, I promise."

"You do love that horse, don't you?" It was Lindsey who was in the stall across from me.

"Yeah, something about her seems to speak to me. Besides, I think she'd be a challenge, and apparently, I like challenges."

"Yup, she's a challenge, but I love riding her, and her canter is amazing. She's fast and strong, needing a firm hand, but you'd love her."

"Do you have a horse here?"

"No. I have one in New Brunswick. She's a palomino. Her name is Larkspur, but we call her Lark. I know, silly Canadian ponies. I don't know where they get these names. Actually, her full name is Fair-weather Flic Larkspur."

"Haha, that's quite a name. My sister's horse's show name was Sugar and Spice, which is pretty boring in comparison. We called her Sugar for short though.

"Yeah, that's a little easier than my pony. Can you imagine being ten and having to say all that? Lark is so beautiful and so much fun to ride. I miss her so much. My dad is actually threatening to sell her since I don't live there anymore, but I can't bear the thought. I've had her forever!"

"Oh, I hope that doesn't happen. I know what that's like. I loved my sister's horse. She was such a lovely pony, but my sister outgrew her, and eventually, we had to sell her. Even though she wasn't mine, I felt the loss, as I was her groom. I helped nurse her back to health when she was sick." I moved around Mia while Lindsey and I were reminiscing. Mia looked a lot like a larger version of Sugar, which was maybe what drew me to her to begin with.

"Well, Mia, I've got to go, but I'll be back." I got a little nudge, and I took that as a favorable response.

"It looks like you're growing on her," Lindsey said.

"I hope so, as I really want to ride her, and if she likes me, that'll help."

"Absolutely, or at least it's a start." We both moved on to our next stalls just in time for Jen to come by with fresh sawdust for the ponies.

"How are we doing timewise?" I asked Jen, as I forgot my watch again.

"Not too bad, although we need to make sure we're done with the stalls before nine. The volunteers can do the blowing. Then we can tack up the ponies. Mind you, most of the people riding today have their own horses. We also need to make room for the people who are bringing their own horses today."

"Well, we only have a couple more stalls to do, then I can take the ponies outside for you," I offered.

"Sounds like a plan. I've written on the whiteboard what horses we need for nine and who's going out. Oh, and, Rain, I don't have the list of people coming today, but Kat will be here soon, so I'll check it over."

"Thanks so much, Jen. I owe you huge!"

"Not a problem. Hey, Lindsey, I hope Beckah comes today as I could really use a coffee."

"Me too. I told Rain about her and told her she needs to get to know her for her coffee alone."

"I do like my coffee too. In fact, Tanis has been nice enough to have been supporting my caffeine addiction so far."

"Yeah, Tanis has been wonderful, especially to runaways like us."

"Agreed," I said with gusto.

We finished our stalls and started to move the horses around to make room for the visitors. As I was taking Nippy out, I saw that Kat had arrived and was going over the camp details with Jen. *Please, please, no Jenna. Although truth be told, I would love to see her. Can she keep her mouth shut about me?*

When I came back into the barn, Jen came back over to me with concern etched into her brows.

"What is it?" I asked.

"Well, I have good news and bad news."

"Give me the bad first. I might as well get it over with." My heart dropped because the truth was, I already knew the bad news.

"Okay. Well, Jenna is on the list for the morning. She should be here anytime as the visitors are here early."

"And what can be the good news?"

"Well, it seems silly now, but I was going to tell you that Yasmin is also on the list for today, but I'm sure that will seem unimportant to you now."

"Yeah, I would have been excited, but how can I earn my keep if I can't be seen?"

"Rain, don't worry about that. We need to devise a plan so that you aren't found here."

"It's not seeing Jenna I'm worried about, but I'm sure she'll be coming up with her mother. Usually, she doesn't stay, so maybe I could even talk to Jenna."

"Or maybe if Ian comes up here with Yasmin, he could take you away for a bit."

"Jen, I can't leave my job. I have work to do, and I can't let Tanis down either, not after all she's done for me."

"Hmmm, look, we're about done here. Go talk to Tanis, and you two can figure out what to do. In the meantime, Lindsey and I will finish up here."

"Okay, thanks so much, and I'm so sorry."

It wasn't more than five minutes later that I saw my stepmother's car, pulling the small trailer behind her, drive into my sanctuary. I put my head down and made a beeline for my trailer, and without a second to spare, I made it inside without her seeing me.

I locked the door behind me, banging it slightly. I then moved quickly and peered out the small window just in time to see my little sister, my reason for living for so many years, get out of the car. That was when I made my mind up that no matter the consequences, I would find a way to talk to her.

Chapter 9

There I stood, rooted on the spot, watching Jenna take out Beanie, her new horse. Beanie seemed to be behaving himself. He wasn't very large at only 15.1 hands, but he was a horse and a step up from her pony, Sugar. I never got to know him much though, so I wasn't as attached to him. He was a good-looking horse, gray with a kind face and a willing nature. He would be a good horse for her to move up in the showing circle. Jenna had always done well, having won quite a few championships, and her room was covered in ribbons. I had actually made her a board in shop class so that she could display her ribbons.

My happiness dissipated as I saw my stepmother come to the side of the trailer that Jenna was on. Fear rippled through me, and I almost jumped as I heard a knock at my door. I knew it wasn't Martha as I was looking at her, but I moved slowly to open my door.

All I felt was relief as Tanis came into view. I ushered her in without saying a word. She closed the door behind her and pulled the curtains closed to block the truth of what was happening in front of me. I turned to face Tanis, who looked as concerned as I felt.

"So, Rain, it looks like your fear has become a reality. I need to know what I can do to help you. I have a couple of ideas, but I want to make sure it's okay with you."

"Well, I know I can't hide out here all day. I mean, how can I earn my keep hiding in here?"

"Rain, that is the last thing on my mind. Never mind about that. I want to keep you safe, and I can see by the look on your face that your stepmother scares the daylights out of you."

"Well, she doesn't usually stay with Jenna. But, Tanis, I really want to talk to Jenna. I miss her so much."

"Can you risk it?"

"She won't tell on me. She hasn't in the past, and she knows all the bad stuff I used to do." I started pacing in my small space. I had to talk to her. There was just no way I couldn't.

"How about I find out if your stepmother's staying? If she doesn't, I'll let you know, and you can make up your mind then. In the meantime, do you want to maybe call Ian and see if he wants to take you out of here for a while?"

"I do have his number, but I heard that Yasmin is coming today, so I could wait on that. Besides, I hardly know him, and I don't want to become a burden to anyone. In fact, maybe I've made a huge mistake. I should just go out now and surrender." There it was, my resolve crumbling.

"No, I will not let you do that. Anything but that. Listen, give me ten minutes to assess the situation. Jen said that you and Lindsey got everything done this morning, and there's lots of people to help. You just take an early lunch break and leave the rest to me. I'll see you soon. Stay put, okay?"

"Okay, I'll stay put. Oh, and, Tanis, thanks for the food and everything else you've done for me." My voice cracked; I couldn't keep it in. My hard shell was crumbling.

"It's okay, Rain." She put her arms around me and gave me a hug. I hugged her back, just being thankful for her. "Now it'll be okay. I'll see you soon, and don't worry. I'll take care of things." I let go of her and watched her leave.

Mary would be so very angry if she knew what was taking place right beside her. Martha, was she still there? I opened the curtains slowly and peeked outside. There was a flurry of activity, but I couldn't see Martha or Jenna for that matter. I did, however, happen to see a certain Impala enter the driveway, and that was it. There went my heartbeat into double time.

"Great, this is just what I needed today," I said under my breath. I walked away from the window and decided to brush out my hair and put on some gloss just in case. How could I be vain amid all the drama happening? It didn't matter. If Ian might happen to see me, I had to be presentable. After brushing out all the knots, I decided to do a low braid, and I changed into my only other top. I was sure I smelled of horse and hay, but a different shirt would help.

I was about to go check out the window again when I heard another knock at my door. Was that ten minutes already? I hurried over to let who I was sure would be Tanis in, but to my surprise, I opened the door to Ian. I was almost too overcome with shyness to even speak.

"Hi, Rain, how are you?" There he was, dressed in fitted faded blue jeans and a dark- and light-blue plaid shirt. I remembered I'd better let him in before anyone saw me.

"Hi, come in, come in."

"Nice to see you. You look nice."

"Well, you may have picked out the top, so you could be biased."

"Nope, you always look nice."

"Seriously, you're too kind. Where are my manners? Come have a seat. Does Tanis know you're here?"

"Yeah. Actually, she suggested I come and see you, which surprised me a bit, maybe seeing as I brought you back unharmed last night. I'm growing on her."

"Yeah, something like that. Actually, Ian, I'm in a bit of a bind." I wrung my hands nervously.

"How can I help?"

"I may need to get out of here for a bit. My past hasn't taken a long time to catch up with me."

"What, is your stepmom here?"

"I'm afraid so." I looked away from him as I was almost embarrassed that my plan had been so faulty.

"You okay, Rain? I mean, are you frightened? Do you want me to go have a word with her?"

"Ha, like that would help. No, no, nothing like that. I'm hoping that she just drops Jenna and then leaves. I have work to do, and I don't want to slough off my responsibilities or be a burden to anyone, especially Tanis."

"Well, I can be your lookout, if you'd like. I can go see what's happening, and I'll repot back like a good Boy Scout."

"Ian, you hardly know me. I really don't want to be any trouble."

"It's no trouble." Ian put his strong hand on my shoulder. Bang went my heart again. Could he hear it? "I'll be back in a minute. Hang tight and don't worry."

I just nodded at him.

As soon as he left, I went back to my post at the window. I saw Martha talking to Tanis and noticed that Jenna had already moved Beanie into the barn. If only Martha would leave, then my plan could become a reality. I watched Ian move by Tanis, looking ever so slightly toward my trailer. I ducked, just in case Martha saw me. I was sure she would be able to sense my presence here.

At least five minutes passed by before I dared look out the window again. It looked as if Tanis was helping Martha remove the trailer, so that could only mean that she was going! I wanted to jump for joy, but I stayed rooted on the spot, almost holding my breath. I guessed that Ian was helping his sister because he hadn't come back into view. I felt so crippled between the fear in my heart and excitement welling up within me with the thought of seeing Jenna.

Finally, I heard a knock at my door. It had to be Tanis. Martha must have left. I opened it up, and it was Ian again. I gulped and smiled at him. "Tell me you have good news for me, please."

"Well, you are no longer a prisoner in your trailer, if that's what you mean. However, I told Tanis your plan, and she's not sure that you're being wise. Are you sure your sister will keep your secret?"

"Yes, yes, she will. But if she doesn't, well, you can get me out of here, right?" Was I flirting now? Jeepers. I was hooked!

"Okay, I surrender, and I'm glad that after one date, I have you convinced that I'm a good guy. Speaking of which, I may have brought you something."

I moved back away from the entrance, and he followed me into the little kitchen. We both sat down on the seat by the table. I tried to dry my now sweaty palms on my jeans. I began, "I do think there's something trustworthy about you, and I'm pretty sure that I've never met anyone quite like you. So it seems you've got me there."

"Good to hear that you've confirmed it. I knew you were a smart young woman." He practically sparkled as he talked. Between his slight accent and his charm, I was fast getting my heart involved.

I was getting more courageous with him now. I was even flirting back. "Haha, yup, and that confirms what I thought about you…"

"And what is that?"

"That you're a charmer."

He gave me one of his sideways grins. "Who, me?"

I chuckled under my breath. "Yes, you, mister."

"Well, on that note, would you like your surprise?"

"Sure, although you've already given me so much with all the clothes."

"It's just a small thing. Here you go."

I took the gift bag that he had been hiding from me. It was simple yet really nice. The bag was a light yellow with pale green tissue paper coming out of the top. I held it gingerly, not really believing Ian's kindness.

"You can open it, Rain."

"Thanks. Okay, here goes nothing." I reached past the tissue paper and pulled out a small box. "What is it?"

"Haha, you need to open it up to see."

I opened up the box to find a beautiful watch with a picture of a horse that resembled Mia on the face of it. "Ian, this is beautiful, but I can't accept it. It's too much."

"Here, let me help you with that. I saw it in a little gift shop and thought that you had to have it. It looks like I was right." He took the box and opened it up for me, setting the time on the watch, while I watched in awe.

"Ian, I love it, but really, it's too much."

"Nonsense. I thought the horse looked like Mia, and you seem to really like her. Here, give me your arm, and I'll put it on you." As stunned as I was, I gave him my right arm, and he put it on for me. "Are you left-handed?"

"No, I'm not, but I think like a lefty, and well, I do things like lefties do."

"Noted. There, it looks great and fits you perfectly."

I admired my new arm candy. It was beautiful, with a brown band and light-colored background behind the Mia look-alike. "Thanks so much." I was so touched that I reached over and gave

Ian a hug, noticing how safe I felt in his arms. I pulled away quickly before he could misconstrue my actions as anything other than friendship. I looked down, embarrassed by my actions, and wished that my hair was down so I could hide my face. When I could look up, I saw Ian was smiling like a Cheshire cat.

"Well, Rain, I have more good news for you."

"What else could top this lovely gift?"

"I offer you the gift of a bit of freedom. Your stepmother has pulled out for the afternoon, so you have options. One is hanging out with me, but the other option, which I don't like much, is you talking to your sister. Tanis said that you can have the afternoon off if you'd like. The clinic is over at four, so you could help with lessons afterward. What do you think?"

"I think I need to see Jenna, although hanging out with you for the day does sound pretty wonderful."

"I'm not going anywhere. Yasmin is going to ride Calvin in the clinic, so I'm here for a while, and if I need to take you out of here, I can. You still have my number, right?"

"Yeah, I do." I looked around, trying to remember where I put Tanis's cell that she gave me.

"Good. It's settled. Do you need to get anything, or are you ready to face the world?"

"I think I'm ready."

"Then let's go." Ian got up and helped me to my feet, not that I needed help. My face flushed at the touch of his hand in mine. I really needed to get a grip and fast. "The girls are just getting tacked up, and Tanis told me you'd find your sister in the big barn down by Mia."

We clambered out of my trailer, which I locked behind us, but all of a sudden, I was weak with the thought of what I was about to do. Was I making the right decision? I moved my feet slowly in the direction of the big barn, and Ian slowed his pace to mine. He must have sensed my nervousness because he put a reassuring hand on my shoulder and whispered that it would all be okay. Where was this kind of protection all my life, and why on earth did Ian care so much? I couldn't speak but nodded at him confidently.

As we entered, I told him that I'd better do this alone. He nodded, although he looked unsure. I continued my slow pace until I came to Mia's stall. Sure enough, I heard Jenna's voice as she talked to Beanie. There was no going back now. My heart soared at the sound of her, my sister, whom I missed so much! I stroked Mia's head softly, willing her strength to help me.

I peered into the stall and saw Jenna decked out in her riding attire, her long blond hair in a braid underneath her helmet. Beanie was tacked up, just waiting for Jenna to put on the bridle. I took one deep breath and stood in her view.

"Jenna." That was all I could muster.

She turned around, disbelief then relief flashing over her fine features. "Rose, Rose, is that really you?" She put the lead rope over Beanie and rushed over to me, throwing her arms around me. She squeezed me so tight I thought I would break.

"Jenna, Jenna, I've missed you so much!" I hugged her back, not wanting to let her go and not wanting to answer the questions that I knew were bound to come. She pulled away and searched my face. I saw all the love in the world in her glistening blue eyes. Then I saw what I was dreading—hurt. It was the hurt that I had caused her.

"Why, Rose? Why did you have to leave me? I have been worried sick about you. We all have. I know you don't believe it, but you are such a vital part of the family. And Dad...Dad has been going out of his mind with worry. We imagined the worst. You've left before, but never like this."

"I know, and I'm sorry. I really am, but I couldn't take it anymore. I know she's your mother, but she pushed me too far. Did you at least get the note I left for you?"

"I did, but I only found it after you'd been gone for two days, and I was already distraught. Rose, without you, life isn't the same. You have to know that."

"I do, trust me. But, Jenna, I can't go back. I just can't. These people here, well, they've taken me in and given me a home."

"You have a home with us, you know, your family."

It was so hard to resist her, but I had to. "Jenna, my family can't include your mother. It just can't. And Dad will never see my side of the story. You and I both know that."

"I don't know what to say. But, Rose, I just miss you so much." She embraced me again, and this time, it was my eyes that filled with tears. Could I really do this? Could I stay away?

Just then, we heard Jen's voice in the barn calling all the advanced students to the outdoor arena.

I let go of Jenna and braved a smile. "You better go. You don't want to be late for Kat. Here, dry your eyes, and I'll bridle Beanie." I picked up the bridle, took off his halter, and got him ready for Jenna. Just like old times, I thought, but it wasn't, as I was now free. "Here you go." I handed the reins to Jenna. "Listen, we'll talk more after your lesson. And, Jenna, my name here is Rain, not Rose."

"Rain? You changed your name?" She shook her head in disbelief, the hurt clouding her expression again. She led Beanie out of the stall, and I followed her, catching up with them.

"It's really important you don't blow my cover, okay?" I said, almost pleading with her.

"Sure, Ro—Rain, whatever." She quickened her pace away from me.

"I'll talk to you soon." I didn't bother to catch up this time. I had to let her go, and as much as I wanted to run from where I was, I stayed put. I decided I might as well be useful. Before I could locate Jen, Ian found me. He seemed to come out of nowhere, but there he was, my protector.

Chapter 10

"Rain, how did that go? Was it like you expected?" Ian asked with concern ringing in his voice.

　I stopped and looked into his brown eyes and tried to decide how much to share. I still hadn't even told him my real name or my age for that matter. I decided less would be more. "It went okay. I guess I didn't realize that she'd be mad at me, but I should have expected that. I think she decided not to tell on me, or at least not yet. I was right about my dad though. I need to let him know I'm okay, but if she tells him today, my cover will be blown."

　"I still disagree with you, Rain. I really think he doesn't deserve to know. But in saying that, I understand, you've been put in an unfair place. To be truthful, I can't see why you won't move out as you're old enough. You've finished school, so what's stopping you from staying here?"

　"It's complicated. Listen, I need to go help with camp, but I'll see you later." I tried to walk away, but not before he took my hand and pulled me a bit closer to him.

　"Rain, I'm here for you. Whatever you need, call me anytime. I don't live far from here, and I'm going to watch Yasmin for a bit, so I'll be around. Hang in there, okay?"

　"Okay. Thanks, Ian. I really don't know why you bother, but I appreciate it. Oh, and thanks again for the Mia watch. I love it!" I gave him a big smile, as I was truly touched by his kindness.

　"You're welcome. Let me know if you want me to take you shopping later or out for dinner or whatever." He let go of my hand, and I mumbled thanks again, as I really had to move, or I was going to get on Jen's bad side.

I passed the outdoor arena first and saw that Beanie wasn't behaving himself very well. Jenna was getting coached sternly by Kat as she had let him get away with something. Sure enough, Ian was watching Yasmin, who seemed to be handling Calvin well. I really hoped that she'd fall in love with him so Mia would stay put. Mind you, who knew where I'd end up in the days to come? I left Kat's group and found Jen in the indoor arena working with Lindsey and the other helpers. It looked like she had things under control. She waved me in and asked me if I could start the lunch feeding as they had gotten a bit behind.

I started back in the small barn, and as I worked, my resolve began to waver again. What would it matter if I went back? Was it really so bad? Maybe I had overreacted to the last fight. Life had never been fair, so why was I determined to live a better life now? I allowed my thoughts to go quiet as I focused on the horses. Each horse had such a different personality, just like humans, I thought. As I was staring into the eyes of Nippy, I heard that voice again, "I will never leave you or forsake you." It wasn't exactly audible, but I heard something. I looked around me, but it was just the ponies and me.

"Who are you, and what are you trying to say to me?" I whispered to no one in particular.

I went back to feeding Nippy, but I heard the same thing once more. I needed to get in contact with my mother as I was sure she would have answers for me. I could 411 her number, since I knew where she lived. All I needed to do was ask Tanis if I could use the phone. I'd do this today, no matter what.

A couple of other camp volunteers came and joined me when I started to feed the horses in the big barn. After we got all the feeding done, I noticed that Jenna's group was cooling out their ponies. I wanted to go walk with Jenna and just talk to her like we always used to do with Sugar. I couldn't though. Time wouldn't stand still, not even for me.

Tanis found me as I was putting the wheelbarrows away. "Rain, how are you holding up? Did you talk to Jenna?"

I dusted off my jeans before answering her. I could hardly look in her eyes as I felt too guilty for putting her in this impossible situation. "Yes, yes, I did speak with her… I tried explaining my side of the story. But, Tanis, she's just hurt and worried. To be honest, I think I may have made a huge mistake."

"Rain"—Tanis touched my shoulder and made me face her—"you have made no mistake. The only possible error you may have made is waiting so long to leave. I hope you weren't wrong in trusting her. I think maybe you should give your real mom a call just to be on the safe side. You need a backup plan in case this all goes badly for you."

"I do need to call my mom, but I don't have her number. Would I be able to use your phone later to find it?"

"Of course. Why don't you come to the house now? We'll find it together."

"Thanks so much. I don't know why you and Ian are helping me when you don't even know me." Tears started to well up in my eyes, but I quickly wiped them away. There would be kids coming back into the barn anytime.

"Well, Ian and I may have different motives." She laughed, and I instantly felt better.

"You may be right about that, although he has been a perfect gentleman."

"He'd better be or else… Anyway, it's the least I can do. Now come on."

"I just need to tell Jen where I am."

"Okay. I'll see you in five at the house." She turned from me and started walking toward the house just when Jenna was bringing in Beanie.

I swallowed hard. Those tears wanted to come back up, but I stayed strong. "How was Beanie?" I asked, whether she wanted to talk to me or not.

"Well, *Rain*, thanks to you, we had an awful ride! How do you think it went after seeing my sister whom I've been so worried about turn up before my lesson?" She walked briskly past me, taking her anger out in her gait.

My mouth fell open in disbelief. Wasn't she a bit relieved that I was okay? There was no way she was going to keep my secret at this rate. Even though I probably shouldn't have, I followed her down to the stall Beanie was staying in. I couldn't bear to leave things that way, especially if I was going to leave permanently. Jenna was busily untacking Beanie when I entered the stall.

"Jenna, I need you to understand that I left to protect myself, not to abandon you. Not a moment has passed by that I haven't thought of you. Don't you think I miss you, miss our time together?"

Jenna put Beanie's saddle down, shook her head, then started crying. All I wanted to do was comfort her, but she had been so angry at me a minute ago, so I wasn't sure what to do. But then she looked up at me, and that was all it took. I went to her and put my arms around her small frame.

"I'm so sorry, Jenna. I really am. It's okay. I'll just come home."

She pulled away from me and sniffed. "It's just...I've been so worried about you. I know you said you'd be okay, but I'd never been away from you for this long. I just miss you so much!"

"I miss you too. You're more than a sister, you know that. My heart has ached every day that I've been away." I tried to dry her tears with my T-shirt. "It'll be okay. I'll just come clean, and we'll figure out how to make life work at home."

This time, Jenna stood straighter. "No, Rose. It's selfish of me. You have to do what's best for you. I can see you're happy here, and it looks like you have people here who care about you. I know my mom hasn't treated you fairly. I'd have to be a fool not to see that, but it's just that I don't know how to function without you. You've been there for me since I was born, and now it's my turn to be there for you. I just need you to promise me one thing."

"Name it. Anything." I was practically reeling from Jenna's change of heart toward me.

"Promise you'll find a way to stay in touch with me."

"That I can and will do," I said firmly and then grabbed her for another hug. "You know, they have sleepovers here, and you could stay with me in the trailer."

"Oh, that would be so much fun!"

We were almost laughing now, that is, until we heard it at the same time—Martha's voice. My heart sunk.

"Do you think she heard us?" I whispered.

Jenna shook her head from side to side and put her finger to her lips. "I'll take care of this," she whispered back to me. She gave me one more hug, then stepped out of the stall.

I moved to the other side of Beanie just in case and made sure his tack was out of the way. I then tried to still my breathing and just listened. Jenna was being a little louder than normal for my own benefit.

"Hi, Mom, you're back already. I just finished riding, but I still have cleanup to do."

"That's okay, dear. I'll wait for you. How was Beanie today? Any better than last time?" she said in her thick English accent.

"He wasn't too bad, but we've got a long way to go." It seemed that Jenna's voice was getting farther away, so I figured she'd be steering Martha out of the barn.

I got up from my awkward position and looked out of Beanie's stall. Sure enough, both Jenna and Martha were out of sight, but what to do now? Martha would for sure come and see Beanie for herself. I was close enough to the far exit of the barn that I figured I could sneak around the side of the indoor arena and back to my trailer. Man, I was going to lose this job if I continued to work this way.

I didn't want Beanie to step on his saddle, so I quickly picked it up and put it outside his stall. That was when Jen spotted me.

"Rain, where on earth have you been? I've looking everywhere for you."

I had to fix this before my other plan would work. Yup, the gig could be up, as I was sure I'd be fired. I walked briskly back to Jen when I saw Jenna, and she saw me, but she quickly steered Martha back out of the barn. "Jen, I'm so sorry, but I'm in trouble. I have to hide. It's the woman I'm running from. She's here!"

Jen gasped. "I'm sorry. I didn't know. Go up to the observation deck. Get Christine to let you into the tack room up there so you can hide there." Christine managed the barn with Tanis and was in charge of the office, so she had keys to all the rooms.

"Thanks, Jen. I can't tell you how much I appreciate it."

"Just go. I'll cover for you."

"Jen, can you tell Tanis where I am, please?"

"Sure thing. Good luck."

I waved at her, ducked around the corner, and ran up the stairs, through to the observation deck. I made sure not to run into one of the many cats who lived in the barn. I knocked on the office door, and thankfully, Tanis had briefed her of my situation, so she moved fast and got me into the private tack room. She gave me a horse magazine to help pass the time. I thanked her profusely but didn't actually breathe a sigh of relief until I was settled in the room.

The whole day had been one of close calls, much too close calls. I was grateful for the small light in the room. The tack room smelled so good, like leather and horses. If I wasn't there hiding, I would have been happy just hanging out in there. I walked around admiring the fine saddles and bridles. There was a wall of ribbons on one side as well, most of them Kat's, but I could tell by the titles that Tanis had won some of them too. I really hoped that Martha wouldn't be suspicious of Jenna. At least Jenna hadn't ever been in trouble in her life, and she wouldn't be now. If anyone got in trouble, of course it would be me.

What would be next? Did I want to keep running like this, or was it time to turn myself back into my prison?

Chapter 11

After what seemed like forever, Tanis came and got me out of the tack room. I hadn't felt comfortable touching anything, so I spent most of the time away just worrying. She brought me back to the house, as she wanted to discuss my options with me. I noticed that Yasmin was still fussing over Calvin. I didn't have the heart to look for Ian.

Although the advanced camp was done for the day, there was still lots of activity at the barn, all of which I wasn't a part of due to my personal problems. I felt like one big burden. I should have just left with Jenna, then everyone could have continued with their lives. And yet there I was, back in Tanis's kitchen again and this time with Kat.

Kat shared much of the same features as her mother, and in fact, they looked a lot more like sisters than mother and daughter. She also had shoulder-length blond hair and really pretty bright blue eyes. She had an athletic build, and I could tell that any horse would have a hard time getting away with anything with her. I hadn't yet been taught by either Kat or Tanis, but I had been told that they were both excellent coaches. Kat's students said that she was a firm but fair teacher and had a way of pushing them outside their comfort zone. Kat had a large following of students, and I knew that she had many who competed in upper levels.

Both Kat and Tanis were in their usual gear, breeches, tall black riding boots, and a black-and-red A&T shirt. Black, red, and white were the colors of the barn. The fun tops they had looked good on almost everyone.

I sat down at the table in the small kitchen and waited for them as they got some drinks together in the kitchen. Finally, they joined me at the table.

"So, Rain, I think I have Martha off your trail, at least for now," Tanis said. Kat nodded her head in agreement.

"Really? What makes you think that?" I swallowed hard, not realizing I had been holding my breath.

"Well, she did ask me about you and said that she was looking for her daughter, and she sounded very worried. The good thing for you, Rain, is that I am not easily fooled and can smell a wolf in sheep's clothing a mile away."

"Yes, that's a gift my mom has passed onto me," Kat added.

"That makes me thankful, as you'd be amazed at how many people she's fooled."

"I believe it. She's a good actress. But even in her concern, I could sense that something wasn't right. Now I also spoke to Jenna and told her if she needed help in keeping your secret to call me," Tanis said.

"Tanis, you really are too kind."

"I don't believe any child or young adult should have to go through what you have. I only know a sliver of your story, but I can tell there is much you aren't telling me. In order for us to keep you safe, do you feel ready to contact your mom?"

"Yes, that would be wonderful! Can I use your phone for that?"

"Of course." Tanis got up and handed me the portable phone and some paper so I could jot down her possible number.

I dialed 411 and gave the operator all the information I could. I waited nervously as she checked through the listings. Then she gave me a number. I wrote it down and repeated it back just to be sure. I thanked the operator and ended the call. I played nervously with the pen Tanis gave me. She came over to me and put her hand on my shoulder.

"Are you ready to call her now, or would you like me to?"

I looked back at her. "I don't know why I'm so nervous, but I am. My mom is a good person, but I'm concerned that she'll want to call my dad. Maybe you can start the conversation, and then I can talk to her. What do you think?"

"I think that's a great idea. Here, let me see the number."

I handed it to her, and without wasting any time, she dialed it. I heard the phone ring and thought maybe I'd actually have some more time to think things through. And then it happened. I heard her voice. I was at once relieved but, at the same time, stressed to my max.

"Hello, is this Ruth?"

"Yes, it is. May I ask who is speaking?" she said with concern in her voice.

"You don't know me, but I know your daughter Rose."

"Is she in some trouble?"

"Not exactly, although it seems as though she has had to leave a bad situation at her home. Actually, she left without telling anyone and landed up at my barn. Please, before you worry too much, I want to tell you that she's okay and wants to talk to you."

"I am quite confused, but I would really like to talk to her, and I am sorry if she has caused you any trouble."

"No. She hasn't caused any trouble. She has actually been a lot of help around my barn. I just thought it was important that at least one of her parents know where she is. Here, I will let her explain, and please feel free to talk to me after or later on, if you'd like."

"Thank you, I appreciate all that you've done."

"You're welcome. Here she is." I heard all the conversation and was still fearful when Tanis handed me the phone. "You can do this," she whispered to me.

I nodded back and took the phone. I sat down and took a deep breath. "Uhh, hi, Mom. How are you?"

"How am I? What has happened? You ran away?" she asked, clearly worried about me.

I filled my mom in the best I could, and she got really upset. She was unsurprised that I was having difficulties. She always knew that there was more going on than what was on the surface. It sounded like she wouldn't tell my dad any details, but she did think it was best to at least let him know that I was alright. I agreed with her, as long as no real information was given. She also wanted to come and see me, which again made me relieved, although somewhat nervous.

By the time we finished talking, almost half an hour had gone by, and Tanis had to get back to the barn. Kat was on her way out to teach, but she waited for me to finish. I ended the call with the promise to call again and with her promising to keep her end of the bargain. I would be okay, I thought. I still didn't know what the future would bring, but for now, I was safe.

Kat looked at me reassuringly. "Rain or Rose…actually, I'll stick with Rain so I don't blow your cover. Why don't you have a lesson with me later? I've had a cancellation, and I think it would get your mind off things. I know you like that Mia, but I need to start you on an easier horse. How about Nippy?"

"Really? I can ride today? I don't know what to say…"

"Just be ready to ride at six. Did you bring any breeches or half chaps?"

"No, just jeans."

"It's okay. I'll lend you something. I'll be right back."

As she left, I pondered my fate. How on earth was I lucky enough to get to ride today? Plus, I got to talk to my mom, who wasn't going to turn me in. I really never gave God much thought, but something my mom said stuck with me. They had been praying for me just as recently as before I called. They thought something was amiss, but they didn't know what it was. Before I could linger on that thought too long, Kat came back with a pair of black breeches and half chaps for me.

"Thank you so much. I can't tell you how you have changed my whole day around!"

"You're welcome. Now come on. Let's get back to the horses."

"Sounds great. I'll just put these in the trailer and see you soon."

We left the house together with her pack of dogs following us. While Kat was pulled away by one of her students, I made a beeline to the trailer.

I had another day of freedom.

Chapter 12

Kat was true to her word. After camp was over and the horses were fed, she told me that I could get Nippy ready to ride. The pace of my heart quickened as I groomed Nippy's light-gray, almost-white body. I spoke to her to take it easy on me as it had been a while since I had ridden. Her ears pricked forward as I conversed with her, sharing with her my fears. She wasn't like Mia, but she seemed like a gentle horse, capable of being a good friend of mine.

I found her tack and got her ready to go. I grabbed a helmet and took a deep breath. The barn had quieted down, except for some of the girls who owned their own horses. I had become acquainted with quite a few of them in the short time I was at A&T as it was probably the friendliest barn I'd ever been to.

I led Nippy to the indoor, and Kat welcomed me in. "Hi, Rain, do you feel ready to do this?"

After the day I had, I was more than ready. "Kat, I am beyond excited to do this!" I practically bounded toward the step to get on. The smell of the arena ignited my senses, and suddenly, all thoughts of Martha were behind me.

"Good to hear. Let's get you two warmed up. You know, Nippy was my first horse and remains one of my favorites. I'm sure she'll be just what the doctor ordered."

I was on and led Nippy around the arena, finding the rhythm of her walk underneath me. Kat coached me to press her on, to tuck my butt under and put my heels down. While she started coaching me, I could tell instantly why she was so loved. She was firm but fair and encouraging when you did what she asked. I hadn't had a lesson in forever, so it felt so refreshing. She had me press Nippy onto a trot, so I put my leg on her and began posting trot. Up down, up down, even the steady motion seemed to calm my nerves. My heart had quit its erratic beat and seemed to still with the presence of Nippy's steady hoofbeats.

"You look good on her. How do you like her?" she asked while watching us.

"She's lovely! I feel so confident on her. Will I get to canter her today?" I asked eagerly.

"Ha, we shall see. How about you show me your sitting trot first?"

I obeyed, willing Kat to see that I was ready for more.

"That's good, Rain, but again, tuck your butt under and keep your hands steady. Find her rhythm as you sit on her. Move your hips in time with her. That's better. How does that feel?"

"That feels good. I just have to relax and trust her."

"That's right. Keep doing it like that, and you'll be cantering in no time."

My face lit up in a wide smile. "Thanks, I love cantering and jumping too," I offered.

"I can see you love riding, Rain, that's for sure. Okay, now using your hips, ask her to canter."

I tried to do what she said. I hadn't managed to get a horse to canter by just using my hips, but I did what I remembered, and just like that, we were cantering around the ring. I was sure my teeth would be brown from the arena dirt from smiling so much. This was living! I could face almost anything if I could continue to ride.

Kat had us canter a few more laps before changing direction. I was still in my glory as she coached me through our movements together. Much too soon, my lesson was over, but I was sure that I would sleep soundly tonight. Kat even said that I could ride with her again. I told her that my goal was to ride Mia, and she didn't even laugh at me.

"You know that Mia is for sale?"

"Yes, Lindsey had mentioned it. But there is no way I can afford a horse, as I can hardly afford what life I have."

"Never say never. If you want something bad enough, you never know."

"Thanks, Kat. You have given me hope."

"I'm glad I could help. Just walk her around a couple more times, then you can jump off her."

"The saddest part of riding is getting off," I said dramatically.

"Haha. Yes, that's true. You crack me up, Rain. I'm glad after the stress of the day that you could have some fun."

"Me too. After that close call with Martha, I was a little worried. I still have to hope that Jenna is true to her word."

"Do you have reason not to trust her?" She walked around with us.

"No, but she'll be worried about our dad, and I don't blame her."

"Well, you've had to make a hard choice, but for what it's worth, I think you made the right choice."

"Thanks, Kat, and thank you for the great ride on Nippy."

"My pleasure. It's that sad time, as you say. Time to get off."

I brought Nippy into the middle of the ring and dismounted, petting her after I did. She was a lovely mare with a lot of spunk in her. I walked her out of the arena and took her for a couple of laps around, cooling her off. I basically wanted any excuse to prolong the experience. The night was warm, and the area peaceful. Gone were all the kids who had been at the barn all day. A feeling of hope bubbled up inside me. This was almost foreign to me.

I was off work for the evening, so I took my time grooming Nippy. While I was brushing her, I heard that voice again, and it said, "I will never leave you or forsake you." I wondered out loud where and who it was talking to me. I forgot to mention it to my mom when I talked to her. Could it be God? I was unsure as I hadn't talked to God in years. I had at one time known or thought I knew who God was, but then my life fell apart. I felt...forsaken most of the time. How could God be with me when I endured daily beatings from Martha? How could he be with me when I wasn't allowed to go to school? No, God or god was not with me, although hearing that voice did come with a strange peace.

I decided to tuck the words away as I didn't have time to analyze how God was or was not with me at present. Instead, I went back to finishing up with Nippy and getting some rest. I was on the early shift again the next day, and needed my rest.

I put Nippy away and gave her some extra treats. I decided to check on Mia before heading back to my home. Mia was in the big barn, so I crossed the parking lot when I noticed a certain gray Impala. My heart began to quicken…and there he was. Ian! What was he up to?

He strode over to me, closing the distance between us in a couple of strides. So much for seeing Mia, I thought. There went my heart again. *Thump, thump, thump… Stay cool,* I thought to myself.

"Hi, Rain, I was hoping that I would run into you."

"Uh, hi, Ian. Well, you did." Seriously, what was I saying?

"I see you like the watch I gave you." He smiled at me.

"Yeah, it's great." I looked at my wrist and again marveled at his kindness.

"So are you up to anything tonight?"

"I just finished a lesson, and I was going to say goodnight to Mia. That's about it."

"Are you working early again tomorrow?"

"Yeah, that's the life of a barn helper."

"So is it too late to take you for a coffee?"

"Well, I do smell like a horse, not that I mind, but you might." I looked nervously around me as a couple of people walked by us.

"Well, we could go for a walk around here if you'd rather…"

"Oh, that sounds good. I wouldn't be able to go for long though."

"That's okay. We could go out back. I've been out there with the dogs while Yasmin rides, and it's quite nice out there." He looked at me pleadingly with his brown eyes.

"Okay. Lead on, and I'll say goodnight to Mia after."

The sun hadn't set yet, so I felt safe yet, unsafe on a different level with Ian. We walked in step as I opened up the gate to the back area of the grounds. I hadn't explored much during my time there as I spent most of my time either working or sleeping. I had heard that there was a cross-country course in the back, and I was interested in seeing it. I was also curious what Ian's motives were in hanging out with me.

"So, Rain, how was your lesson?" he asked as we walked farther into the back.

"Good, actually, really good. Have you ever ridden before?" I looked sideways at him.

"Not really. I leave that to my sister, although I'd be willing to try it."

"Oh, you should. It's so much fun! There's really nothing like it." I smiled broadly more to myself than to him, remembering cantering Nippy around the ring.

"It does seem to bring out the best in you, Rain. I mean, I think I would try it just to see you smile like that," he said sheepishly.

I was sure my face turned red as a beet, and just then I realized that I must look like a mess. I absentmindedly tried to fix my hair back into my ponytail.

"Anyway, isn't it beautiful back here?"

I nodded in agreement. The sun was slowly setting, and we had passed the outside paddocks and were nearing the beginning of the jump course. Ian motioned to a large log that we could sit on. I smiled and followed his lead. My palms started to get sweaty, so I wiped them on the breeches I was wearing. "You're right. It is amazing out here, and you know, I have never experienced a sunset like this."

It looked like there were at least five acres of beauty. The grass was plush and still green from the previous rains we had experienced. There were all sorts of different-sized logs, as well as tire jumps and trees that were able to be used for challenging cross-country jumps. We hardly covered the space on our short walk to the large log.

We both sat down on the log. I made sure that there was some distance between us. I really couldn't get involved with someone when my life was in such disarray.

"I saw Tanis, and she mentioned that you talked to your mom today. How did that go?"

"It went all right, although I feel bad about laying my burden on her."

"Rain, no mother would see your problem as a burden. I am sure that she feels terrible for not knowing what you've been going through. Will she come and see you?"

"She wants to, but first, she wants to talk to my dad, and I'm sure that won't go well."

"So do you at least feel a little better than you did earlier? It seems that you're safe here, and soon your dad will know that you are okay." I nodded weakly. "Does your sister know how to contact you?"

"No, she doesn't, but her lesson didn't go so well today, so I'm sure that Martha will make sure that she gets enrolled in another camp. And as for feeling better…I don't know. I just feel guilty so far. Sorry, Ian, I'm not much fun to be around tonight." I looked away from him. My heart was still beating irregularly, but I had to push past it and see him as just a friend.

"Rain, it's okay. I like you, and I enjoy hanging out with you. If I can be of some help, then great. You don't owe me anything. Do you want to take a walk back in the clearing?"

"Sure, and leave this comfortable log?" I laughed and jumped up.

"See, you can be fun. Let's go." He wiped the dirt from the big log off his dark jeans, and we started following the path to the back of the cross-country field.

There were more jumps around us, and the low-lying trees seemed to beckon us forward. We walked close beside each other, and I had the distinct impression that Ian wanted to hold my hand. He brushed my hand more than once, but I didn't make any movement to encourage him. We found a clearing that opened up to a pond. The whole area was so inviting. I used to journal a lot, and this would be the perfect spot to continue that habit. There was a small pathway over the pond, and I made a mental note to come back here and explore.

"Looks nice, doesn't it?" he asked.

"Yes, so peaceful."

That was when I heard that voice again, "Peace I leave with you. My peace I give to you." It startled me and reassured me at the same time. Ian must have sensed a change in me.

"Rain, what is it? Are you okay?" He touched my shoulder gently.

"Yes, it's just that every so often, I think that God may actually be speaking to me. Doesn't that sound weird?"

"I don't think so. I believe that God is as close to us as we let him."

"Well, thanks for not thinking I'm crazy. The thing is, I'm not religious, and I haven't been raised religious, but I do remember knowing that God is real at a young age. I haven't really thought about it until now."

"Maybe you haven't had time to think about it until now."

"That's a good point, as most of the time I was too exhausted to think."

"It sounds like this place is good for you, Rain."

"I think so too." I smiled at him and, for an instant, felt a warmth pass though us. The sun was continuing its descent, which meant I had to get to bed. I didn't really want this night to end, but 5:30 a.m. came far too early, and I really had to make up for today.

"I guess we need to make a move back, don't we?" I nodded and turned away from the pond. "But we can pick up this conversation, say, tomorrow? After I take you shopping...," he said with a sly grin on his face.

"Yes, that would be fine, but after work, of course."

"Of course, I actually have to go to work too. I don't get to bring my sister up here every day."

"Yeah, I don't think I even asked you what you do."

"I'm in lumber sales with a partner of mine named Ron. We work for Irly Bird."

We had walked past the first set of cross-country jumps and were nearing the large log.

"Do you like it?" I inquired.

"I do, actually, but what I like best is Ron. He treats me so well, and I get to learn so much from him." Then just as we passed the log, he took my hand in his, and I didn't flinch. "Is this okay?" Again, I saw the twinkle in his brown eyes.

"Yes, as long as you let go before we get to the outdoor arena. I don't want to start any rumors. Besides, I've never had a boyfriend, and I'm not sure now's the time to start."

"How about we enjoy the moment and figure the rest out later?"

"Deal."

I thought we were both a little giddy, as we walked a little slower than necessary to where I was presently living. And true to his word, before we were spotted, he gave my hand a squeeze and let go. He walked me to my door and, before leaving, picked up my hand once more and kissed it. My face was flushed by this gesture.

"Until tomorrow, Rain."

"See you tomorrow." I closed the door behind him and sighed. This was going to be an interesting summer, I thought to myself.

Chapter 13

The next couple of weeks passed without incident. I had talked to my mom again and knew that she and John were planning on coming to see me. As of yet, they hadn't picked a date. I did find out that she had told my dad that I was all right but that she was not happy with the lies and deceit that she had uncovered. As for me, I was happy keeping a low profile.

The one thing that had changed in the past few weeks was that Ian and I had seen a lot of each other. I still hadn't told him my real age, but I hoped that when he found out, he wouldn't care too much. I still wasn't ready to call him my boyfriend, but he continued to hold my hand when we were in private. I had confided in Tanis, as she had done so much for me already that I thought I'd better be honest with at least one person.

I had been able to ride Nippy a handful of times, and Kat said I could give Mia a try this week. Not that there was any way that I could afford her, but she seemed to call to me. She was still my favorite horse to be around. Another one of my favorite animals was a little black cat called Patio Kitty. I wasn't sure who gave her this name, but I just loved her. If I could stay in this world that I had created, I would remain happy.

I heard there was another advanced camp on today, and so far, I hadn't seen Jenna's name on the list. I did ache to see her, but even more, I wanted to keep things at status quo. I looked at my watch on my nightstand and saw I was up before my five thirty alarm. I stretched contentedly in my comfy pj's, which I had bought with one of my first checks. Even though Ian was incredibly generous, I insisted on paying for as much as I could. I did let him help me get set up with food and such, but I was actually getting by with what I was making.

I breathed in the scent of fresh coffee, one of the luxuries I bought, a small coffeepot with a delay brew option. I found out that I loved waking up to the smell of fresh coffee, and in fact, this woke me up before my alarm almost every day. I turned off my alarm and pulled the covers off my small bed.

I was told a girl who had previously worked at A&T was coming back. I was pretty sure her name was Alicia. I hoped that we would get along, as so far, Lindsey, Jen, and I had become pretty close. I was even on Beckah's coffee routine. Today I was to work with Lindsey and Alicia, and although that didn't cause me much worry, there was still a little nag of concern in the back of my mind. I shook it off and decided to get on with my day.

I opened the small curtains and saw that the sun was up. The outdoor arena and large parking lot looked peaceful. I poured my coffee and added the necessary cream and sugar to make it the way I liked it. I didn't putter around for long though as 6:00 a.m. would come way too fast.

I saw a blue Aveo pull in just before six, so it was time to meet Alicia. I decided to wear my breeches as I hoped I'd get to ride by the afternoon. I was ready and out the door before six. I walked briskly to the big barn. It was a sunny morning, but I still wore my faithful gray hoodie to keep the early morning chill away.

As I entered, I saw a pretty young woman who looked to be in her early twenties. She was slim and was also in black riding breeches and a hoodie. She had long blond hair that she wore in two braids and had cute black glasses that suited her small face perfectly.

She heard me enter and turned to me and stuck out her hand. "Hi, I'm Alicia. You must be Rain, the girl I've heard so much about." Her voice held a note of authority but also kindness.

I shook her hand and smiled. "Yes, nice to meet you. I heard that you worked here a long time ago and are back now."

"Yes, I've done a lot of traveling, but it feels good to be home. And you're living in the trailer right now?"

"Yes. Without A&T, I don't know where I'd be."

"You're not the first person to say that, and I can guarantee you won't be the last. I guess we'd better get to work, but I look forward to getting to know you, Rain."

"You too. I usually start in the small barn. Do you want me to do that today?"

"Sure, and I see Lindsey just pulled in. We'll feed the big barn and meet you there."

"Sounds good." I left Alicia and walked back across the parking lot to the small barn, waving hello to Lindsey.

I just loved the smell of fresh hay in the morning and the satisfying neighs of the ponies.

The day seemed to fly by as we got the stalls all mucked out and filled with new sawdust. It must have been around ten when the three off us were going to go for our breaks when I saw it—the station wagon with the trailer that I knew so well. It was Jenna and… could it be my dad? I ducked behind the large arena door, but I was sure Jenna saw me. I peered out, and there she was. Martha!

I was trapped. I couldn't just stay in the arena all day. I didn't have my phone on me, and I didn't have a plausible way out. I could, however, walk to the back of the arena and hide in a stall, or I could just come clean. Was I strong enough?

Lindsey came around the corner and saw me hiding. "You're in trouble, aren't you?"

"Yes, and I'm about two seconds away from coming clean. I can't keep hiding every time Jenna comes up here," I said frantically.

"Are you sure you can handle your stepmother?"

'No, but she'll be unloading Beanie any minute, so I might as well get this over with"

"Listen, I'll help them get settled. Why don't you go out the back? I'll cover for you, and if you still want to confront her, you can when she picks up Jenna."

"Okay. You're probably right. Thanks, Lindsey. I appreciate it."

"No problem. Now go quickly, and I'll help your sister. I'll come and get you when your stepmother's gone."

"Thanks again. See you soon." I moved quickly. I still felt like I was taking the coward's way out but realized that Lindsey was right.

I made a right turn out of the arena and was able to make my way to my trailer without being seen. I noticed that Jenna was glancing around nervously, most likely looking for me. I really hoped that she wouldn't be distracted as she rode.

I watched from my window, feeling like a trapped bird. There she was in all her glory, Martha, and she also seemed to be looking around a lot. I hadn't realized that I had been holding my breath, and it wasn't till I saw her moving her car that I began to breathe again. I sat down in my little kitchen and just waited.

After what seemed like an eternity, I peered back out my window. She was still there! In fact, she had parked to the side and had gotten out of her car. What was she up to? She must have known that something was up. I watched as Tanis came out and greeted her. Tanis was shaking her head as Martha was talking to her. I wanted to be a fly on the wall. The waiting was killing me.

I decided to give Ian a quick call to let him know what was going on. I was thankful that he picked up on the second ring.

"Rain, how are you doing today? I was just thinking about you."

"Hey, Ian, I've been better... Martha and Jenna are here."

"Oh no. Where are you?"

"I'm hiding out like a frightened child instead of confronting her like an adult."

"As much as I really think that at your age you should be free of her, I'm not sure that you should face her alone."

"Tanis was just talking to her, so I'm sure I'd have protection."

"Please talk to Tanis before you do anything rash, okay?"

"Deal. I'd better go. She must be gone by now."

"Okay. I'll see you after work today."

"See you then." I pressed End and took another look at the parking lot. She had left the trailer behind, but her car was gone; so it looked like I had another day of freedom ahead of me.

I didn't wait. I was off to find Jenna.

I almost burst out of the trailer with the excitement I felt. Yes, I had made the right decision, for now at least. I was oblivious to the group of girls gathering outside the arena, and it wasn't until I saw Tanis flash me a warning look that I stopped short. What was it?

Then I saw it, her ugly station wagon. Martha hadn't left but had been around the corner waiting. My jaw dropped, and it was the first time that I saw Jenna making her way to me, shaking her head. I remembered I had to protect my sister. Martha couldn't know that Jenna had found me.

Tanis intercepted Martha and tried calming her down, but there was no way. Martha had never wanted to make a scene in all the time I had known her, but she was quickly losing her cool. I didn't want to make a scene either, as I wanted to be the independent Rain and not the meek Rose. But there went my life flashing before my eyes.

Martha's mouth went off like a burst dam! "Rose Stevens, what do you think you've been playing at? You didn't think that I'd figure out that you and Rain were one and the same? Your father almost had a heart attack worrying about you! Selfish, that's what you've been!"

It was then that she appeared to remember that we weren't alone. She took a deep breath and changed her tone. She put on her sweetest British accent. "Rose, we have all missed you, especially Jenna. She hasn't been able to cope without you."

I still hadn't the guts to speak. The guilt from the exchange was weighing me down. That was when Tanis spoke up.

"Martha, you are upsetting Jenna, who is almost in tears, not to mention that we have camp on. Why don't we take this conversation to the office?" Tanis then started to walk toward the big barn, and it looked like Martha was about to follow when she looked at Jenna.

"Jenna, dear, why don't you run off to camp? We've got this. Don't worry, dear. Rose will be home soon." Her voice was dripping with her enhanced English accent for show.

That did it. The fight in me started to rage. "Martha, you have no guarantee that I am going anywhere with you. In fact, my *real* mother will be here any day now, and you'll have to face her for all the awful things you've done to me!" My legs moved me onward toward the big barn and to the office. I didn't walk but rather stomped. I happened to notice both Lindsey and Jen giving me two thumbs up. All the while, Alicia was trying to get the kids organized with the help of two other counselors. I had caused a scene with my outburst, but Martha needed to know I wasn't going to take things lying down anymore.

Jenna seemed as mad as I was and soon caught up to me and took my arm. I had ruined camp for her. I felt bad about that, but she loved me, and that counted for something. I squeezed her arm and wanted to hug her, but I was still in business mode. Martha had no choice if she wanted a conversation with us, so she followed along.

Martha had never been particularly pretty while I had known her. In her younger days, she was called a beauty. I had seen pictures of her as a young woman, and she was pretty in her own way. She had gray hair cropped short but without any real style. She had small skinny legs but had always struggled to keep weight off her midsection no matter how hard she tried. She looked older than her years but didn't seem to mind. Her eyes were a light blue, and although they could look kind, I usually saw them when they wear filled with disgust and anger. All this added up to a woman I didn't want to look like or become like. She had a will of steel. There was no way to bend her. She could appear weak, but it was always for show.

If Martha had been a kind woman, I would have admired her strength. But as she was usually in a rage, I'd learned to fear her. Even if she was kind to me, I would walk on eggshells as it could change in ten minutes. One minute we could be laughing together, and the next she was angered by one of my comments. I trained myself to stay quiet. Being told not to speak was common in my life, so much so that I went years without talking to people. Thankfully, something changed in the past couple of years, and I had found my voice. It was still a struggle with any sort of authority figure, but at least I was speaking.

All this led to me being strong for small bursts and meek for long stretches. I would rise up and then, just as quickly, turn into a mouse. I still hadn't found my true self, but being at A&T was a step in the right direction. This was why I had to stay.

I was deep in thought as Jenna and I passed the horses in the big barn. We rounded the stairs and proceeded to the office. The smell of the barn as we walked through calmed me down. Some of the young girls who hadn't witnessed the recent exchange smiled at me and said hi. I smiled in return and held on tighter to Jenna.

Tanis was ahead of us and entered first. I was sure that Tanis must have texted Christine as to what was happening. Christine whispered "Good luck" as she passed me. I smiled weakly at her. I hoped to finally get some closure and face my fears.

Tanis opened the door for all of us, and Martha begrudgingly came in. She didn't wait for Tanis; she just started talking. "Tanis, you have things all wrong. I'm not sure what Rose has told you, but she is dearly missed at home, and she needs to be where she belongs." Martha laid it on thick, but Tanis looked unmoved.

"Martha, Rain, or rather, Rose, is an adult, true?" She eyed Martha with a coldness that I had never been able to muster.

"Just an adult. She was eighteen as of April. And you and I know that it takes more than an age to say one is an adult. She doesn't even drive for goodness sake, and she has no money. Now please don't argue with me. Rose, you need to pack up and come with me."

"No. I am not going." I was so tempted to just run to the trailer, but I decided I needed to stand my ground for once. With Tanis with me, I felt braver than ever before.

"Your father will not be happy knowing that not only did you run away but that you won't even see him. And he is sick. Do you know why he is sick?" I shuddered inwardly as I had heard this line of thought before. "Because of you, Rose. He was devastated not knowing where you went."

"Martha," Tanis interjected, "Rose is employed here. She is earning her keep, and I would suggest that you and her dad come visit her here. You will see that she isn't breaking any laws and has settled in nicely. I am sure you want her to be happy, and from what I can tell, she is. She hasn't shared all the details with me, but I am sure she wouldn't have left if she hadn't thought she needed to."

Martha was not amused, and she was fighting to keep up what little patience she was pretending to have. My resolve was shaking, but then I heard that voice again, "Fear not for, I am with you. I have called you by name. When you walk through the waters, I will be with you. When you walk through the valley, I am there." That voice, what was it?

Both Tanis and Martha were now looking at me. Had they heard the voice too? I was suddenly all too aware that I needed to assert my adulthood then, or I'd be branded a child in both of their eyes.

I cleared my throat. "I am staying here, Martha. If you can please tell Dad to come and see me, I will talk with him and go from there. In the meantime, I have work to do. I will see you when you pick up Jenna, but I will not be going home with you." And with that, I left an open-mouthed Martha, turned on my heel, and left the office.

My legs were shaking as I went to find Jenna. I made my way down the barn aisle and, I almost ran right into Lindsey.

"Are you okay?" she asked with concern written all over her face.

"Yes and no. I faced the beast and survived." I suddenly smiled at her.

She laughed and gave me a side hug. "Spoken like a true horse girl. Are you looking for Jenna? Oh, and are you staying?"

"Yes on both accounts."

"Good to hear. After I heard your stepmother, I have to admit, I was worried. Having Tanis on your side definitely helps though, doesn't it?"

"I couldn't agree more."

"Well, Jenna is in the arena warming up, but I think it would do her nerves good to see you."

"Thank you. Where do you want me after I see her?"

"I'd check with Jen. All the ponies are tacked up for camp, but you may need to water the horses in the outdoor paddocks again."

"Thanks. I'll see you in a few."

I left her and went back to the outdoor arena, and sure enough, Jenna was walking Beanie around, but she looked far from relaxed. I waved at her, and when she saw me, relief washed over her face. It wasn't her fault that she was in the middle of the mess I had made.

"Rose, I mean, Rain, are you okay?"

"It's okay, Jenna. As much as I actually prefer Rain, you can go back to calling me Rose seeing as your mother has found me. And I'm alright. I'm not unscathed, and I'll make it."

"So are you coming home?" she asked shyly.

"No. I'm sorry, Jenna, and if I was, it would only be because of you."

"I didn't think you would be, but I miss you. I won't be selfish though, as I can tell you have a good thing going for you here."

Just then, I heard Kat calling all the students to go into the middle of the ring. "You better go. We'll talk later. Have fun, Jenna, and remember to relax and breathe."

"Thanks, sis. Talk to you soon."

I watched Jenna and a couple of the other advanced riders gather around Kat. I was slightly jealous, as I would much rather be riding.

I decided to stay busy, as I didn't want another confrontation with Martha. I found Jen and told her I'd take care of the paddocks outside. I figured Martha wouldn't bother me out back.

I had, however, underestimated Martha's persistence. There she was coming toward me, looking angrier than I'd ever seen her. I put the hose in the large water bucket; I didn't want to be tempted to cool Martha down with it…or did I? She marched up beside me and grabbed my arm roughly.

"Rose, I don't know what you're playing at, but you will not get away with this! Your dad will see to it that you find yourself back home where you belong."

I shook free from her hand and stood my ground. "I am not going anywhere with you! When my mother comes to see me, I'd like to see how you're going to smooth everything out."

She leaned into my face and barked, "I am not done with you!" At that, she shoved me toward the fence and stormed off.

I breathed out for the first time since Martha's car pulled in that morning.

Chapter 14

I busied myself with chores around the barn all day. The whole day had just brought back ugly memories of the past number of years. I hadn't been around when Jenna was picked up, and Jenna was actually too busy preparing for the upcoming show to visit me. It was probably for the best. I had wished that she'd be able to spend the night with me so we could have one of our long sister chats.

Ian was supposed to come and see me that night, but I assumed I'd be no company and he would just worry. I was in the small barn watering the horses when Tanis surprised me.

"How is my hardest-working girl doing now that the drama of the morning has come and gone?"

I dropped the hose in Nippy's big bucket before answering her. "If you're referring to me, I'm fine, albeit slightly embarrassed."

"There's no reason to be embarrassed. I'm just relieved that you aren't second-guessing your decision. I also have some cool news for you, but I need you to come into the house. Finish with Nippy, then come on over." Her eyes sparkled mischievously, which caused me to wonder what on earth she was up to. "I am so proud of you, Rain. It took a lot of guts to do what you did today. I'll see you in the house soon, okay?"

"Thanks, Tanis. I really appreciate all that you've done. I would never have stayed away had I not found your barn."

She came over to me and patted my arm. "It's worth it seeing you stand up to Martha. Now come on! Shut the water off; the surprise is anxious to see you!"

"I'll be there in a minute."

She left me and walked back to the house. I lifted the hose out and bent it, trying not to spill water everywhere. I turned the tap off and rolled the hose back up again.

Who was anxiously waiting for me? It had to be Ian, but if it was, he would have just found me as he always did. Hmmm, maybe it was a lawyer trying to get me free. On that thought, I tried to tidy my messy ponytail and smooth down the flyaways. I then made my way to the house.

As I was about to open the door, it swung open. There standing in front of me was none other than my mother! She had her arms wide open and had tears streaming down her face.

"Oh, Rose, it is so good to see you!" She grabbed me in a big hug and squeezed me so I could hardly breathe. I was so shocked that I hardly had time to register what was happening. My mom, my real mom, was here in Ontario! I hugged her back, and it was hard to hold back the tears.

The next thing I knew, my stepdad, John, joined us. He wrapped his arms around both of us. Why had I waited so long to get them involved with my plight? For the first time in my life, the love seemed to come without strings.

Before I pulled away, I heard that small still voice again, "I will never leave you or forsake you." I thought that voice was somehow tied to my mother.

After what seemed like seconds, my mom and John pulled away. My mom held me at an arm's distance and scanned my face. It was as if she saw through me. That did it. I lost it too. I let out the tears that I had been holding in.

Tanis, sensing that we needed this time, held back. I was slightly conscious of the people coming and going in the parking lot next to the house. I pulled away and laughed nervously. "We should probably go into the house, or we may cause a scene."

My mom joined me in my merriment, and we closed the door behind us and walked into the kitchen where Tanis was.

"I must say, Rain, or Rose, that there is a vast difference between Martha and Ruth. I have a hunch that you will make the right choice in what you do next. Now, John and Ruth, I have a pot of fresh coffee on, and after your travels, I am sure that you'll need it. Also, Rain has her own accommodations, but they aren't large by any means."

"That's okay, Tanis. We've booked in a hotel nearby. We were just so anxious to see Rose and to come in person to thank you for your help."

"Tanis, you knew they were coming?" I asked, astonished.

She smiled. "Yes. Your mom and I have had a few conversations, and I was right that Martha was getting closer to finding you. Unfortunately, the horse community can be a small one, especially with Jenna riding with Kat. Now come on, let's go into the living room and I'll bring the coffee. Rain, you can show them the way. Ruth, I just realized that I'm calling her the wrong name. It's just that I've gotten used to it."

"That's okay. She did it to stay safe, which I admire. Besides, it's a pretty neat name, if I do say so."

"Thanks, Mom. I've always been a bit on the creative side." I looked into her clear blue eyes that seemed to look happier than I'd ever seen.

"Yes, that's true," John joined in.

"Come on, you two, I'll show you the way. Tanis, I still can't believe you did all this, but thank you again."

"You're welcome. I'll be there in a minute." She turned to get busy with the coffee, and I led my parents into the front room.

John leaned over to me as we sat on the couch and took my hands. "It is such a relief to see you, Rose. Your mother, she has just been going a little crazy since she found out the truth of what had been happening to you."

John's eyes were the most earnest eyes I had ever seen. They were brown, but it was the sincerity in them that had always touched me. He didn't have to love me, but he chose to love me. He was quite a bit older than my mom, but he had the nicest silver hair anyone could ask for. At sixty-nine, he looked way younger than he was. When I first met him at seven, I felt instantly at ease with him. My life would have been so different had I been raised by him and my mom.

My mom joined him on the couch. She, too, looked at least twenty years younger than she was. I really hoped I'd inherit that gene as I got older. Right now, it was a bit of a pain always getting asked if I was lying about my age. I never had even thought of it till recently.

My mom had short blond hair, which added to her youthful appearance. I had yet to see any gray on her head. John, on the other hand, had thick silver hair. When he grew his hair a little longer, it curled at the nape of his neck. They were both in pretty good shape and complemented each other. My mom had the sought-after classic hourglass figure, and John was barrel-chested and strong-looking. This was just another attribute that made me feel safe when I was in his arms.

Tanis entered the room with a tray full of coffee mugs and cream and sugar. I stood up and helped her with it. We soon all had our caffeine, and the conversation flowed naturally and easily. I noticed that John was looking a bit tired.

"Mom, do you think you two should get some rest? I'm not going anywhere, and Martha has gone for the day. I wouldn't be surprised if she returns tomorrow with Dad, but that's for tomorrow. Before you go, I'd love to show you around if you're up for it."

"Do you like horses, Ruth?" Tanis asked.

"Like? Yes. But obsessed like Rose? No." We all laughed at that.

"Well, I have to say, I fall into the same category as Rose on that one."

"I think it's your mutual love of horses that brought Rose to you. This place was like a beacon to her, I am sure of it. You sniffed this place out, didn't you, Rose?"

"It's only the best-smelling place I've ever come across, Mom."

"And this is coming from the girl who mucks out stalls in the morning, Ruth."

"Ahhh, heaven." I chuckled.

"Yes, yes, take us to see your heaven. Tanis, thank you again. I really don't know what I would have done had I not been able to find out that Rose was safe. Now the next big question is how to get Ivan, her brother, as well." My mom looked sad for the first time since I had seen her. It kind of broke my heart.

"Mom, at least he's already out of the house, and if I can be free of Martha, so can he."

"You're right." She paused before going back to her happy demeanor. "Now, Rose, let's see this paradise."

I nodded. We all got up. I moved the cups to the tray and thanked Tanis again. We left the house and walked over to my little trailer. I really wished my mom could stay with me as there was so much I wanted to ask her. I didn't know if she'd be comfortable on my little bed, and I was sure she needed her sleep.

After I showed off the trailer, I took them to the barns and the hayloft, where I had first hidden. There was still activity bustling around the barn. I think that was one of the things I loved about being there; life never stopped. I knew my parents weren't real horsey people, but they oohed and aahed at most of the right times. Before they left, I had to show them Mia.

"Now I know this isn't very exciting, but I have to introduce you to my favorite horse. Her name is Mia, and she is beautiful!"

"I'm sure she is, dear," my mom said without a lot of conviction.

"She is." I practically skipped to her stall. "Here she is. See, just gorgeous."

Mia, noticing that we were paying attention to her, poked her head out as if to say, "Here I am."

"Hi, girl, how are you tonight?" Instantly she went looking for the carrots I almost always had on me. "No, no carrots tonight. Tonight you are meeting two special people. Mia, this is my mom and John."

"Does she actually understand you, Rose?" My mom stroked her bay face.

"Yes, she does. She understands me more when I give her carrots. I've even taught her a couple of tricks. She now gives me her hooves for treats. And Kat says that after a few more lessons with the other horses, I'll get to ride her."

John cleared his throat and got my attention. "Rose, your mom and I want to offer you a proposal." He paused. "We want you to come home and live with us. I know you may not have thought of this as a choice, but it is a real option. We want Ivan to come home too."

I couldn't look at John or my mom as he spoke. I kept stroking Mia. To give up my life at A&T, what would that look like? And Jenna and Ian. I couldn't answer.

"It's true, dear. I was going to wait to ask you, but we would love to have you, to have the chance to get to know you. Can you look at us?" she asked quietly.

I gulped but then turned to face them. There was so much love in their faces that it was hard to say no, but I wasn't sure. "I don't know what to say. I really don't. You see, I've started a life here. I'm finally happy."

"You could come for a trial period and see if you like it. If you don't, I'm sure that Tanis would give you your job back," my mom offered.

"Please, honey, think about it," John added.

"I will think about it. I can't afford a ticket though, as I haven't made that much yet."

They both smiled at that and in unison said that there was no way I would have to buy a ticket. John squeezed my shoulder and said, "Oh, you funny girl. Please come home so we can be a family."

"I promise you, it's a strong possibility." Mia, sensing we weren't paying attention to her, tried to nibble my hand. "Hey, girl, you're important too. Don't worry."

"Rose, we should probably get going to our hotel, but we will be back to see you in the morning."

"I'll walk you to your car."

I kissed Mia good night and led my parents back to their rental vehicle. We hugged again. I reminded them that I worked in the morning, and when they come to see me, they could be assured that I would be smelling strongly of horse. That didn't seem to faze them.

I watched their car leave the farm. Within two minutes of their leaving, the one person who would make this decision a whole lot harder pulled into the driveway. Sigh. Ian, what was I going to do with Ian?

Chapter 15

Ian parked his car, and I walked over to him. My heart always beat faster when I saw him, but this time, it was different. I knew I was in trouble when I met him, and now I would be proven correct. Ian got out of his car, looked at me, and gave me one of his most heart-fluttering grins. I smiled back and absently smoothed down my still messy hair.

"Hey, Rain, nice to see you on this fine night." Fine...it was not fine... Ian looked good as always. He was in light jeans and a loose-fitted white T-shirt. His hair was freshly cropped and was shorter than usual. I smiled at him, pushing past my insecurities and fears. It was time to tell Ian the truth.

He gave me a hug, and I didn't resist even though we were in the parking lot. As we pulled away, I looked into his brown eyes and took a deep breath. "Ian, I've got quite a lot to talk to you about. Would you mind skipping our outing and instead going for a walk out back?"

"Sure. Are you okay?" He looked concerned and kept his hand on my shoulder.

"I am just okay. Come on, I'll explain when we're not in the parking lot."

Ian nodded, locked his car, and followed me to the back area of the property. I was walking slightly ahead, but he pulled me back and took my hand. No, this wasn't good. I smiled weakly at him, and he squeezed my hand.

As it was a warm summer evening, the horses were able to stay out in the paddocks overnight. We passed Lain, the young draft horse, and his best buddy, Diesel. They were an unlikely pair; as Lain looked almost double Diesel's size. We passed the two foals and their moms that were in two of the large paddocks while they were enjoying their evening snack. Each step reminded me of how much I loved it here. If my mom had come before I had run away, I would have left without thinking, but now it would be hard.

"Penny for your thoughts," Ian asked quietly as he swung my hand gently.

"I was just thinking how much I love this place and that in such a short time, it's become home and how…" I couldn't finish that sentence yet.

"And how?" Ian pried.

"And how…how can I possibly leave?" I said in barely a whisper.

"Leave?" Ian stopped abruptly, which caused me to stop.

"That is what I needed to talk to you about, but first, let's get to our log." *Our log, how can we have a log when I am about to tell him I'm leaving? Have I made up my mind?* I didn't even realize that I had. Ian agreed, and we stayed quiet as we passed the other paddocks.

"Here we are, Ms. Rain, our log. Now sit down. Please start at the beginning, as somewhere between 'I'll see you tomorrow' and seeing you now, something has obviously changed."

"Okay. I'll try to tell you as much as possible, but it may take a while." I sat near the stump, and Ian joined me.

"I'm in no rush, take your time." He smiled at me reassuringly.

"Well, first, you need to know that my stepmother found me today."

"What, she did? Why didn't you call me?" Ian tensed, ready to defend my honor.

"Because Tanis was here, and for the first time in my life, I actually stood up for myself."

"That's great, Rain. Way to go. I'll try not to overreact and let you talk," he answered sheepishly.

"It's all right. Actually, I appreciate that you care, which is why telling you some of this is harder than expected." Ian took my hand and urged me on. "As I was saying, Martha came here today. We had it out, and I told her I wasn't coming home. I actually did it. I didn't back down!"

"I am so proud of you." He turned slightly so he could see my face better.

"Thanks. She actually showed some of her true colors today, which was helpful. Tanis saw that I hadn't been lying about my story. I haven't told Tanis everything, but she knows enough to know that Martha is bad news. Jenna was here too, and she was quite upset, but I settled her down. Then a little while later, Martha left, but not before she threatened to stick my 'sick' dad on me. And just as I was thinking my day was ruined, my real mom showed up with my stepdad."

"They showed up here? Wow! What a crazy day you've had. I now see why you didn't call. What happened when they arrived?"

"I was blown away, to say the least. I had no idea that they had been in contact with Tanis and had organized all this. They're both pretty mad at my dad and Martha that they've been lied to for years. To be honest, my mom just found out that Ivan, my brother, isn't living at home."

"I've got to say, Rain, that is messed up. No wonder you ran, but to think you lasted almost twenty years, there is a miracle, to say the least."

"Yeah, about that. Ian, I need to come clean with you about a couple of things. Afterward, you can decide if you still want to be my friend." I looked beyond where we were sitting and gazed at the sun that was beginning to make its descent. I needed to be braver, or I would never tell him the truth.

"Rain, I am sure whatever you have to tell me, I'll still want to be a part of your life. Now you've got me curious, so please continue."

I looked back at him and turned to face him, letting go of his hand to adjust my position. "First, my name is Rose. Rain was the name I chose when I ran away. Secondly, I am not twenty. In fact, I was eighteen as of April." I gulped, but Ian actually was smirking. "You think that's funny? I thought you'd be mad."

"Well, I haven't been entirely honest either. You see, I'm not twenty-five but rather twenty-eight, and Ian wasn't originally my real name either… It was Anton. I changed it during a brief stint in the military."

"What! You lied to me too?" I couldn't help it. I laughed out loud and then laughed some more. Ian joined me as we both thought our situation was pretty hilarious. "What kind of people are we that we both lied about the same thing?" I said after I caught my breath.

"I don't know. Creative?" Ian answered while shrugging his shoulders. Ian took hold of me and gave me a hug amid our laughter. "Rain, or Rose, whatever, you're a little nuts. So we're ten years apart. What do you think about that?" He let me go but held me at arm's length.

"It's too late. I like you already. But what about you? What do you think?"

"It's too late for me too, but I have a feeling your parents may not agree."

"Actually, John is seventeen years older than my mom, so we're all good there. But we have a bigger problem."

"And what is that?"

"Well, my mom and John want me to move to Nova Scotia with them, and I feel tempted to go. We're actually going to try to get Ivan to come too." I had filled Ian in about more of my life over the past couple of weeks, so he knew how badly I missed Ivan in my life.

"Have you made up your mind about this already?"

"No, but I do think I need to consider it, especially since I haven't lived with my mom since I was five, and I'd love to get to know her better."

"I can't compete with that, although I'd hate to see you go, but I understand, that's for sure."

"You understand?" I was kind of disappointed that he wasn't fighting a bit harder for me to stay. But how could I get mad at Ian for being a gentleman?

"So when do you have to make up your mind?" Ian asked in a slightly clipped tone.

"No time limit. It's just a possibility. Ian, the thing that makes it harder"—I sighed—"is you." It took all my courage to say that, but what did I have to lose?

"Rain, or Rose, what can I say? I haven't even asked you to officially become my girlfriend, so what hold do I have on you? I have to try to support what is best for you, and at eighteen, the world can be your oyster."

"I don't need an oyster. I don't even know what I want to do with my life. I do know if I stayed, I'd like to see more of you." Where was I getting this courage tonight?

"Yeah, I'd like that too. So you're not in a rush to go?" Ian asked with a smile.

"No, I'm not in a rush." The sun had now set, and the darkness was starting to envelop us. My heartbeat quickened as Ian leaned closer to me.

"Seeing as you're not in a rush, there's something I've been wanting to do for weeks now." Ian touched my face with the back of his hand and drew me closer to him. Before I knew it, his lips touched mine. If I thought my heart was beating quickly before, it was in overdrive after he kissed me. This wouldn't make leaving any easier.

We kissed until we both needed a breath. As he pulled away, I started to laugh lightly.

"That's not a good sign," Ian said while trying not to join me.

"It's nervous laughter… It wasn't funny. Don't worry."

"Good to hear. I thought I had lost my touch."

"I don't have a lot of experience in the kissing department, but I'd say that just made my decision even harder."

"I'd like to say that doesn't make me happy, but it does." Ian kissed me once more until we were interrupted by Murphy, Tanis's black lab. "Easy, boy." Now Ian was laughing. "I guess I should be a gentleman and walk you to your door." Murphy jumped off Ian's lap and joined us, running around our legs. He got up and offered me his hand. "My lady."

I jumped off the log and petted Murphy's head. I had a bit of a challenge trying to find my shaky feet. It wasn't every day that I got kissed at sunset on a farm. In fact, I had never been kissed like that, period.

"I have another question for you, Rain. Actually, first, would you rather I call you Rose?"

"To be honest, I've gotten used to Rain, so let's not confuse everyone." We had started to walk toward my little home again, passing the horses neighing on either side.

"Rain, as I was saying, I have to ask you something, and seeing as we've already kissed, I hope you say yes." I waited, anticipation growing in my chest. "Will you be my girlfriend, even if you leave me for Nova Scotia?" We had stopped, and he turned me to face him. Murphy had run on in front of us, giving us some space.

"Ian, I want to say yes, but are you sure?"

"Yes, I'm sure. That is, if you say yes?"

"Yes, I will be your girlfriend, even if it's just for a short time." He gave me a quick kiss to seal the deal. "But, Ian, maybe don't tell the world, okay?"

"Who would I tell?"

"Just saying. I'm new here, and I don't want people to think I'm using you."

"Okay. Yeah, you're using me. Got it, Rain."

It was now dark out, but we could see Murphy ahead of us wagging his tail. I was sure that he thought we had food. He would be disappointed that we were empty-handed.

Ian got me to my door, true to his word. We said good night, and seeing as my door wasn't facing the parking lot, I got another good night kiss from him. I would tell Tanis and maybe my mom about Ian, but I wanted to keep things quiet.

I didn't know how I would sleep after all the excitement. What began as a nightmare of a day ended in an incredible way. After getting showered and changed for bed, I lay on top of my covers just reliving the evening. I had a boyfriend, and I had been kissed. Furthermore, I might be moving to Nova Scotia. What a day!

Chapter 16

After the crazy day that I had lived through, I was sure that sleep would come. However, somewhere after kissing Ian good night and waking up, I had been plagued with terrible guilt. The memories of what I had lived through came back at an alarming rate—memories of Martha's arms raised and spanking the life out of me, Martha sending me on the task of finding the right stick to be hit with, the blows to my head and then the rare times when I thought she cared for me. I had more concussions because of her, not to mention stitches and a scar on my leg from where she once cut me. Even though the blows hadn't been as bad as I grew older, the images were hard to escape.

My father had a passive-aggressive way of trying to be in charge, which never lasted more than a fleeting moment. Then there was the decision I made to stand up for myself in order to be able to go to school. If I hadn't, I would never have passed high school. There were years of my life that I stayed home to care for Jenna instead of going to school. I couldn't believe that I lived through what I used to think was normal—having to sneak out of the house in order to see friends, not to mention never being allowed to have a life that didn't involve taking care of the family.

Why was I overwhelmed with guilt? Was my dad really sick, and did I make him sick? Then there was Jenna, whom I had raised since she was a baby. Could she survive without me being there to mentor her? There were more questions than answers to my quandaries.

I thought of Ivan and how we saw a window for one of us to escape. We agreed he should take it. This meant he got into foster care. And in all this, I wasn't allowed to get my mother involved. In fact, I wasn't even allowed to call her. I knew she had tried to call me, but Martha, in her sincerest English accent, had told her that I was out playing with friends. Friends, what friends? The only friends I could have were the ones I had to practically hide. Two of my best friends, Sandra and Daryl, had both been so wonderful and patient with me. In fact, Daryl and I had dated for a short period of time, but both of us thought we were better as friends. He had been there when I had run away from home previously, but without success.

I didn't know what time it was. I hadn't heard my alarm or any cars drive into the lot. I wished it was time to get up in order to leave all my dark thoughts behind me. I hadn't seen Ivan in what seemed like forever, and I missed him so much. It had been so good to see my mom and John, but I needed more. Could we really be happy together in Nova Scotia?

Curiosity got me up to check my alarm. It read 3:15 a.m. I still had a couple of hours till I had to get up. I lay back down, willing the bad memories to leave me. That was when I heard it again, "I will never leave you or forsake you." I sat bolt right up in bed.

"Who are you?" Nothing. I heard nothing… "God, is that you?" I didn't get an answer, but a sense of peace washed over me. "I'm not sure who you are, but thank you for the peace."

After that encounter, I fell back asleep. That was until my 5:45 a.m. alarm went off.

"No, no, no…I'm not ready for today!" Was there camp today? Was Jenna supposed to be there? Where was the peace I had felt last night?

I had to move quickly as I knew Jen and Alicia were on that morning, and neither of them stalled for time. Even when their friend Beckah came up with coffee for them, they only stopped momentarily. I brushed out my long hair and threw it up in a ponytail, then put on my breeches, boots, and one of the T-shirts Ian had given me. I got some breakfast and a glass of water and was out the door.

Jen, Lindsey, Alicia, and I worked together like clockwork now. There were also some of the other young boarders who gave us a hand for credit. I would usually start feeding in the small barn, although I always managed to see Mia before my day began. Whether or not I would be leaving, I hoped I'd still get to ride her before I left. Since I was able to trade some of my work for lessons, there was still hope.

I had asked Jen if there was advanced camp on, and I was thankful when she told me there wasn't. Finally, just maybe I could catch a break. I knew my mom and John would be confronting Martha and my dad today, and I was anxious to learn the outcome. I figured my mom would come up around lunchtime. Although Tanis was flexible, I wanted to make sure that I got my job done before they came.

I worked like a woman on a mission to prove I was worthy of the chance I'd been given. We managed to get both barns done by 9:00 a.m., so we were on track. With the sun shining, it was so much easier, as many of the horses were able to stay out at night. I had told Jen that I'd get the waters done outside. I was due for a break, but I didn't really want one. I knew any minute things could go south.

When I came in, I saw Kat talking to the girls. Kat looked especially sun-kissed, and her blond hair looked even blonder than before. She always preferred to teach outside, so it was no wonder she was so tanned. She turned and waved me over as I came closer to her.

"Hey, Rain, I've got some good news for you." She beamed.

"You do?"

"Well, you know how badly you've wanted to ride Mia?" I nodded. "I think you're ready. What do you say, after work you get on her?"

"Really? That would be awesome!" I couldn't believe my luck.

"Yeah, I've got an opening at one. Does that sound good?"

"Sure. Thanks so much! I just hope nothing disrupts our plans."

"If you get any unwelcome visitors, we'll usher them away. Don't worry."

"Easier said than done, but I like your confidence. I can't wait!" I was giddy with excitement.

"See you at one. I've got to jump on Diesel, so I'll see you then."

I nodded and smiled from ear to ear. I then went to tell Mia the great news.

I had finished what was required of me, so I decided to freshen up in my trailer. As I was trying to make some sort of sense out of my hair, I heard a knock at my door.

"Please don't be Martha," I whispered.

I opened the door up to see my mom and John standing outside. What a relief! I let them into the small space. After we'd exchanged hugs, I got them seated at my little table.

"It's so great to see you both! I was worried it was Martha when I heard the knock at the door."

"We are both so glad to see you," my mom said in a choked-up voice.

My mother had a musical voice. It was almost as though she sang as she talked. Seeing that she was an accomplished singer and pianist, not to mention teacher, I assumed she'd learned how to properly use her voice. John, on the other hand, had a slight Cape Breton accent. He didn't actually let his words run together, mind you, but you could tell he was from there. Both of them came dressed for the barn. I don't think John ever wore jeans, but he was casual in his beige khakis. My mom had just discovered that there were jeans that looked good on her and sported a nice peach top to go with them.

"How did you both sleep?" I asked while getting them each some water. I still didn't have much to offer guests in my trailer, not that I had many guests.

"We were comfortable. But, Rose, to be honest, we were mostly worried about you," John said.

"How about you, dear?" my mom offered.

I joined them at the table and sat across from them. "You'd think after all the excitement of yesterday I would have been out cold. To be honest, I was awake at three with awful memories—memories I thought I had run away from." I shook my head, trying to forget.

"I'm so sorry." My mom reached over to me.

"It's okay. I heard something or someone, and well, I had a real peace come over me." I looked up as I remembered the good part of my sleep.

"What do you mean?" asked John.

"Actually, maybe you can help me understand. I heard this voice that said, 'I will never leave you or forsake you.' Have you ever heard that?" They both smiled at me and seemed to look at each other knowingly. "What, you both know what that is?"

"We have been praying for you, Rose, and even more so since we found out about the truth of your situation. It seems God is answering our prayers," my mom answered in a hopeful voice.

"Do you think it was God? How would he know what I needed? I never asked for his help." I was stunned, to say the least.

"Yes, dear. God knows what you or I or John need way before we ask him. You may have forgotten, but when you were five, you gave your heart to him." She looked at me tenderly.

"I did? Oh, was it after you read me a story from the Bible?" It was all coming back to me. I had been alarmed at the picture of Adam and Eve being turned away from the garden of Eden because of their sin. How had I forgotten? I don't think I had read the Bible in over ten years.

"You remember?" my mom asked encouragingly.

"Yes, I remember." I smiled weakly. So that was what had been happening recently. "I've heard his voice several times since I've been here, but I didn't know it was God."

"I'm so thankful God has heard us. Rose, we need to tell you some other things." My mom's voice took on an urgent tone.

"What? What's happening?" I looked at my watch. It was quarter past twelve. I didn't have a lot of time before my lesson.

"Well, we went and saw your dad and Martha this morning. We weren't invited, but we showed up. We have also made arrangements to see Ivan later today."

"And how did it go?" I took their water glasses, got up, and placed them in the sink. I couldn't help it; I was nervous about their meeting. I looked out of the little window and held my breath.

"It went as you would expect. They denied a lot of things, and your dad pleaded ignorance."

"But, honey, we want you to know that we believe you and are on your side," John added.

"I don't know. I feel so guilty, and if my dad is really sick, then how am I supposed to stay away?" I turned away from the sink.

My mom had left her chair and closed the space between us. "You have nothing to feel guilty about. You were a child. Now you're an adult and can choose your own life."

"But at what cost?"

John got up and joined us. There sure wasn't a lot of room in my place, but they created a united front with me at the center. John looked deep into my eyes, his brown eyes practically sparkling with kindness. "Rose, you have nothing to fear, and you did nothing wrong. Those people, especially Martha, are evil. I told your mother that after today, I am never setting foot in that home ever again, nor is she. You were brave to run and thankfully you found this place. We are so grateful that you came to a place where people genuinely care about you. You are finally safe."

I gulped. I was about to cry, and I didn't have time for tears. I could cry later when I was all alone. I switched gears. "Listen, you two, I don't mean to change the subject, but I have a lesson at one. I finally get to ride Mia. I can't be late, as Kat will be waiting for me. Do you both want to watch me? I have to warn you that it'll be my first time on her, and I'll be nervous, but it'll be fun."

"Sure thing. We'd love to watch you ride," my mom said and smiled at me, her blue eyes shining.

"You came dressed for it, and if either of you ever want to ride, let me know."

"Sure, dear." John laughed, and my mom joined in.

"Come on. You can learn how to tack up a horse!"

As I was already dressed to ride, all I needed to do was find a helmet and get Mia ready. I checked my watch again. Twelve thirty-five. I could do this.

The three of us moved quickly. I even had them help me brush Mia. I managed to be ready for Kat right on time. I was outside waiting with horse in hand. I was thankful that Mia and I had already been working on her stall manners, as it made getting her ready so much easier.

Kat came toward us, and I noticed she was wearing her usual cutoff jean shorts and an A&T red shirt and runners. She had her hair down but had on a ball cap to shield her from the sun. She greeted us happily as she saw all of us together.

"Hi there," Kat said cheerily. "I'm Kat, Rain's instructor." She stuck out her hand to my mom and John.

My mom took it and smiled at her. "It's so nice to meet you, and we both want to thank you for all that you've done for Rose, er, Rain, while she's been here." John shook her hand too and repeated the sentiment.

"We've loved having her, and if she leaves with you two, she'll be missed, that's for sure. Now, Rain, are you ready to finally ride Mia?"

"Yes, yes, I am," I answered excitedly. I moved Mia closer to the mounting block and tightened her girth.

"Great. Get on and let's get started. Ruth and John, there's a bench right outside the riding area. Feel free and make yourself at home."

"Thanks. And, Rain, good luck," Mom said, walking out of the pen.

I smiled at them, then proceeded to get up onto Mia. She was so much bigger than Nippy, so I was a bit nervous. In fact, the butterflies danced like crazy in my chest and stomach. As I sat on top of her fixing my stirrups, Kat had to remind me to breathe. I was sure that wasn't the last time I'd hear her say that.

I started to walk Mia around the outside of the ring and took in the scene around me. There was my mom and John watching me. It was kind of surreal to think of what was about to unfold.

The outdoor smelled so good—a mix of freshly cut grass and the scent of horses. The summer's heat bore down on us, but I didn't care. I was finally on Mia. Kat brought my attention back to the task at hand as I steered Mia around the ring. I tried to match her rhythm with mine. She was slow to start, and Kat kept telling me to wake her up. After we were warmed up, I was able to trot her. Mia's stride was so big that I honestly felt like I had never ridden before.

"Now keep her trot steady, butt underneath you, and your hands need to be still. That's better. Now just remember that you're not having tea. Keep your thumbs up and pinkies down. Good, Rain, just like that."

I tried to concentrate on all the things Kat was coaching me on—butt under, thumbs up. I felt more confident than I had at the start. That was until Kat asked me to do sitting trot. Oh, how I hated sitting trot. I looked like a sack of potatoes on a very pretty horse.

"Move your hips, Rain." Kat got off the rail and came to the center of the ring and tried to show me how to move my hips. "Like this, Rain. Find her movement, then try to match it." Kat moved her hips as she demonstrated what I needed to do.

I took another deep breath, concentrating very hard on Mia's pace, and then for a moment, we had it. "Like this?" I asked excitedly.

"Yes! Now keep that going. Good. Now back to posting trot," she said encouragingly.

She kept us alternating between the two, and I had moments of greatness and moments of feeling like I had no control at all.

"Now bring her to a walk using your body. Sit down deep in the saddle. Try not to pull on her mouth. That's it, like that."

"This is hard," I called back.

"I know, but you can do it."

"I did it!" Mia and I were back to a good walk. She was amazing!

"Good. How do you feel about cantering her?" I moved Mia closer to Kat and just beamed.

"Really, can we?"

She laughed as she nodded. "Okay. The plan is a slow canter. Steady your breathing. Get her back to trot, and I'm going to get you to canter her by just using your hips. Mia is really good for this. Now start sitting trot, and in the next corner, move your hips with her and get her to canter."

I started sitting trot as I brought her up the side of the fence. I tried to match her hips again as I struggled to sit. Her hooves were kicking up the dust, and the air was thick with warmth, but nothing mattered as my heartbeat quickened. I listened to Kat coaching me on. I was in the corner, and I moved my hips in time with her, trying to get her to canter. At first, she just trotted faster. Shoot, I couldn't get her to canter.

"Just bring her back to a slow trot and try again in the next corner." Kat continued to watch us from the middle of the ring.

I slowed her trot, and this time, as I reached the corner, I made a more pronounced movement with my hips. She listened. She was cantering, and it was incredible! "She feels amazing!" I was sure my teeth would be brown from smiling so much from the dust in the ring.

"Good job, Rain. Keep her going using your hips. Keep those hands steady and your butt tucked under you."

I tried to listen, but all I could think was how amazing the feeling of cantering Mia was and how I would do whatever I could to keep riding.

Kat had us canter the other direction and work on slowing her fast pace. I was in heaven. While riding, I had totally forgotten about Martha, my dad, and the possibility of leaving Ian behind. I had forgotten it all, until I saw a gray Impala pull into the driveway.

Chapter 17

My wonderful lesson and escape was over. It was now reality time. At least it was Ian who pulled in and not Martha. I was walking Mia out when Ian waved at me. I waved back but kept walking. Kat was still giving me some more pointers on my ride. I really hoped that I could keep riding if I left A&T.

I saw that Ian had introduced himself to my mom and John. I was sure they'd be as charmed by him as I was. I then shot Ian a look of panic that I hope said, "Don't you dare tell them you're my boyfriend!" He smiled at me, which wasn't reassuring at all. Kat brought me back to myself as I had missed answering a question she had asked me.

"Sorry, what did you say?" I slowed Mia's walk down and gave Kat my attention.

"I just asked if riding Mia was all that you were hoping for." She walked toward us, and I stopped Mia.

"Oh yes, yes, it was. I love her canter. It's so smooth." I petted Mia's long bay neck as I purred my thanks to her.

Kat joined us and petted her too. "It's a pity you don't know if you're staying, as maybe you could save up and buy her." Kat smiled at me, her blond hair moving slightly in the warm summer breeze.

"You know, it's getting harder and harder to make up my mind as to what to do."

"Does Ian have anything to do with that?" We were at the far area of the riding area, so Ian couldn't hear us, but I lowered my voice just in case.

"I hate to admit it, but yes, it does. Ian and all of you. I have never been treated so kindly in all my life."

"Your mom and stepdad seem like great people though, and if you have a chance to get to know them better, then you probably should. There will always be other horses and other Ians."

"I hope you're right." I wasn't sure though as I had never met another Ian, and well, Mia was amazing too.

"I've got to go get another lesson going. You can hop off and go enjoy your time with both your parents and Ian."

"Gee, thanks." I laughed.

"Good luck." She moved away from us, and I just shook my head.

I moved Mia to the middle of the pen and jumped off her. "Good girl," I cooed to her. "I hope we get to do this again." I walked her over to the gate where my entourage was waiting for me.

Ian opened the gate, smiling at me. "Hi, Rain, I thought I'd surprise you and take you for lunch, but it seems I've been beat. I met your parents. They're both so nice." He closed the gate behind us.

I stopped Mia and turned her large bay body around to see everyone. "What did you think, Mom?" I stroked Mia's neck. I was a little out of sorts having Ian and my parents there.

"You both looked lovely, although I was a little nervous when I saw how fast you were going." John nodded and added his appreciation. "So we've met your friend Ian while we were waiting for you." My mom moved closer and gave Mia a pat while Ian came and took up a slightly protective stance by my side. I wanted him to know that I was totally fine with this set of parents, so I smiled at him reassuringly.

"Yes, Ian has been very helpful while I was trying to get settled in here. He's been a great friend to me."

"Hopefully, a friend she doesn't want to leave," he added.

"Well, I'd better get Mia untacked and put away, as I still have some things to finish up. Mom, John, are you two going to wait for me?"

"We want to, but we have a meeting with your brother's social worker. We also want to meet with your dad. Why don't you finish up here? We'll be back to take you out to supper. And, Ian, you can still take her for lunch." My mom gave Ian a warm smile. This brought me some relief.

"That works for me if it works for all of you," Ian said confidently. "I have to get back to work in the afternoon, but I have a break till two."

"It looks like we have a plan," John added. He came over to me and gave me a side hug as I was still holding onto a slightly impatient Mia.

"See you later, Ro—Rain." My mom also gave me a hug and then gave Ian her hand. "It was very nice to meet you, Ian."

"Likewise." He shook both my parents' hands. This was all so weird. I'd never had a boyfriend, and now here he was meeting my mom of all people.

I moved Mia back into the barn, and Ian came with me. I was sure people already knew that we were an item; why else would he be hanging out with me? Mia moved quickly down the aisle, and I had to stop her a couple of times. She was lovely, but she could be so rude. I noticed Roxy, one of the other mares, wanted to take a bite out of her butt, so I moved her swiftly away from her. "Easy, girl. It's okay. You're fine." She slowed down a bit as we got her to a set of crossties. The camp kids were in the indoor arena, which I was grateful for. Mia could be a pain when there were lots of kids around. I took off Mia's bridle and put her halter back on her. I tied her up to the crossties and started putting things away.

Ian was standing nearby observing me. "I had an idea," he said.

"Yes, and that is?" I hoped it wasn't telling my parents about our new status.

"As you are clearly in your element here, and I don't want to rush you, why don't I go and pick up a couple of burgers? We can enjoy them out back." He stroked Mia's neck as he talked to me.

"You know, that sounds great. That'll also give me a bit of time to clean up."

"I'm getting used to you always wearing the same perfume."

"And what is that?" I cocked my head toward him.

"Eau de horse."

"Very funny." I mock threw Mia's brush at him.

"Hey, I didn't say I minded it, but please don't hit me." I threatened him again, but he grabbed the brush from me and grabbed hold of my arm. "I'm a little stronger than you are, Rain." He kissed me on my cheek.

I pulled away abruptly. "Secret, Ian, remember?" I untangled myself from his hold.

"Oh yes, 'secret.' My bad, there's no one around, Rain."

"The horses have eyes and ears." I laughed in spite of myself. Besides, I didn't want to offend him.

"Yes, yes, I forgot about that. Seeing as I can't be trusted around the horses, I'll be off. And no, I won't kiss you goodbye," he whispered into my ear. That just caused me to have goose bumps down my arms. I was sure he knew it too.

I again pushed him playfully. "Okay, go, but hurry back, I'm hungry." Mia swished her tail in agreement. "And so is Mia."

"Fine. I'll be back soon, and I'll pick up carrots for Mia too."

"We both thank you." I bowed.

"Bye, Rain. And bye, Ms. Mia." I shook my head, then went back to taking care of Mia.

I had almost finished brushing her when I saw Jen. "Hey, Jen, how's camp going?"

"Good, good. Hey, I've got a question for you." She walked over to Mia and me.

"Yes?" I paused my brushing as I gave her my attention.

"I noticed Ian was up here again, so what's up with the two of you? He's a little old for you, isn't he?" She looked at me, her face furrowed in concern.

"Well, he's a really good friend, or he's been a really good friend to me." I was sure I was blushing, and I was a terrible liar.

"Friend? Are you sure that's it? He's never been up here so much since he met you."

I looked around, and it looked like we were pretty much alone. "I'll tell you, but you have to promise not to say anything to anyone. The only other person I'd probably tell is Lindsey."

"I promise, cross my heart." She crossed her heart as she looked earnestly at me.

"So we talked last night, Ian and I, and it seems that we both like each other. I know there's not much point, as I'm most likely leaving, but we decided to be boyfriend girlfriend for the time that I'm here."

Mia was stomping her feet in impatience again. She could be such a diva.

"I knew it. Lindsey said I was wrong, but I knew. So you do like him." She paused and looked at me more intently. "Rain, you are going to get into trouble before you go, if you go."

"No, I'm not." I put the lead rope on Mia's halter, unclipped her from the ties, and led her back to her stall. I wasn't sure why, but what Jen said bothered me, but it did. What did she mean anyway? I closed Mia's door behind me and gave her a kiss on the nose. Jen had followed me to her stall.

"I'm sorry. I didn't mean anything by that. Just be careful. I've seen Ian up here with his sister before, and the girls like him. I'm not saying that he's dated anyone from here before, but I'm sure he's had lots of girlfriends. You told me you haven't even dated, so I couldn't help but be concerned."

"Thanks, Jen. I do appreciate the concern. I'm sure we won't date long enough to get into trouble, but I'll be careful. He's coming back to take me for lunch, so I've got to clean up and get ready."

"If you ever need anyone to talk to, Rain, you know you can talk to me, okay?"

"Thanks again. There's a lot going on right now, and I may take you up on your offer. But as for now, I've got to go."

"See you later. You're on the morning shift, so I'll see you then." She turned to go back up to the observation deck, and I left the barn to go to my trailer.

I decided to stay in my breeches, as I couldn't bear to be out of them yet. I had pure helmet hair, so I undid my braid and put my brush through it. It didn't help much, so I put it in a ponytail. I didn't like that either, so I tied it up in a bun. I loved riding, but I was never crazy about what it did to my hair.

I washed my face, put on some ChapStick, and changed my top. I was wearing one of the tops that Ian gave me, which made it look like I tried to be presentable. I wasn't sure how much of my heart I should be sharing, but trying to look decent was being respectable. I still had to think about my decision. I really thought I already knew what I was going to do, hard or not. Maybe Ian and I could do long distance, then again, maybe I'd enjoy the summer and never see him again.

I was about to go wait for him outside when I heard a knock on my door. I opened it up, and there he was with his hands full of McDonald's takeout. Mr. Trouble himself. I was excited and panicked all at the same time.

"Your lunch awaits, Ms. Rain."

I guess I wasn't that panicked. "Let's go have our picnic. I'm starving."

We walked to the cross-country area, and of course, we passed Jen on our way. She waved sweetly to us. We both juggled the food, and I had taken a towel from my supply to make it feel a bit more like a picnic. I hoped the dogs wouldn't be out and about, or it would be hard to enjoy our lunch while trying to fend them off.

I lay the towel over our usual log, and we both took a seat. Ian divided up the food, and I inhaled the smell of the burger. I knew it was so bad for me, but after the past forty-eight hours, I needed some comfort food. I took a swig of my Coke before deciding on doing some quizzing.

"So, Ian, you never told me, but have you had a lot of girlfriends?" I could tell he wasn't expecting that as he nearly choked on his pop.

"What brought that question up?" He tried to recover his lost drink.

"I was talking to someone earlier, and they were trying to warn me about you." When had I gotten so bold?

"I am not sure what they are talking about as I have had a few, but not more than most my age." He said this with believability, but I was still unsure. I knew he was charming and kind, so of course, girls would like him. The question was, Did it mean that I would like him any less? "Is that the only question you have for me on this beautiful summer day?"

"I'm sure I have many more questions to ask you, but until I eat, they may not make much sense." I bit into my burger and allowed the food to help my mood. "Did you tell my parents anything I need to be worried about?"

"Of course not. We said it was a secret, and it is safe with me. They do seem really concerned for you. I know you've told me some of what you went through, but I have a feeling there's a lot you're not telling me."

I took another swig of pop before answering him. "Yes, I suppose there is a lot you don't know yet, but to be honest, I don't want the past to ruin my present."

"That sounds fair. I guess, as you're going out with them tonight, you'll all be discussing the big move."

"The bigger problem is that I know I will have to face my dad, and I am not looking forward to that. I'm surprised Martha hasn't dragged him up here already. I am worried about my mom and dad's confrontation. If I were to stay, I would be in more trouble than I could tell you, and no amount of Jenna's interfering could save me this time."

"Rain, if you need any help at all, please let me know." He put his arm around me, which, contrary to my earlier emotions, made me feel secure.

"Thanks, Ian." We had both finished our lunches and put the garbage in one bag. I noticed Ian looking at his watch. "Do you need to go?"

"Unfortunately, yes, but not before I do something." He smiled at me deviously.

"And what do you have to do first?" I asked, my heart a flutter.

"This." He leaned closer to me and kissed me. This time, the kiss lasted longer than the night before. I kissed him back thinking that I could get used to this, until I heard the panting of Murphy, the black lab, jumping up on our laps, coming to say hello. "Well, hi, Murphy. Don't you have great timing?" We both laughed.

"Better him than a camp full of kids or Jen," I added.

"What, you mean she doesn't trust me?"

"Should she?" I laughed at him getting mauled by Murphy.

"Why, of course. I'm a perfect gentleman. See, even the dogs agree. But I do have to go." He got up, and Murphy went around him, clearly feeling a bit put out. "One more thing though." He pulled me back off the log and gave me one more kiss. "Until we meet again, Rain."

I kissed him back. "Until then," I said breathlessly.

Chapter 18

I had a pretty good day despite having some big decisions to make. It was late evening, and I had enjoyed a pleasant dinner with my mom and John. Things had been a bit harder than they thought with the meeting with the social worker. I promised my parents that I'd give my side of the story if that would help. I still hadn't heard from my dad, which I thought was odd. My mom said that it looked as if he and Martha were avoiding the conflict, which was sure to arise.

So far, they had a tentative meeting set up for the following day. Since I was legally an adult, I could do as I pleased, whether it was agreeable or not. I guess my mom just needed to set Martha straight. *Good luck,* I thought.

I was puttering around in my trailer when I heard the all too familiar station wagon pull into the barn. It was after nine, but the gate was still open. I hoped with all my being that my dad was with her, but a feeling of dread overwhelmed me. I knew the sound of her car anywhere!

I peered out my window, and sure enough, I saw Martha getting out of her car. I was all alone; I was vulnerable. Where was Tanis or Ian? Could I stand up to her on my own? That was when I heard that voice again, "Fear not. I am with you. Be not dismayed, for I am your God."

"God, if you are with me, I need your help now!" I said, hoping that the god of my mother would hear me.

There was a knock on my trailer. Martha knew I'd be inside. Where else would I be? I would have to open the door, but I wanted to hide. I had to face her. I could do this. I opened the door, and there she was in all her awful glory.

"Rose, I have a bone to pick with you!" She let herself in and bounded past me. Martha's larger-than-life personality quickly filled the space of the trailer.

I closed the door behind me and whispered, "Please, God, help." I met her in the little kitchen. She was standing there in her baggy blue shorts and awful blue-and-white shirt that looked like it belonged to a man.

"Rose, you have gone behind my back, and because of you, not only has your dad become more ill but we now also have child services at our door. Do you realize that Jenna may lose both her parents because of you?" Her English accent seemed to cause a tremor throughout my little home.

I steeled myself, finding strength from somewhere. I spoke up, "I have not done anything but run away, and you always told me that you'd be better off without me. I have, in fact, done you a favor."

She came closer to me, which caused me to shrink back. I hadn't been hit in a long time, and I wasn't about to let it happen tonight.

"Don't play innocent with me, young lady. I know that you blabbed lies to Ruth and that she met with Ivan's social worker."

"And? If you have nothing to hide, then you have nothing to fear. Now you and I know you have a lot to hide and, therefore, a lot to fear." Where was I getting this boldness from?

"Don't speak to me in that tone of voice!" She shook her fist in my face.

"You barged into my trailer uninvited, and you kicked Ivan out of the house. I did you a favor by leaving, so I don't see why you need to be so upset."

"You have left Jenna devastated, not to mention what you have done to your father's health."

"Jenna is fine, and as for my dad, why isn't he here trying to get me back instead of you?"

"He is too sick," she said, frustration growing in her voice.

"Well, it looks like I'll be seeing him tomorrow with my *real* mother."

"Real mother? You call Ruth your real mother? Who do you think raised you, you ungrateful child!"

"You call what you did raising me? Ha, that's ludicrous! As for me being a child, I am an adult, free to make up my own mind about where and who I want to live with!" My voice was building now. I was sure that we were going to draw some attention to ourselves if we kept this up. I also knew that the gates got locked at nine thirty, so someone would be around.

"You ungrateful little piece of shit! Ruth did nothing but marry John and move halfway around the world. She was no mother to you!" Martha was getting closer and closer to my face, and I was trying hard not to shake from the emotion of the exchange. I had gone this far; I wasn't going to back down.

"Ruth is my mother, like it or not, and you never were and never will be." That did it. She snapped and smacked my face with her hand. It stung, and I could feel a large welt forming. "You get out of my trailer, and don't come back!" I shoved her away from me, and as I did, my trailer door opened. It was Tanis.

"What do you think you are doing here, Martha? I thought I had told you to stay away from Rose."

"I was just leaving. Goodbye, you ungrateful child." She pushed past Tanis. Two minutes later, I heard her car come to life.

Tanis came over to me where I held my cheek. "Are you okay?" She removed my hand and looked at my face. "I'll get some ice for you." She walked toward my fridge, opened the freezer, and emptied some ice into a baggie. She also poured me a glass of water, which I sipped carefully. "Here, sit down, Rose."

I moved toward my table, still shaking. I sat down and tried to get my bearings. I held the ice to my face, which, although really cold, felt good.

"I'm so sorry that I wasn't here earlier. I saw a vehicle pull in, but it didn't register as to who it belonged to. Then I heard voices coming out of your trailer when I went to lock up, and I feared the worst. I see I was right to be afraid. What did she do to you?" Her blue eyes were so kind, and she tried to soothe me as she spoke.

Even though it was still warm out, I was shivering. I took a moment before answering her. "She wanted to warn me about what I had done. I wasn't really scared, but I really didn't think that she'd hit me again." I continued, reliving the scene, "She had stopped that, so why now?"

"I'm so sorry, Rose. What can I do to help?" She looked at me earnestly, her blond hair falling toward her face.

"You got her out of here, so I'd say you already helped a lot. I don't think she'll be back, at least not tonight." I tried to sound hopeful, but I was probably not convincing either of us.

"Do you want to sleep in the house tonight?"

I took a sip of water before answering. "No, I don't want her to win, and besides, she's not going to get me out of my home. My mom will be here tomorrow, and I'll get her to take me to see my dad. Then I can get to the bottom of things."

"Can I give you some advice?" Tanis moved away from me slightly, and I nodded. "I know you love it here, and trust me, we love having you here. I also know you like Ian, but...I really think that you should go and get to know your mom better in Nova Scotia. You'll have a fresh start, and I think it would be good for you."

I swallowed before I answered her. "I think that you're probably right. Maybe I could stay till the end of August though. Would that be okay?"

"That would be just fine." She smiled at me, which helped to ease the shaking I had been doing. "Okay, I need to get to bed, but do you need anything?"

"No, I'll be okay." I really wanted to call Ian, but if I told him anything, then he'd be here in a flash, and what company would I be for him tonight?

Tanis got up and gave me a hug. "Get some rest, okay?"

"I'll try to."

"Do you need me to find someone to work your shift tomorrow?"

"No, I'll be there. Besides, if I'm only here till the end of the month, then I need to make sure I make the most of it."

"Okay, I understand. I'll see you in the morning. And, Rose, if you need anything, just call or come to the house." She let herself out, and I locked the door behind her.

I had been ready to sleep before Martha barged in, but now... now there was no way I could sleep. I decided not to tell Ian about

Martha's coming over, and I also decided I wasn't going to tell him my decision to leave until I had to. I did, however, decide that I'd call him just to hear his voice. What harm could that do? I pressed his number, and after the second ring, the sound of his voice helped still my fears. I lay in my bed looking at the ceiling as we chatted, enjoying the escape of my current reality.

Chapter 19

I wasn't sure how I had fallen asleep. In fact, I hadn't even set my alarm. I was sure I had missed feeding the horses. I found my loaned cell, but the battery was dead. Had I fallen asleep while talking to Ian last night? I was a mess. My hair was everywhere, and I felt like I had traveled back to my house during the night. *Martha.* Martha had actually entered my safe haven last night. Her awful scowl clouded my morning. "Ugh, that was real."

I found the watch that Ian gave me. It was only 5:30 a.m. I hadn't missed my shift. That was a miracle. I knew that Tanis would let me have the morning off, but I didn't want that. I needed to move and lose the memories that came with the awful visit. Then I remembered. I felt my face. There was a welt on it. I brushed my face with the back of my hand. I wouldn't allow self-pity to overwhelm me.

"God, the god of my mom, you said not to fear. It looks like you were wrong." I had never been much for talking to God, but I was so sure that there was someone looking out for me recently. I waited to see if I could hear the voice that seemed to be speaking to me a lot lately, but nothing happened.

I figured I might as well embrace the day, but for some reason, I ached to see my dad. It had been too long. Why hadn't he come for me? He had never been able to stand up for me and my brother. It was almost as though he wasn't allowed to. Ack, there it was again. I had to stop thinking.

I threw the covers off me, plugged in the cell, and started getting ready. In no time, I had made a peanut butter sandwich and a cup of instant coffee. I put on my T-shirt, along with my breeches. Maybe I'd get to ride again today. That would brighten up my day. I tried to put my brush through my hair, but it wasn't successful. I gave in and just put it up in a messy bun. While I was looking in the mirror, I wondered what I could do to hide the welt.

I wanted no one's pity, but I didn't have any makeup. I knew that Jen or Lindsey wouldn't bring makeup to the barn either. Maybe Tanis could lend me some, but that would have to wait. I'd tell the girls if I had to, but everyone else would have to think I had an accident involving a horse.

I left my trailer and walked slowly toward the big barn. The air was fresh, and I breathed it in deeply. It was another beautiful summer morning. We were fortunate to have the weather we had all summer. The gravel crunched beneath my feet. I said a silent prayer that I could stay there just a little longer.

I opened up the large doors and drank in the horsey smells of the morning. One had to be a horse person to think that waking up to this was wonderful. I was greeted with neighs and whinnies. I flicked on the main lights so I could see where I was going. I looked at my watch. I was still a bit early, so I decided to give Mia some love before I began work.

I grabbed a handful of hay for good measure. I said hi to all the horses on my way to her stall, but as soon as she heard me, her bay head popped out of her window. I scratched her head and gave her the hay. I let myself into her stall and began stroking her beautiful long face. "Hey, girl, how are you today?" She answered me back with a nudge of her head. I reached up and gave her a hug as she sniffed me for more hay. "Don't worry. I'll bring you your breakfast. Hold on." She looked around my back to see if I was hiding anything. I gave her another hug and kiss on the nose and let myself out of the stall. "I'll see you soon, Mia." She kept her head out of her stall as if she weren't sure if I were telling the truth. The great thing about having a relationship with a horse was, you couldn't lie even if you wanted to.

I was busy filling up the wheelbarrows with hay when Jen, Lindsey, and Alicia came to start their shifts. I said hi, but I kept my head down and focused on the job at hand. I didn't realize that there were so many of us on.

"Hey, Rain, Tanis told me that you needed a day off today," Jen asked, coming closer to me.

"Uh, I changed my mind, or well, I wanted to help, if that's okay." I grabbed the list of horses and the portions they got, not that I needed it anymore. I tried to maneuver myself away from Jen, but she came up beside me.

"Can I talk to you for a minute?" She turned toward the others and told them to start in the small barn while we feed in the big barn. I waited for her, not liking where this would eventually have to go. "Rain, Tanis didn't tell me much, but she did say that Martha was back up here last night. Are you okay?"

I didn't have any way to hide my face, and it was obvious I wasn't okay. I could tell the truth to her. "Jen, the truth is, well, she gave me this." I pointed to the side of my face. "It was a rough night, that's for sure."

"I'm so sorry, Rain. Really, that's awful. You can't stay here, you know." She put her hand on my shoulder.

"I know, but I'm not in a rush to leave. I don't want to run away again. This time, I want to stand up for myself."

"Do what you think is best, but please have protection. Call Tanis or your mom or even Ian if you need to." She looked deep into my eyes with so much concern. "Okay, Rain?"

"Okay. Thanks, Jen. I really don't want to be any trouble today, but honestly, I can't just sit still."

"I get it. Just let me know if you need a break. Actually, there's a huge camp today, so that's why there's so many of us here. It'll be busy, so I appreciate the help."

"Well, my mom and John should be up here today, but I'll help until then."

"Okay. Thanks. I'll go get the grain, if you want to do the haying."

I smiled at her. "It would be my pleasure." She smiled back and gave my shoulder a squeeze. It was truly odd to have people caring the way they did at A&T. If only I could pick up this barn and move it to Nova Scotia.

Jen and I worked in peaceful silence. The horses were the ones that seemed to have the most to say, especially Diamond. Diamond was a new Appaloosa pony. She was so cute with her light-brown body and spotted behind. Considering how small she was, she made a large amount of noise. It reminded me of a hungry cat. After feeding her, she quieted some. Mia was the opposite. Although she was hungry, she took the hay in a very refined fashion. She was such a feminine horse. I had never met such a dainty horse with a deceiving diva quality. I assumed that was why I fell for her.

I was happy to have the distraction and quickly fell into my morning routine with the girls. I knew I would have to face some sort of decision and consequence for last night, but around the horses, I felt safe.

It was just before 9:00 a.m. when we finished our morning rituals. With having four of us on, we cleaned up well. The barn looked ready for advanced camp, which started at nine thirty. I was sure that Martha wouldn't be sending Jenna no matter how hard she begged to come. I decided to get cleaned up before everyone arrived, as I knew my mom and John would be up to see me soon.

The lot was filling up with kids and trailers. One by one I scanned the faces and waited to hear the sound of Martha's car in case I had assumed incorrectly. I recognized a lot of the kids but sighed with relief when Jenna wasn't among them.

I let myself into my trailer and checked my now charged cell. I had a couple of texts from Ian asking me how I was doing. I had a voice mail from my mom telling me to get ready for an important meeting. She'd be up to see me by ten. I didn't have a lot of time, so I quickly showered and changed into the best I had.

I tried to dry my hair, but it was just too hot out. Maybe it was time to lose the long hair that had been my signature look for so long. I had decided to grow it long when at sixteen, I finally got control of my hair. Martha had made sure I was as ugly as possible growing up, so she kept my hair in a boy haircut. It worked; I sure didn't have a lot of boys asking me for dates. I was also really chubby until I hit thirteen, when I decided to do something about it. Working at the barn all summer had helped me turn my once loose arms into much more of a defined look. Maybe that was part of the reason I actually had a boyfriend.

I braided my hair back and put on some ChapStick. I was in my only pair of jeans, and again, thanks to Ian's generosity, I had a nice top. I looked over at my paddock boots and shook my head. "Oh well, you can take the girl out of the barn, but you can't take the barn out of the girl."

As I was shaking my boots outside my door, I noticed my mom's rental car pulling in. *Just in time,* I thought. I put my cool horse watch on and grabbed my cell and made it out to the lot just as Tanis was coming out of the house. *Did she tell them about last night?* I wondered.

I walked up and gave John and my mom a hug and looked sheepishly at Tanis. I asked Tanis if I could talk to her before she said anything. I just didn't want my mom to take me away from A&T before I was ready. As I pleaded my case, Tanis begrudgingly agreed to stay quiet, but she made me promise to tell them what happened. I thanked her and went back to my mom to find out more about this important meeting.

"Mom, what's happening this morning?"

My mom was dressed in beige summer pants, brown sandals, and a pretty coral top. She had curled her hair slightly so that it framed her soft features. "Well, Rose, we are meeting with the social worker who handled your brother's case. We are also going to meet with your dad."

"With my dad? Does that mean that he will be alone, or will Martha be there too?" I couldn't help but hope that I could see only him.

"Most likely it will be both of them," she answered disappointedly. "Now come on. We need to go."

I got in the Malibu feeling like I was leaving my safety net behind. I wanted so badly to see Ivan and my dad, but the rest I could do without.

Chapter 20

We walked into a cold-looking building. I wasn't on trial, but being there made me nervous. There were doctors and nurses passing us, all engrossed in conversation. The three of us remained silent. I was sure my mom was as jittery as I was.

Finally, we entered a room with the name Child and Family Services on the door. I remembered that I had one visit from them when I was in grade 4. Martha had been too angry with me and stabbed me with a steak knife. Although it had been years, I still had the scar on my thigh. I wished that I hadn't had an altercation with Martha last night. I shuddered involuntarily at the thought.

I took a seat on an uncomfortable office chair, as my mom and John checked us in. I was told that after I saw the social worker that I'd finally get to see Ivan. It had been so long since we'd spent time with each other. I was excited, but nervous. Had he changed? I knew that I had.

I looked about the room and saw posters about how child and family services could help you. *They never helped me,* I thought. Then again, I lied whenever anyone asked me about my life. Maybe things would have been different had I told the truth, but there was always Jenna.

Mom and John came and sat down beside me. I looked over at my mom and asked, "What is the point of this meeting? I mean, I've already left, so why go through with this?" I shrugged.

My mom cleared her throat before answering. "To set things right. You have a chance to tell the truth. No one will hurt you, Rose," she assured me.

"That's not true." I touched my face absentmindedly. I told them what had transpired last evening on the drive to our meeting.

"I know, honey, but that won't happen again, not after today."

"I hope you're right."

John looked over at me. "Have you thought any more about our offer to come home?"

"I'm tempted, that's for sure."

"So that's a yes?" He smiled at me with his eyes taking on an unearthly quality.

"It's an almost yes." I smiled back at him weakly. What would my life be like not having to run from pain?

Just then, I heard my name being called.

"I guess this is it. Are either of you coming with me?" I looked expectantly at both of my parents.

"No. It's important that you do this on your own," my mom replied.

"Okay. See you soon." Both of them hugged me. It was as if I were leaving for longer than a few minutes.

I followed the counselor to an office that looked a lot friendlier than the waiting room. She made some idle chitchat with me as we got seated. The room was painted in a light-blue color, and there were even stuffed animals in a corner. I felt like I could use one of those to hold on to. The chairs were more like a comfy sofa, except for hers, which was a black office chair. She offered me a seat and then offered me her hand.

"Rose, my name is Edna, and I am hoping that I can help you today."

I appraised the woman who appeared to be in her late forties. She had short blond hair and inquisitive blue eyes. She smiled and seemed genuine enough. I still wasn't sure what I was doing here. "I'm Rai—I mean, Rose, as you already know, and I don't know how you can help or how I'm supposed to help."

She leaned forward in her chair and began, "Rose, your brother Ivan has been here a few times and has told me about your life growing up. I wanted to ask you some of the questions that I asked him. I want to know what happened with you as well. You see, we have a record of counselors coming to your house a few times. The problem is, most children don't feel comfortable telling the truth. I am hoping now that your actual mother is here that you will feel safe enough to confide in me."

I nodded at her, pretending to understand what she needed.

She continued, "Rose, I have been told that you have recently run away. Can you tell me why?"

"Um…" I looked down at my paddock boots and tried to decide how much to tell. "I had finally had enough," I said, finding my voice.

"Enough of what?" she asked softly.

"Enough mental and physical abuse. Martha, my stepmother, had pushed me too far."

I continued to explain what happened over the course of several years. Once I started, it was as if a dam burst open, and I couldn't stop. I had no idea how much time had passed as Edna just let me keep talking. By the end, I felt like more of a victor and less of a victim.

Edna got up and walked over to me and put her hand lightly on my shoulder. "Rose, I want you to know what you did today was really brave. I also want to tell you that you have told me the exact same story as your brother. What do you wish to do?"

"I want to leave and not come back. That is, unless I want to come back." I stared straight ahead, ready to fight for my resolve.

"Then I will help you do that. Since you are eighteen, you are legally an adult and can do what you want, but I want to do more." She walked over to her desk and found some papers, then turned back to me. "Rose, do you wish to press charges?"

"Are you serious?" *There is no way,* I thought.

"Yes, very serious. We have a solid case, including all the times that we visited your house. I am also sure your teachers would confirm your story."

"I don't know. I don't want to hurt my sister Jenna."

"It's up to you. I won't press you, but I would hate for the two people whom you have called your parents for so long to get away with what they have done to you and your brother."

"Can I see Ivan?" I asked, realizing that I needed him.

"Yes, of course. He's waiting with your parents. Rose, here's my number." Edna handed me a card with two numbers on it. "My cell is on there as well. I want you to know that you can call me anytime, okay?"

I took it. "I appreciate your listening, Edna." I faltered.

"Of course. But, Rose, I don't want to just listen. I want to help bring justice to your situation." She spoke with such determination that it was hard at that moment to say no to pressing charges. "Now let me get Ivan for you." She got up from her chair, squeezed my shoulder again, and left me alone in the office.

I stood up and paced. I was exhausted and exhilarated all at the same time. I was so glad that I actually had the courage to run away. I hadn't seen Ivan in months. Martha wouldn't let him visit often, and my dad didn't fight to change the arrangement.

I moved back over to the doctor's desk, really wanting to look through the notes that she had been taking while we were talking, but I resisted. I heard the door open, and there he was. I crossed the room quickly and threw my arms around my brother. We laughed at the sheer excitement of seeing each other. I didn't want to let go, but as we were being watched, I finally did.

"You look amazing!" I exclaimed in shock. I held him at arm's length and took in his changed demeanor. When he had left Dundas, he was scrawny, his blond hair poorly cut, and his eyes held no confidence. Now he had filled out, his hair was cut short, and his light-blue eyes almost shone. I could tell he had more confidence now. As I looked deeper, I could still see the hurt, but it wasn't like before.

"You look pretty good yourself, sis, and I heard you actually ran away."

I grinned. "Yes, that I did."

"I'm impressed. I wish I'd done the same."

I put my hand on his arm. "Hey, at least you got out." He smiled in return.

The doctor, closing the door, interrupted our reunion. Edna motioned for us to sit back on the couch; she sat across from us at her desk and gathered her notes.

"Ivan, Rose, you both have a decision to make. Either way, with what you've told me, I can at least make sure that they don't have the chance to hurt anyone else. I still need to confirm a few things, but I was serious when I asked you if you wanted to press charges on both your dad and Martha."

I looked at Ivan. "Are you wanting to pursue this?"

"No, not really. I'm out now, and to be honest, as long as there is a record of it, I'm happy with that. I also don't want to see the two of them in court. How about you?" He turned toward me.

"I feel the same way. I'd rather be one day further away from my past." I turned back to Edna. "It looks like you have our answer."

"I am sorry for that, but I understand. You two must be pretty special young people to just leave this behind you. I hope that you get rewarded for it. I'm going to get your parents now. And, Ivan, as you are just sixteen, you can decide to move with your mom and John or stay in foster care. In meeting your parents, I would advise going with them, as not many kids get the chance to start over again."

"Thanks, Edna. I am definitely considering it." He ran the palms of his hands over his green shorts. He appeared a bit nervous.

"I'll be right back to help you facilitate the next step." She got up and left us alone, and I was glad; I wanted to find out how Ivan had fared in the outside world.

"Would you really consider moving to Nova Scotia, Ivan?" I hoped he would, as it would be so much easier if we both went.

"Ever since Mom came to town, I've thought about it. But, Rose, I've built a life in Stoney Creek in the last year. I have a girlfriend. Heck, I have friends!"

"You're allowed to have friends now, eh?" I laughed.

"Yeah, and I'm not a loser anymore. It will be hard to leave the life I've created for myself."

"I know. I've only been on my own for a bit, but I've made friends, and I kind of have a boyfriend too. But I've always wanted to get to know Mom. I've also always wanted to leave this place, and well, Nova Scotia is pretty far away."

"That's for sure. Rose, why did you finally leave? I mean, I got shoved out. I know I shouldn't have stolen, but it wasn't as if you hadn't stolen before... They just caught me and pinned everything on me." Ivan looked away, his blue eyes clouded over with the hurt I knew so well.

"It was just one day. She pushed me too far, and the abuse that I thought had disappeared started to come back. I left that night. I didn't know where I was going, but I figured I could die on a road somewhere or I could die at home. At least I'd die fighting."

"You were always a fighter." He looked back at me. "I didn't learn how to fight."

"It was because you were too young when they took you from Mom. I was at least five. I had been fighting all along. A lot of good that did me. I would have been hit a lot less had I not fought back."

"That's not true. I didn't fight, and look at the beatings I got. You know, besides my foster parents, no one knows about my past. I've been seeing a social worker, and she knows, but I've kept my past hidden. When they said they didn't want me back at the house, I didn't ask why. The truth is, I missed you and Jenna a lot. My feelings for Dad were different. I missed him, but all I saw was disappointment whenever he looked at me."

I ached for Ivan. I wanted to cry but stuffed it down. Now wasn't the time. "Ivan, are we doing the right thing not pressing charges?"

"I don't know. After talking to you, I'm not sure." I turned from him and over to the clock. What would it prove? "I'm glad we seemed to have the same thoughts on it though."

"Me too." I smiled at him reassuringly. I didn't want to say goodbye to him. "Do you think we can go out for a bite to eat with our real parents?"

"I hope so, but I'm not sure, Mom said something about another meeting with Martha and Dad."

"Ivan, Martha came to see me last night. She threatened me. I do not want that meeting," I said sternly.

"You'll be okay. Mom and John will be with you, right?"

"Right." I heard their voices at the door, and we got up to greet them.

FALLEN PETALS

"Rose, Ivan, it is so good to see the two of you together," my mom said warmly and came over to embrace the two of us. We both sank into her embrace. I felt safe, and I had never felt safe.

Chapter 21

We finished up with Edna, but sure enough, our respite would be short-lived as we had a meeting with Dad and Martha. I still hadn't seen or even talked to my dad since I left. I couldn't believe that now that he knew I was okay, he hadn't made any move to see me. My resolve to stay away strengthened as I mulled this over.

We did get to go for some lunch before the meeting, but my stomach was tied up in knots, so I spent more time in the bathroom than at the table. I thought that Ivan might have had similar sentiments, but he was never one to pass up food. We had been tormented even when it came to eating regularly, so I couldn't blame him.

I thought that my mom laid out a pretty good case for Ivan to move to Nova Scotia, but only time would tell. He was still in high school, so if he was going to move, he'd have to make up his mind quickly. It was still August, so there was a bit of time. In the end, Ivan agreed to go for a visit while I was there so he could check it out.

I don't think I had ever seen my mom so happy before. She had always dreamed of getting to know her kids, and it was finally happening. She kept saying how God had promised her certain things. I was still doubting that God was a part of all the planning, but after hearing what could have been his voice, I wasn't going to argue. Both Ivan and I thought that if God was so involved that, he could have made a move sooner.

We drove to the next meeting place. It was another social worker's office, but I was assured that Edna would be there to facilitate. The whole thing just felt surreal.

"Do we really have to do all of this?" I asked from the back seat of the rental car. "I mean, I'm old enough to make my own decisions, and they pretty much kicked Ivan out. What do they have to gain or lose for that matter?"

My mom turned around to us and said, "Honey, they have everything to lose. What they have to gain is nothing, but we have much to gain. It'll be okay. We have the truth on our side."

"The truth hasn't helped us, at least not yet." I tried to hide my sarcasm, but it seemed impossible. "Ivan, are you as nervous as I am?" I looked over to him, and I found myself admiring his stylish haircut and healthy-looking face. Gone were the days of his looking homeless.

"I don't know what I feel... I'm not sure if it's nervousness, but it is unsettling. I just look forward to getting this over with. Do you know Dad hasn't even tried to contact me since last Christmas?" Ivan turned his eyes back to the road.

"Well, he's a fool!" I spat out. I always wanted to protect Ivan but was never able to.

"I agree," my mom stated.

The car came to a stop, and that was when I saw the ugly station wagon. She was here, but I wasn't alone this time. There would be no slapping my face today.

John turned to us and spoke with authority, "Kids, I promise that if you move in with us, you will never doubt that you are loved. I, we, will take care of both of you. You will not wonder where you stand. We can do this together. Finally, the truth will come out, and we can build a new life together. Your mom and I love you so much and want to get to know you both better."

"Thanks, John." Ivan nodded in agreement. "Let's get this over with and get on with the rest of our lives."

"Amen," Mom chimed in.

We clambered out of the car and walked toward the front door of a gray building. That was when I heard it again, "I will never leave you or forsake you."

Inwardly I said, "God, if you get me through this, then I will learn more about what you are about." After that, I felt such a wave of peace come over me that if I wasn't experiencing it, I wouldn't have believed it. "Thank you," I whispered.

I caught up to Ivan and pulled his ear to me. "It'll be okay, I promise."

He smiled at me, a real smile that reached his eyes. "I believe you," he answered me.

We would get through this and leave this place to start a new life. I could feel it just as I felt the ground beneath my feet.

We got to the room that was set up for us, and sure enough, Martha and my dad were already seated across the table from where we were supposed to sit. I looked at my dad and had to swallow hard. He didn't look well. Could Martha have been telling the truth? Was he sick? His light-blue eyes that usually sparkled with humor looked faded. His laugh lines looked deeper. He appeared to have aged ten years since I'd seen him. Before I got too caught up in my emotions, I looked over at Martha. She was presenting herself as a weak woman. She was such an actress, but I knew her emotions were made of steel.

My dad got up and came around the table to me. I was sure this was an act of defiance as Martha seemed to wince. I felt Ivan tense beside me, but I received my dad's hug. I had missed him. I was a part of him. It was never him whom I wanted to run from, but unfortunately, he was part of the package.

"I'm so sorry," he said in a quiet, broken voice.

"You didn't even come to see me when you found out where I was." I tried not to sound judgmental, but I was hurt.

"I didn't know till last night where you were." He was crying, but I didn't let his tears reach my soul. I couldn't.

"Martha knew." I pulled away and looked into his tired face.

"I'm so sorry."

"I know, but it may be too late for that. She's your wife."

The room was waiting for our exchange to be over. We would have to continue this later, but for now, at least I'd been honest. I moved away from him. He tried to hug Ivan, but Ivan just stood stiffly. I was right. It was too late.

I remembered how a year ago I had poured my heart out to my dad. I told him every detail of the abuse, the lies, and yet he still married her. They had lived together common law for so many years. I was sure after learning the truth, he would end it, but he didn't. That was the day I realized that Martha was more powerful than I realized. I would try to forgive, but I wouldn't stay in this province.

We all got seated, and Edna explained why we were there. I listened, staying close to Ivan, who was visibly shaken seeing Martha again. I steeled myself to look her in the eyes, those angry gray-blue eyes that could love one minute and be cold as ice the next. I trusted that Edna could handle her and, even more than that, that God somehow had his hand on us.

Edna asked all of us questions throughout the next hour. Both Ivan and I tried to stay on course and not let our fears derail us. I was so grateful for John, who was the backbone for all of us. Finally, after what seemed like forever, Ivan and I were asked to leave so that the parents could work out the details.

Ivan and I left the cramped office and past the reception desk. We decided to get some air. Both of us were visibly shaken. He was the first to speak. "Rose, if we don't see her ever again, it'll be too soon."

"I agree. She acts so innocent. I tell you, when she smacked me last night, she was not innocent."

"So you've made up your mind? To leave, I mean."

"I think I have. Have you?"

"I'll visit and see how that goes."

I grabbed him and gave him a huge hug. "Want to get out of here?"

"And go where?"

"I don't know. I'll leave a message for Mom to call my cell. I saw a coffee shop across the way. I just know I can't handle seeing Dad like that again."

"Okay, let's do it."

I laughed for the first time all day. "I'll be right back."

I left a message with the young woman who was at the reception desk. She informed me that the meeting would continue for some time. I hoped my mom would be okay, and then I remembered the peace I felt earlier. My mom had that peace, lived that peace. She would be fine, and once more, we would be too.

Ivan and I left the office, and I made sure that my phone was on. I didn't want to add more worry to Mom.

I think Ivan and I practically floated with giddiness. To be free was a wonderful thing. We weren't totally free yet, but we were actually able to hang out together without the restraints we were so used to. In fact, we had never been able to hang out like this. I had a feeling that even though I'd have to say goodbye to my new A&T family and Ian, I would be walking toward a new life.

Chapter 22

My mom and John found us at the coffee shop. They both looked like they had been through a war. The happiness I had been feeling moments earlier quickly dissipated. Ivan and I got up to greet them. I gave my mom a hug, then pulled a couple more chairs at our table. The store was busy, but there was enough room for all of us to sit together.

"What happened? You both look awful," I asked earnestly.

"Well, Rose, it was terrible. Martha threw all the dirt of the past at us. I have to say, if it weren't for John and Edna, I would have buckled over in guilt right there," my mom shared.

"But you have nothing to feel guilty about. In fact, Ivan is already in a foster home, and I'm old enough to make my own choices. What they say is null and void, right?" I searched my mom's eyes for answers.

John took my mom's hand and looked into both Ivan's and my worried faces. "What you say is true. I think she just wants to destroy us in the wake of losing both of you."

"Losing us? They kicked Ivan out, and as for me, they never had me!" I had raised my voice, so a few onlookers took me in. I quieted my voice and continued, "Why do they want to destroy you, Mom? It's not as if she hadn't tried to destroy Ivan and me for the last thirteen years."

"I know, honey, but that's what evil does."

Ivan had been pretty quiet during this exchange, but as he hadn't decided where he was going to live, he was in limbo. "What happens next?" Ivan offered.

"Well, Ivan, as you are already in care and you are your mom's son, there is nothing stopping you from coming home with us. Rose, as you stated, you are of age, so you are an adult in the eyes of the law. Our plans don't have to change."

"Okay then, let's make our plan. Mom, John, Ivan has some news for you both." I looked expectantly at my brother and smiled at him.

"Rose and I were talking, and we thought it would be a good idea if I came home for a week so I could test things out. That way, I could find out what it would be like to live in Nova Scotia as a family. What do you think?"

I looked at our parents. The battered look was gone, and in its place, they both looked like they'd been kissed by the sun. Mom rose from her chair and came around and hugged Ivan. "That is wonderful! Rose, you're coming too?"

"Of course."

John joined in on the hug. We were making quite a scene in the café, but we didn't care. Happiness, was this really what it was like?

"Let's get things going, you two. We have tickets to buy and plans to make," Mom said excitedly.

The rest of the day flew by as we dropped Ivan off at his foster parents' place. We also got to meet his girlfriend briefly. We had to rush back to get me to the farm. Although I wasn't on the night shift, I really wanted to help, as my time there was coming to an end. I also needed to talk to Ian and figured that if I had the excuse of working that I could put it off for a bit longer.

By the time I arrived, Jen and Lindsey had finished work, but Jayden, one of the young eventing riders, was on shift that night. She was thankful for my help, as it meant she could ride Ellie after she was done with work. I ached to ride Mia again, but with all the kindness of Kat and Tanis, I didn't want to push my luck.

I had texted Ian to say when I'd be done, and always the gentleman, he didn't complain. He had to work a bit later too. I knew that we had spoken briefly about my departure, although now that there was a date attached to it, I assumed he wouldn't be happy. For the first time, I was sad that Ontario and Nova Scotia weren't closer.

I was feeding the horses their nightly hay in the large barn when I was surprised at seeing two familiar faces. "Jenna, what are you doing here?" Jenna was in Calvin's stall with her good friend Mya. Both of them looked extremely guilty. "Jenna, answer me. What are you doing here, and why are you in Calvin's stall?"

Her usual bright blue eyes were clouded over with moisture, and she couldn't really look at me, but in a small voice, she began to answer my question, "I kind of ran away."

"You what?"

This time, her face held a sort of determination. "That's right. Like you, I ran away. You can do it, so why can't I?"

"And you, Mya, why are you here? I know you don't ride, so I'm a little confused."

Jenna answered before Mya had a chance, "Well, I needed a ride, and Mya's brother offered to drive us."

"But I assume he doesn't know your plan. What about Dad? Did you tell him where you were going?"

Calvin continued to munch on his hay as the three of us were crowded in his stall. Before Jayden came to feed him his grain, I had an idea.

"Listen, you two, we need to continue this conversation, but we need to get out of here, and I need to finish my job. Come on."

I opened up Calvin's stall door wide enough for all of us to get out. He looked at us briefly and then went back to his dinner. The horses around us, sensing they were being forgotten, started creating a ruckus by banging their stall doors with their hooves. None was worse than Dakota, who seemed to find precisely the metal spot of the door and knocked it with his hoof. Mia, on the other hand, just looked longingly at the hay with her brown ears piqued in interest.

"Jenna, why don't you and Mya help me feed that side of the barn?" I motioned to my left. "And I'll feed this side. Just follow the hay plan on each stall door. Jenna, I know you've done this a hundred times before. Mya, if you don't feel comfortable, then just wait for us over by the stairs."

"I'm comfortable," she said in her strong voice. She piled her long, thick blond hair in a ponytail and gave me a large grin. I had always liked Jenna's best friend; she never seemed to take sides when it came to our family. She and Jenna had become instant friends after I introduced the two of them when I was younger.

"Jenna, after this, we can go to my trailer, and I'll talk some sense into you and Mya. I hope your brother can come back for the two of you. If not, I'll get Ian to take you home. Got it?"

"We'll see," Jenna said defiantly while turning to the hay in the wheelbarrow.

I had no time to argue; I really didn't want to cause a scene. Jayden was halfway down the barn with feeding the horses their grain. Thankfully, Jenna had started with Dakota, so the racket was dying down. I took Mia's hay inside her stall and stole a quick hug. While hugging her, I breathed in the smell of her coat. What was I going to do with having Jenna and Ian there at the same time? I was grateful that I wasn't getting together with my mom and Ivan till the next day. With all that I had to do, I didn't have time for too much drama.

I reluctantly moved away from Mia and finished my side. At about the same time, Jenna finished hers. The two clean girls I had encountered just minutes ago were now covered in hay. "You both look marvelous. Gee, no one will know you've been hanging out at the farm, won't they?"

"We probably look the same as you, smart aleck," Jenna piped out.

"Hey, we all look pretty good," Mya added with her brown eyes sparking.

"I never knew that under your city girl exterior, you were a horse girl, Mya. It looks good on you."

"Thanks, Rose."

"I told you her name is Rain up here," Jenna corrected her.

"It's okay. Seeing as your mom has found me, the cat's out of the bag. Mind you, up here, I'm still known as Rain."

"Okay, Rain, where to next?"

"You both stay here, and no hiding. I have to return the wheelbarrow, and then we can go." They both nodded and turned their attention to Mia, who seemed to be enjoying the extra interaction.

I put my tools away, then met up with Jayden. She was thrilled that I brought more help and was looking forward to riding. I could understand, but riding for me would have to wait. I still wasn't given unlimited access to any one horse.

The barn was pretty quiet when we got back to the trailer. There were only a couple of lessons on the go and a few boarders taking advantage of the long summer evening. Summer was always such a crazy time with camp, but the quiet evenings were nice. I checked my watch. Shoot, Ian would be here soon, and I wouldn't be ready. He was almost always early too. Sigh, I would do what I could.

The trailer was crowded with the three of us, but I had both of them sit at my little table while I thought about my next move. I got my phone and saw I had missed a text from Ian. He was on his way. I would have to be short and sweet.

I turned back to the two happy and content girls. "You both could have a sleepover here as long as someone knows you're here. Also, they have to know when to pick you up."

"I guess we could work with that," Jenna suggested.

"The only caveat is that I kind of have a date tonight."

"A date!" the both squealed in unison. This caused me to laugh.

"Yes, a date. A lot has happened since I've been gone. Anyways, this isn't an easy date but one that has to happen. Jenna, there's a lot that is about to happen. If you want, when I get back, I can fill you in."

"My mom says that you've been really unfair to Dad."

"Well, she's lying. Look, I really have to get ready so I don't smell like horses. You can both make yourself at home here while I'm gone. Don't move anything though." I heard my phone go off. "One sec, I'll be right back." I picked up my phone and saw it was Ian. He was almost there, and I was totally not ready. Maybe we could just stay at the farm so I wouldn't need to change. I hung up with him agreeing to take my lead.

As I entered back into the kitchen area, I saw that Jenna and Mya looked like they were up to something. "You guys behave," I called over my shoulder as I went into the bathroom to get myself spruced up. I took down my hair and tried to get out all the knots.

I decided to use the baby powder trick, and it didn't look too bad. I changed my shirt but stayed in my jeans and boots.

It was still a warm night out, so it would be perfect for a walk. It was just getting dark, which suited me just fine. I heard a knock at the door, took a deep breath, and went to answer it. My breath caught in my throat. It wasn't Ian. It was Martha.

"What are you doing here?" I managed to choke out. I refused to be afraid of her, especially when Jenna was present.

She pushed her large body past me and seemed to squeeze all the air out of the trailer. "Jenna, what has Rose done? What are you two doing here?" She then turned her steely blue eyes in my direction. "Now you want to try to pit Jenna against me?"

"Hey, they are here on their own accord. If you'd ask them, they'd tell you that I told them it was a bad idea." If Ian came and Martha was here, I wasn't sure what he'd do. He knew enough not to like her. I peered my head out of the trailer but didn't see his car. I closed the door. I had to get them all out of here. "Jenna, Mya, I know you wanted a girls' night, but it seems that will have to wait. Go ahead, Martha, take them home."

She continued to glare at me. I wondered, if the girls weren't there, would she try hitting me again? I shook off the thought and walked next to Jenna. "Get your stuff, you two."

"But, Mom, can't we stay? Rose told us that we shouldn't have come, but we wanted to see her. Puleasssse."

Martha always had a problem saying no to Jenna, but I was sure she'd do it this time.

"Jenna, after all that Rose has done to your dad, you need to come with me. Get your stuff and let's go."

Jenna looked so crestfallen, but after seeing my insistence, she moved to get her bag. Mya followed her to my room. They hadn't been gone a minute when I felt a pressure on my arm. Martha was squeezing it hard.

"You, Rose, don't think you can get away with this. You will not get your way in court. You are a sniveling little child who knows nothing." She was so frightening, and she yanked my arm one more time for good measure. Then she turned her act around as she saw

Jenna coming. "Let's go, girls." She was back to her "sweet" English accent.

She walked out just as I heard another car pull into A&T. I knew it was Ian. They couldn't meet. I ushered Jenna and Mya out and told them to be good. I felt my arm. There was a bruise forming. Why couldn't I have fought back? Was I playing the victim by leaving? I wanted to call my mom or curl up in a ball and cry. I was tired of this life in Ontario, that's for sure.

My trailer was empty. The night that had started fun had ended in disaster. I'd call my mom tomorrow. First, I'd begin my journey to my new home.

Chapter 23

I met Ian outside, as I suddenly felt claustrophobic. I also wanted to make sure there was no confrontation with him and Martha. Ian didn't seem like a violent man, but he was protective of me.

I was so happy to see his smiling face. I felt safe with him. I'd miss him, that's for sure.

"Rain, how goes it?" He gave me a quick hug but noticed I wasn't myself. "What's wrong?" He held me away from him. I averted my eyes from his, but he saw the bruise on my arm. "What is that? Did you have an accident riding?" He touched it gingerly.

"No. Nothing like that. It's worse actually, but let's go to the back."

"Okay. I brought you a snack. It's in my car. Give me a sec to grab it." Ian walked over to his Impala and retrieved a wicker picnic basket that looked perfect for the summer evening. He was so thoughtful. If only his work could take him to Nova Scotia. "Let's go." He looked around, and as most of the girls were in the barn, he boldly grabbed hold of my hand with his free one.

There were horses outside in the riding area. They looked so peaceful, the opposite of how I felt. The ground crunched beneath our feet as we passed more horses outside in the paddocks enjoying the summer night. I just loved the smell of horses mixed with summer. My mom thought I was a little crazy, but she was supportive of my passion.

We went to our usual log, and Ian put the basket down. I was glad that the resident barn dogs seemed to be elsewhere, for now at least.

"That looks like the perfect idea." I smiled at Ian.

"It will be, but first, come and tell me what happened. I have a feeling I won't like it."

I sat down beside him, and he took my hand, which gave me the strength to continue. "Did you see the station wagon that pulled out when you pulled in?" He nodded at me. "Well, Martha was driving it, and she's not happy with me."

"So she gave you that bruise!" Ian said in disbelief. "Who does that?"

"Someone who's not getting her way anymore. We got some good news today, and it'll make her and my dad's life a lot more difficult."

"Well, good. She deserves it. You could press charges if you wanted. My brother knows a great lawyer." He had let go of my hand and was up on his feet, giving me his impassioned plea.

I shook my head. "No, no, I don't want to do that. But, Ian, you will understand that I need to leave here. I can't live like this any longer, and I don't know if it's the coward's way out or not, but I'm leaving at the end of the month." There, I had said it. It was final.

Ian sat back down beside me. "I knew you were thinking of it, but you've made up your mind?"

"Yes, it's the right thing to do, and my brother is coming to visit as well. I can't tell you how I've missed him."

"Well, Rain, Rose, I am going to miss you, but I get it." He paused before continuing on. "So what do we have, a week before you go?"

"Something like that…" I looked away, feeling slightly guilty, but as if he could read my thoughts, he brought me back to the present.

"It's okay. If we're supposed to be together in the future, we will be. Are you okay? I mean, is your arm okay?"

"Yeah, it's just that she's so dishonest. One minute she's doing this"—I pointed to my arm—"and the next she's being all sweet. I hate the lies!"

"Rain, I think you know the best way to get back at her is to live well and to become a success at whatever it is you want to do. Have you thought about what you will study or what you want to do?"

"No, actually, I haven't. My whole goal this past year was to get out of Dundas. Oh, and to not get a boyfriend." I laughed, and Ian joined me.

"Sorry, I didn't mean to ruin that plan of yours."

"It's all right. I still managed to get out of Dundas, and well, you aren't too bad for a boyfriend." I blushed and tried to turn away from him, but he pulled me close. He smelled so good. I wasn't sure what cologne he wore, but the smell of him mixed with the night air was stirring up emotions I wasn't used to having.

"Not too bad, eh? I mean, I did provide you with a picnic."

"Yes, you did."

We were sitting pretty close to each other on the large log. He looked around, checking to see if we were alone. "I guess as I only have a week, I'd better take advantage of the here and now."

Again, my heart was full of butterflies. He leaned over and kissed me. As I was pretty sure we were alone, I kissed him back, not worrying about my troubles. After much too short a time, I heard someone hooting at us. We pulled apart. It was Jayden and one of the other girls. We had been caught in the act.

We both laughed. It was a risk trying to find privacy at the barn. Ian waved them away in a good-natured fashion. "I guess it's picnic time, eh, Rain? By the way, that shade of red looks great on you."

I knew my face was as red as a beet. "I can't help it. I haven't ever been caught kissing someone."

"Oh, so there was kissing involved back in your old life, eh?" Ian teased.

"Not much, and no real boyfriends. So anyway, about that food you keep promising me."

"Yes, I almost made it myself too." He pulled out a couple of sandwiches clearly marked Subway.

"Yeah, almost made them. So you're a gourmet cook, are you?"

"Almost. I'm spoiled. My mom's a great cook. She takes care of me whenever I get home."

"So you have a good relationship with your parents?"

Ian handed me my food and took his. "They're the best. That's why I can't understand why your dad isn't protective of you. I like your mom and John already, but that father of yours, well, that's another story. Tell me about the good news from today. I also think you going to live with your mom and John is good news, even though I'll miss you like crazy."

"Thanks for being so generous." I leaned into him. "Do you ever get to Nova Scotia for work?"

"Not yet, but I'll try. We may actually be opening up a new store in BC, just in case you ever think you'd want to move there."

"Oh, good to know, although I'm not sure why I'd ever move there. I guess only time will tell."

"Just thought I'd keep my options open with you. I've never met anyone like you. But I want to see you be all that you can be, with whatever you decide to do. Rain, you can call me anytime if you need help, okay?"

"Okay. Thanks. I really do appreciate it, and it's not easy to leave you."

"Is it because of my charm?" He moved his face closer to mine.

"Yeah, that's it. Or because of your cooking skills."

"Good to know. Eat up. I brought some cokes too." He leaned down and produced our drinks.

We both ate, content for the moment. I saw Jayden one more time bringing in a couple of the horses, but she pretty much left us alone. I was sure if we started kissing, it wouldn't be the case.

I ended up telling Ian about how the social worker had put my dad and Martha on Ontario's list of dangerous parents. He was pleased, even though it happened by accident. I loved hanging out with Ian and thought that it was probably a good idea that I hadn't met him earlier, or it would be too hard to leave there.

We went for a walk farther back into the cross-country area. It was thrilling to think of cantering over the jumps in the back. I was sure it wouldn't happen for me now that I was leaving, but I hoped that I could at least watch some of the girls do it. At least I had ridden Mia and had experienced the thrill of her stride.

We ventured by the small stream that was behind a few of the larger jumps. The sun was starting to dip, and it was another stunning sunset. Sunsets at the farm never got old to me. I always wished I could paint them, but I wasn't skilled in that department.

Neither of us seemed to be in a rush to get back to normal life. I actually didn't have to get up early to feed in the morning, which made the idea of staying out even more tempting. There was also a sense of freedom bubbling it's way into my spirit. I wasn't sure if it was Ian or just the fact that Martha was soon to be out of my life. Either way, I felt I was on the edge of a precipice.

"It's so nice here," Ian offered. "Yasmin used to drag me here, but it seems you may have converted me to more of a horse guy. I don't need to ride them though."

"Oh, but would you want to go riding with me? It would be so much fun!" I turned excitedly to him.

"If you think it's a good idea."

"Oh yes! We've got adult rides here, and maybe Alicia and Lindsey will ride with us too."

"But you're all pros, and I've never been on a horse."

"You can ride Toby. He's so good and quite gentle. Please, can we do this before I leave?"

"Okay. If it means that much to you."

"It does! Oh, thank you. It will be a perfect goodbye gift."

"I know another little gift. Is there anyone else around?"

"No, I don't think so."

"We got interrupted earlier. Shall we try that again?" He brought me to him and again kissed me. It felt almost sad though. It was going to be harder to leave than I thought. I kissed him back, and this time, we weren't interrupted.

We spent the next couple of hours talking and planning for him to come visit me. There seemed to be ample time to savor each other's lips.

The sun had set, and there was a cool breeze starting. We both knew I had to get back. The night had been wonderful, and I didn't want it to end, but reality would come soon enough.

When we walked back to our picnic area, I really hoped that Jayden hadn't told anyone about where we were. I assumed Tanis would figure it out after seeing Ian's car in the parking lot.

"Ian, your car. Tanis and whoever will know you're still here."

"It's fine, but let's get you back." Ian picked up the picnic basket and walked me back to my trailer. I was sure I'd have a message or two from Tanis.

As we came to my door, we made sure not to linger. He did promise to see me almost every day before I left, as long as I didn't get sick of him. I was pretty sure I'd be able to handle that. Two weeks at the longest until I left this world behind me. On one hand, it was terrific; on the other, it felt frightening. It occurred to me that for the first time in my life, I felt like a typical teenager.

Until I turned off my lights and tried to sleep…

Chapter 24

My night was bad. In my dreams, I was back in the evil house, and Martha was hitting me with wooden pieces of broken furniture. In reality, I always had to pick out the sticks or wooden door stoppers that she would use to beat me. I tried to have a system so it wouldn't hurt so much, but that never worked. It always hurt.

It had been years since I had felt the sting of wood on me, but the bruise on my arm was a reminder of how powerful she was. She had fooled the judge when I was five. She could fool them again. It was as if there were an evil presence inside her. How my father could never see that, I couldn't understand.

My father and Martha had attended church regularly, and I was told that years earlier, they had been part of a church plant in Winnipeg. I actually had some recollection of that. I remembered dancing in the aisle at church. I hadn't been to church in years. It wasn't that I didn't want to go, but I didn't know how to make the move to go. I also didn't understand how you could seemingly praise God on Sunday and yet beat the kids on Monday.

They quoted scripture to me all the time, but when I started looking through one of the Bible I found lying around, I learned a few things. They were pretty surprised when I started quoting verses back to them. I only learned the ones that seemed pertinent to me, but it helped a bit. Until I brought up their affair, which I wasn't supposed to know about.

My sister Jenna was actually my half sister, although no one would own up to that. That bothered me all the time. I had extremely great hearing, and neither my dad nor Martha knew the things that I found out just by listening. I actually knew about my mom and dad's divorce long before they decided to tell me about it. I was also a good snooper. I found multiple letters containing the lies that were passed back and forth between Martha and Paul, Jenna's supposed father.

Yup, I knew too much. What would they think would happen now that we were being reunited with my mom and John? "I bet they're worried," I said to myself.

I was still in bed. I could tell it was early, but I didn't realize how early until I checked my watch. It was 3:00 a.m. Why was I up now? The whole evening with Ian seemed to fade under my current thoughts. Had I really spent that time with him?

I got up and grabbed a glass of water. I looked outside, and it seemed too peaceful. I really wanted to go snuggle up to Mia. As all of a sudden, I was afraid of what else I would face before I left Ontario.

The counselors had been so positive with Ivan and me, but I was worried that they'd still want us to testify against my dad and Martha. I wanted Jenna to have a normal life, even though I didn't get that privilege.

I went back to my bed with a sense of unrest. "What am I supposed to do?" I wasn't looking for an answer, but I heard one.

"Trust me." It was that voice that seemed to come when I was troubled. I had heard this voice throughout my life, especially when things became unbearable. I needed to know more about this. My mom had said it was God, or Jesus, who was speaking to me, but how could it be?

I then remembered a time when I was five and my mom had been reading me a Bible story. My life was still good then, as I had both my parents together. In the story, there was a sinful person and a person who didn't want to sin anymore. I had said to my mother that I wanted to be the person who didn't sin anymore. In fact, didn't I ask Jesus into my heart? I had forgotten that I could do that…

"Jesus, is that you who has been speaking to me?" I asked

I sat bolt right up when I heard, "Yes. It is I."

"The same Jesus whom I knew as I child?" I waited… I waited some more.

"Yes. Trust me," I heard in a still small voice that was more in my spirit than audible.

"Okay. You've got me. I'll trust you, as I know I can't trust myself. Come back into my heart and stay," I said as I bowed my head.

Then again, in that sweet voice, I heard, "I never left."

That did it. I began to cry softly at first, then the floodgates opened. I asked for forgiveness for all the lies I'd told, even when they were to get out of trouble. I asked forgiveness for the things I knew were wrong and for the things I didn't know were wrong.

My tears started to subside. I was filled with such peace—peace I didn't know was possible. I was still at a loss at what was next, but I knew I wasn't going to face it alone.

Chapter 25

I awoke to the bright sun streaming through the small window in my trailer. I had slept, and not only had I slept but I also felt lighter than I had in years. I was grateful to have another day to really live.

I jumped out of bed and started to get myself ready for the day. I checked my phone and saw I had missed some calls from my mom. I quickly called her back. She sounded so worried when I called and asked if something happened to me last night. It seemed that she had also been up at three, praying for me. I really wanted to tell her in person, but I needed to tell someone in order for it to be real.

"Mom," I said excitedly, "I remembered what happened when you read that Bible story to me when I was five."

"You what?" She sounded confused.

"Remember about the sinner and the one who asked not to sin? Well, I remembered I didn't want to sin anymore. And I asked Jesus to come into my heart again. Do you know what he said?"

"What?" she asked through what sounded like tears.

"That he never left. Can you believe that?"

"Yes. Yes, I can. Oh, honey, that's wonderful! No wonder I woke up at three." She was laughing now and calling John, telling him the great news.

"Mom, I'm not sure what today brings, but I know we aren't alone in the battle." I really didn't want to bring up what happened that night with Martha. She didn't need to know. I switched the subject. "Mom, when do we leave?"

"I hope it's okay, but we booked your ticket and Ivan's for a week from today. Ivan's is a one-way ticket too, as I am so hoping that he'll agree to stay."

"I hope he does too. I have a good feeling about that."

"Good. I do too. John and I are booked on a flight tomorrow already. We have a few more things to do at the lawyer's, but since you're eighteen, it's easy. With Ivan, it takes a bit longer. His foster parents have encouraged him to come to visit at least."

"Do we need to do anything else?"

"No, but I hope you get to see your father alone before you leave."

"I do too, Mom." I paused. "Martha, she's bent on destroying us." I sighed.

"I know, honey, but in a week, we will all be together. Before we say goodbye, have you talked to Ian?"

"Yes, I talked to him last night. I wasn't sure how much time we have, but he knows it's not much."

"Just be careful. Even though you know you're leaving, just be cautious."

"I will, but honestly, he's a perfect gentleman."

"Even so, don't spend too much time alone with him, okay?"

"I can't promise that. Mind you, that's hard to do at this place anyway."

"Well, at least that's good."

Trying to move on, I asked, "When are you guys coming over?"

"In a couple of hours, and we'll try to pick up Ivan as well."

"Sounds great. I'm pretty much off today, but I may beg Kat for a ride."

"Of course you will. Please be careful."

"Mom, I'm really not used to being worried about, but thanks. Kat would never get me to do anything that I wasn't ready to do."

"Even so. I'll call you when we're on our way."

"Okay. Love you."

"You too, so much."

We ended our call, and I knew I'd need to tell Tanis about leaving and try to locate Kat. I had some money saved up now, so I could afford a lesson. I also needed to book the group lesson with Ian, and I hoped that Alicia and Lindsey would be around today.

I finally got out of the trailer after eight, which was late for me. I headed to the big barn as I knew they'd be done in the small barn.

I really wanted to see Mia too. I walked in and was immediately greeted by the chorus of Lindsey and Alicia asking me about my hot date last night.

"Jayden, she told you." I blushed.

"Told us what?" they said in unison. They both laughed at their cleverness while spinning their shovels.

"Um, she may have caught us kissing," I owned up.

"Yeah. I heard it was pretty passionate," Alicia added.

"Come on, you guys. He's like my first real boyfriend."

"I told you to be careful of older men," Alicia said.

"Yes, I've heard it already from my mom today. Thanks."

"Well, I bet she's got a reason to worry, "Lindsey said, her brown eyes twinkling with mischievousness.

"Ahh, I knew when Jayden saw us, I'd hear about it." I tried walking away from them, but they were still teasing me when Tanis came into the barn.

"Hey, girls," she said brightly. She wasn't in her riding gear and had her blond hair tied up off her face. We all answered back our hellos. I was grateful for the diversion. "Lindsey, I'm going to take Kier out. Are you able to help tack him up while I talk to Rain?"

"Sure," she replied back. "Are you wanting the jumping saddle?"

"That would be great. I've got a lesson, and I'm pretty sure we're jumping. Rain, do you have a minute for me?"

"Of course," I said nervously.

"Let's go to the house. Girls, I'll see you soon."

I turned, leaving a couple of good-natured chuckles behind me.

We passed Kat on our way into the house, and I checked to see if I could get in a ride today. She said that she'd check to see if there was a spot for me. There was at least hope. If I was leaving in a week, I'd try to get in all the riding I could before I left.

We walked into the house. I was too nervous to start any small conversation. I was sure she found out about Ian last night, and I really didn't want to hear another lecture on him. Besides, I knew that I wouldn't put myself in danger.

"Want a quick coffee?" she asked encouragingly.

"Sure, that would be great." I didn't realize that I was hungry until I smelled fresh banana bread coming from her kitchen.

"And help yourself to the fresh bread." She busied herself pouring us two cups of coffee. I helped myself to the bread.

"This smells delicious. Thanks so much!" We took our cups and bread and sat down at the small kitchen table. We both took a couple of bites and enjoyed our coffee. I was still curious as to what this was all about, but I was momentarily distracted.

"So, Rain, I heard you had a visitor last night." She turned her brown eyes on me.

I gulped. I had many visitors. "You mean Ian?" I put my cup down.

"No. Oh, that's why you look so nervous." She paused. "I like Ian, and in fact, I think he has your best interest at heart. I meant Martha. I heard she was here and that your sister tried to stay over."

Relief flooded me. "Yes, I found Jenna and her friend hiding in the big barn. Martha found out that they were here and came to take them home."

"And is that why you have a large bruise on your arm?" I covered my arm, feeling ashamed, but I didn't answer her. "I thought so. Listen, Rain, I'm going to ban her from here. I don't want anyone like that around any of my girls. If Jenna wants to continue to do clinics here, I'll consider it, but Martha is off-limits."

"I really didn't mean to cause any trouble, and I know the horse community isn't that large."

"Rain, it is by no means your fault. I just want to make sure you are protected while you are still here. Did you tell your mom about it yet?"

"No, not yet. I really don't want to." I took another sip of coffee, as my nerves weren't as bad as they had been moments ago.

"Well, it's up to you. Has your mom booked your ticket home?"

"Yeah, it's in a week. I haven't got the ticket yet, but when I talked to her this morning, she mentioned it was booked."

"We're going to miss you, but I am happy for you. I bet Ian will miss you as well."

"I'll miss him too." I blushed again.

"I've never seen him up here so much since he met you."

"He might even do the adult night with me."

"Really? He's never been on a horse here before."

"I think it would be fun. I was going to try to get my mom to go for a ride, but I don't think she'll have time."

"I'm sure that's the problem. It's funny. I wonder from where you got your love of horses. I've talked enough to your mom to know it's not from her."

"She said something about my great-grandfather loving horses."

"That could be it, as you definitely have the horse craze gene."

"That's true. It's saved my life more than once, that's for sure." I finished my coffee and thanked her for it.

"I'd better get ready for my lesson. Rain, just know if you need anything or if she tries to hurt you, find me. Actually, I have something for you." She got up from the table and grabbed a canister of something. "Here, it's pepper spray. She won't be expecting it, and it will help to make sure you don't get any more bruises."

"Thanks. I've never used this before." I shook the container and looked at it carefully. "Won't this hurt her?"

"Yes." She looked at me intently. "Therefore, it won't be you getting hurt."

"I'll keep it safe, but if I use it, I may need your help."

"Anytime. I promised your mom I'd look out for you."

"This is a new world for me, but I think I'm going to like it." I smiled widely at Tanis.

"I think so too," Tanis returned the smile.

I helped her put the coffee cups in the kitchen. We both left her house, and she headed back to the barn.

I put the spray into my trailer and decided I was going to see about that lesson.

Chapter 26

The day continued on in my favor despite all the teasing I got. Next time Ian and I got together, I was going to make sure he took me somewhere other than A&T. There was no way anyone was going to catch us kissing again.

I got my lesson, and Mia was a superstar. Kat even let us jump! Mia had such a large takeoff point, but by the end of the lesson, we were starting to feel in sync. I wished I could take her with me to Nova Scotia. I had been to my mom and John's place before, and although it had a large backyard, it didn't have enough room for a horse. Mia was just special. There was something about her that clicked with me. I was told she didn't have a smooth past before coming to the barn, so maybe that was it.

I was getting ready to see my mom and John when I heard a knock at my trailer. I just hoped it wasn't Martha. I picked up the pepper spray from the table just in case I needed it. As I opened the door, I was shocked to see my dad. I looked around him for Martha, but he was alone.

"Hi," I said weakly. "You're alone?"

"Yes, I am." He smiled at me, but the smile didn't quite touch his eyes. "Can I come in?"

"My trailer's small. Why don't we talk outside?"

"Okay. As long as we can talk."

"Yes, we can talk."

I could count on one hand the number of times my dad and I had been allowed to spend time together. It was almost as though we were strangers, yet I had grown up with him. My mother, on the other hand, even though we had maybe spent two weeks together in a row since I was five, I felt close to her.

I wasn't sure where to take my dad, as I didn't want us to get interrupted. I figured we could leave the property and find some space. I left the pepper spray but took my cell. I didn't want anyone worrying about me.

My dad, although kind, had a sort of meekness about him. I knew at times people misunderstood it for weakness, but he could be strong. I had seen him fight for Jenna and for others in our family, but I had never seen him use it for Ivan and me.

We moved away from my trailer, and a few of the students waved at me. I saw Tanis coming out of her house. I figured I might as well get the introductions over with. I turned to my dad before introducing him though and gave him a warning about not getting too warm a welcome.

Tanis met us halfway in the parking lot and smiled at me, but she looked accusingly at my dad. I couldn't blame her.

"Uh, Tanis, this is my dad, Mike. He's just come up to talk with me about a few things."

Tanis, in spite of having opinions, was always the professional and reached out and shook his hand. "Hi, I'm Tanis. I have been one of the people who have been making sure that Rose has been kept safe."

"Thank you," he said. I was shocked. "It's nice to meet you. I know how much Rose loves horses, so I'm sure she has been in her glory here." They let go of each other's hands. You could have knocked me over with a feather.

"Mike, I hope that you encourage Rose to do what's right, even if it's difficult." He just smiled at her. "Rose, I'm sure I'll see you later. You're on the schedule early tomorrow, right?"

"Yes, I sure am. I'm meeting my mom and John in a bit, but I'll be back early."

"Sounds good. Well, I'm off to meet Todd." I had heard she had a new guy in her life, so I presumed it was Todd. "I'll see you in a bit. Mike, take care."

"It was nice to meet you, Tanis, and thanks again."

I seriously didn't know my father at all. One minute he was all mad and hurt, and the next he was thanking Tanis.

"She's very protective of you, isn't she, Rose?"

"Yes. She is the one who helped me out of my muck of a life. Let's go down the road, Dad."

"You lead. I'll follow." I had a dozen questions to ask him, but I didn't know where to start.

We walked past the gate and turned right. The road was quiet except for the horses on either side. Murphy and Cammie, Tanis's dogs, followed us as we left. It warmed my heart that these dogs I'd known for such a short time seemed to follow me around. I assumed I'd have to start the conversation, but for once, I really wanted to be the child.

"So, Dad, what brings you out here?"

"I didn't want to leave things the way we did at the meeting. There are things you don't know, Rose. There are reasons that I left your mother and got full custody of you."

I stopped and turned to face him. "Dad, I have heard those stories all my life! I am done listening to them, you understand? I am not saying she is perfect, but I can guarantee in the short time I've known her that she would have never beaten me. So you can tell me all you want about how and what you did to protect me, but there wasn't a day where Ivan and I felt protected!" I walked away from him. He could catch up; I didn't care.

"Rose, wait, slow down."

I slowed down, but there was no way I was going to continue to listen to those lies anymore. "What do you want? Are you going to change your tune now?" I suggested.

"Rose, you know that I was unaware of what you and Ivan went through."

"Yes, but after I told you what we went through, you still decided to marry Martha."

"And you can't forgive me for marrying the woman that I love?"

"I don't know. Maybe one day I can, but honestly, if it were someone who had beaten Jenna, would you act differently?"

"Rose, you are my firstborn, and I love you. I am crushed that you felt you had to run away from us. I am also hurt that after spending ten minutes with your mother that you are throwing away all the things Martha and I did for you." He was beside me now.

"I am not throwing everything away, but I am your daughter, so one would expect some things. Besides, I was the one who took care of Jenna and forfeited school. It was a miracle that I passed high school."

"And Martha helped you. She helped you apply for colleges, or have you forgotten?"

"And I made you stay home that one fateful day two years ago in order for me to go to school. Or have you forgotten that?"

"I haven't forgotten that, but she also let you go to horse camp with Jenna. She also made sure that you had a horse to ride."

"Dad, I am not saying that it was all bad, but I am saying that I sure had to fight a lot in order to have any type of life. If you look at the other kids and you look at Ivan and me, you will notice a great deal of injustice."

"Does this mean that there is no way that you will drop the 'most dangerous parents' thing?"

"So that's what this is about? That's why you took time out of your busy schedule to come see me?"

"No, that isn't why I came, but I did want to ask you about that."

"That wasn't either of our idea, but the social worker wanted justice. It was her idea seeing as we don't want to go to trial. We just want out of this life." I felt my phone buzz. I looked and saw it was Ian. I wasn't really in the mood to talk to anyone, and if he heard my mood, he'd know something was up.

I looked back at my dad. We were both off to the side of the road. The dogs had gone ahead of us, assuming that we'd follow. I could tell he was struggling not to break down, but I didn't need his tears. I needed resolution.

"Dad, I'm sure there will come a time when we can talk in a much less heated manner, but it isn't today. I need to get back. Mom is picking me up."

"And you're sure you are ready to leave all this behind and move halfway across the country?"

He had me there. It would be hard. I felt I was on the right track though, and when I prayed, I had peace, so I steeled myself and answered, "Dad, I know what I am doing is right. I don't know how long I'll be in Nova Scotia, but I want to give it a shot. You've had me for eighteen years, and now it's time for me to get to know my mom. Unfortunately, because of Martha, we have wasted a lot of the eighteen years we've had together. We all have regrets, but I don't want to live my life based on them."

"Okay, I understand."

That was it? I still wanted him to fight for me. Not in my whole life did I see him fight for me. And as much as he was agreeing with me, his passiveness irked my soul. I sure didn't feel like I had given anything to God, for at present, I was just angry.

"Rose, does that annoy you?" He must have read my face.

"Yes, that annoys me, but it is what it is. Let's head back."

The dogs made their way back to us and led the way.

"I didn't mean to upset you."

"Did you know that your precious wife was here the other night threatening me?" I wouldn't look at him as we walked side by side.

"She said you had threatened her."

"And you believed her?" I gasped.

"I didn't think she had reason to lie. I mean, you've left, so what does she have to gain?"

"What do I have to gain? She even tried to physically hurt me. Still to this day, she tries this. What do you have to say to that?" I looked at his face, but he was starting to well up again.

"I'm sorry, Rose."

"So you believe me?"

"I believe that Martha and you bring out the worst in each other."

"That's not the same thing, and you know it."

We had reached the gates again, and I felt worse than before we had talked.

"Dad, you are living in a fool's paradise. I'm sorry, but that's the truth. We will have to agree to disagree. When you are ready to talk truth, call me. I'll stay in touch with you, but as of now, I don't consider Martha my mother anymore. I have a mother, and I look forward to getting to know her better. I am leaving at the end of the month. You can come and see me, but please don't bring Martha."

I didn't know when I'd see my dad again. I should hug him, but I was still too riled up. We lingered at the gates as the dogs passed us and ran into the yard. My dad seemed to have difficulty speaking, so I waited. I kicked the stones nervously. Silence and I weren't friends.

"Rose, I am sorry, and I will tell Martha not to come up here again. I understand why you're doing what you're doing. I wish it was different, and maybe one day it will be. I love you, and I already miss your presence at home." He reached out and hugged me. I hugged him back as the little girl in me still wanted to be loved and accepted by him. I would never be fully loved by him till he opened his eyes.

"I love you too, Dad, and I wish things weren't this way, but they are."

He squeezed me one more time and let go. "Stay in touch, Rose." He patted my shoulder, and his light-blue eyes were full of tears.

I gulped, willing my tears to stay down. I just nodded and left him. I didn't look back but shut myself in my trailer and let my tears pour down my face.

Chapter 27

I cried myself to sleep, and when I awoke, my cell was going off like crazy. My hair had knotted itself around my face. What time was it? I was supposed to meet my mom and John. I was sure I was late.

I plunked myself on my bed when I came back, and I wasn't sure where I had put my phone. There it went again. "Where are you?" I felt around the bed, and sure enough, it had fallen between the sheets. I didn't have time to check the ID before answering. "Hello," I said groggily.

"Rose, oh, Rose, what did you say to Dad?" It was Jenna, and she sounded desperate.

I shook my head awake and took a deep breath before answering her. "Jenna, what's wrong? I didn't say anything to Dad that he didn't already know."

"He's really upset, and Mom says it's because of you."

Of course it is, I thought. "Jenna, your mom is just trying to rewrite the past."

"She says because of you that Dad might lose his job and that we might lose the house."

She was so upset, and every bone in my body wanted to scream how unfair this was. I didn't. I stayed calm and gathered my wits about me. "Jenna, I wish we could talk in person, but since we can't, I'm going to have to ask you to trust me. Do you remember when I asked you to come to the basement when your mom was about to hit me?"

"Yes," she answered quietly.

"Well, it seems that the social workers now know about that. It wasn't me who brought it up, but both Ivan and I had the same stories, so they know it was true. I tried to leave it, but the courts want to make sure they get punished. But, Jenna, it isn't my fault that they are now being held accountable for their actions." There was just silence on the other line. I knew she knew that I was right. "Jenna, are you okay?"

She sniffed. "I'm sorry, Rose. I'm sorry that I couldn't protect you."

"Jenna, it's not your fault. Please don't be upset. It was in the past, and I'm ready to move on. She's your mom. You can't take sides. I understand that. I love you and know that you are a wonderful sister."

"But…" She was trying not to cry.

"But nothing. It's okay. Listen, come visit me in Nova Scotia, and please give Mia some love when you come up here. I'll see you before I leave, I promise."

"Okay. I love you, Rose, and I'm going to miss you so much!"

"You too! This isn't easy, but I feel it's the right thing to do. Try to come up and sleep over, okay?" I knew that would be next to impossible, but I had to try.

"I'll try."

"Get Mya's brother to bring you up. You can both stay. Just don't disappear so I don't get in more trouble."

"Okay." She laughed. "Love you. Thanks for helping to raise me."

"Love you, and you were the best part of growing up. I've got to go and get ready, but I'll talk to you soon."

"Deal. Have a good night and say hi to Ian."

"Very funny."

"I heard you got caught kissing." She snickered.

"Yes, yes, and the world now knows. Bye, Jenna."

"Bye, Rose."

We both hung up, and I took a look at the rest of the missed calls. Sure enough, my mom had tried to get hold of me, as had Ian. I needed to shower before dinner, and I wanted to fit in a visit with Ian too.

I called my mom, and she informed that they were already on their way. I also quickly called Ian to see if he wanted to meet afterward. I was delighted when he said yes. I'd have to tell him we'd need to go somewhere other than the back cross-country field.

I took the time to get presentable and managed to get a brush through my messy hair. I was expecting my mom to be at my trailer when I heard a knock at the door. I was surprised to find Jenna there when I opened the door.

"Jenna, did you get the okay to come over?" She grabbed hold of me and hugged me tight. "What is it?" I hugged her, but I was concerned as she couldn't get to the barn by herself. "Jenna, you're worrying me. Are you okay?"

She let go of me and turned her blue eyes to face mine. "Please forgive me, but Mom wants to talk to you."

Instantly I was full of dread. "Where is she?"

"She's waiting for you down the road." Jenna looked guilty, but she was so young, and it wasn't fair for her to be used like this.

"And she knew she couldn't come here. Figures."

"She asked me to get you, and seeing as I won't get to see you anymore, I jumped at the chance. I really wish you'd stay." Jenna's eyes were full of sincerity, but my mind was made up.

"Will she talk to me in front of you?" I already knew the answer, but I asked it anyways.

"She asked me to give you both ten minutes."

"Of course she did. Come in for a sec. I'm just going out."

Jenna moved from the tiny doorway and sat down at the kitchen table. I grabbed my cell and called my mom. She was furious, but I told her I'd be okay and to come pick me up. They were ten minutes away. The worst that could happen was that Martha could plead her case one more time.

I put on the watch that Ian had given me as it helped to remind me that I was no longer a victim. I'd go see Martha, as she couldn't hurt me anymore.

My hair was still damp, so I pulled it into a loose bun. Hopefully, by the time I saw Ian, it would look nice.

I met Jenna back in the kitchen. I knew Martha wouldn't come to the trailer as Tanis had torn a strip off her the last time she saw her.

"Well, here goes nothing. My mom will be here soon, so your mom doesn't have a lot of time."

Jenna got up and made her way outside. I followed her and locked the door behind me.

"Jenna, it's not your fault, okay?" I hugged her small frame. "Try to come up without Martha one more time before I go."

"I will. Love you."

"Love you, too. Go say hi to the horses." We parted, and I figured Martha had about five minutes to talk to me now, which was better than ten.

I was tempted to knock on Tanis's door, but as my mom was almost there, I decided against it. I left the property and saw that her station wagon was parked up the street. I hated that station wagon. It represented my bondage of a life.

I saw her gray head in the driver's seat, but I wasn't about to get trapped by her. She saw me coming over and motioned me to come in. I shook my head and went to her side.

"Hi, Martha. I don't want to go anywhere with you, so I'll talk to you outside the car."

"It would be better if you got in, Rose." Her British accent seemed thicker than normal that night, but I pushed past the intimidation.

"No. I'm getting picked up in a few minutes." I made the mistake of leaning into the car, at which time she grabbed my arm.

"You will get in, do you hear me?" She began twisting my arm again.

"Fine!" She had nothing on me. I was almost free of her, but I got into the passenger side.

"You don't need to hurt me anymore. I'm not your problem now. You should be elated. I'm out of your hair."

"You have destroyed your dad, Rosie." I hated that name. No one called me that name since I turned fifteen. I cringed. "I don't know what you did to him, but he's very depressed, almost suicidal. I know you hate me, but I thought you loved your father."

"I do love him. All I did was tell the truth. It's not my fault that you kept me home from school, that you beat me. I raised Jenna. You know that. How on earth can you say I'm the one who's unfair?" I was yelling. She always brought out the worst in me.

"You're not acting very Christian, Rosie."

"Christian?" What did she know?

"Yes, that's what I said. You're supposed to honor your parents." I was flabbergasted, to say the least. "You're not being fair to your father. He could go to jail because of you."

"It is not because of me! It is because of you and all that you have done to me."

Martha grabbed my arm again, and the blood rushed to my hand. I wasn't thinking, but in one swift movement, I hit her with my free arm. She let go of my arm, shock registering on her old face.

"Don't you dare hit me!" she screamed.

"Then don't hit me." I matched her steely blue eyes with my dark blue ones. "I am out of here. Don't try to stop me."

At that, I opened the door and slammed her ugly station wagon, just in time to see my parents' rental car pull into A&T. I fled her car and ran to my mom. My eyes filled with tears. I had tried to stay strong, but this time, I couldn't do it.

"What happened?" my mom asked through my sobs.

"Martha happened," I choked out.

"What did she do to you?"

I pulled away from my mom. John had joined us now and had placed a protective arm on me. I looked up. "She tried to say my dad is suicidal because of me. She was about to hurt me again, so I slapped her." I tried wiping my tears.

"You did what?"

I was sure I saw a smile starting to form at the corner of my mom's mouth. "I hit her. She had grabbed my arm, like she always does. I was done! So I surprised myself and slapped her face."

"Oh, Rose, you fought back. Good for you." Mom hugged me again. "I'm proud of you, honey."

I had forgotten about Jenna and the fact that Martha needed to pick her up. I saw Martha's station wagon out of the corner of my eye.

"Mom, I need to go get Jenna."

"You go. John and I will handle her."

"She's banned off the property."

"Good," John answered. John suddenly seemed so much larger. He was mad. I had never seen him so mad before.

"You go, Rose. Take your time." My mom gave me another protective hug.

"Thanks, both of you. I am so glad that I'm leaving."

"So are we," she offered.

I left them and went to find Jenna. *The sooner I start my new life, the better,* I thought.

I found Jenna talking to some of the girls from camp. She brightened as I came toward her. She had no idea. How much did I need to share with her? I wanted her to know that it wasn't my fault. I also had to make sure that she'd still grow up humble and kind. She had a beautiful heart and was so different from the spoiled child that her mother had tried to raise. My heart started to feel the ache of losing her again. I'd have to trust in the God, whom I had reconnected with, to keep her safe.

"Hey, Jenna, are you ready to go?"

"If I have to." She was currently snuggling O'Henry, one of the school horses.

I joined her. "He's pretty cute, isn't he?"

"So cute." She looked up at me. "Rose, now that all this bad stuff has happened, I'll probably have to get a new coach. I won't really be able to bring Beanie up here anymore."

"I know. I'm sorry for my part in that."

"It's not your fault. It's just too bad. I was talking to Maggie [one of her older sisters], and she filled me in on a few things. She told me that she had seen Mom beat you before."

"It's true, Jenna."

"Why didn't you tell?"

"I didn't want to stir up trouble. I didn't want to leave you."

"How can she be so sweet to me and terrible to you?"

"She's your mom. As for me, I'm a reminder of my mom. Now that I've gotten to know her a bit more, I see why. My mom and I are so much alike. It's not my fault, but she didn't like it."

"Can you promise not to forget me?"

"Of course." I grabbed her small shoulders and gave her a hug. "I love you, Jenna. That will never change."

She hugged me back. We both started to cry. What a sight. I still had a short time before I'd be leaving, but for us, this could be goodbye.

O'Henry nudged us, which caused us both to laugh.

"I think you'd better go, Jenna. I didn't tell you what happened, but it wasn't good."

"Do you want to tell me?"

"No, it doesn't matter. Your mom will spin it that she was the victim. She probably won't try hitting me again though."

"That's good, isn't it?"

"I think so. Come on."

We left O'Henry's stall and walked hand in hand out to the parking lot. I was surprised to see the ugly station wagon still parked outside the gates. I wish I could have been a fly on the wall for John, my mom, and Martha's conversation. It must have been short as they weren't with her now.

I walked Jenna to the edge of the gate. "You have my number. Use it. Call me anytime. Remember that I am not the perpetrator, no matter what anyone says."

"Okay. Love you."

We hugged one more time before she returned to the station wagon of evil.

Chapter 28

I came back to where my mom and John were next to their rental car. They both looked as if they had just fought a war. My mom's face was almost white, but John still stood tall. He had an air of gallantry about him. It was no wonder my mom had married him after marrying my real dad.

"Are you both okay?" I asked, concerned.

"She is a terrible, evil human being. I am so sorry that you have had to spend so many years with that woman," John offered. "Once you come home, you don't ever have to come back here."

"Thanks, John. And, Mom, how are you?" I put my hand on my mom's shaking arm.

"She brought up so many things from the past. There are things that she has so distorted to make me look like the bad parent."

"I'm so sorry, Mom. You know I don't believe anything she says."

"I know, but I hate the lies she tells. She's probably even told the others her made-up lies."

"Well, ten minutes ago, she was trying to hurt me. I mean, physically hurt me! This is the one woman people looked up to in churches. Come on! She's evil!"

"I couldn't agree more. I feel sorry for your father."

"How can you, Mom?"

"He was a good man once. You don't remember, but he was a great father. He loved you and Ivan so much. He played with you like no one else did. He was fun. It all changed, but our first years together were really happy. You and Ivan were so happy. You had such a beautiful room of dolls and toys."

"I remember some of that. But, Mom, that's never been my reality here."

"I know that, dear. And it's time to make up for some of that lost time."

"Ruth, we need to get the rental car dropped off." They were set to fly out tomorrow. I really didn't want to be without them, but I had my ticket, so I knew I wasn't going to back out now.

"I don't feel good about leaving."

"I'll be okay. I've got Tanis and Kat, oh, and Ian. They're all looking out for me. It'll be okay."

"If our flight wasn't so early tomorrow, I'd ask you to come to the airport."

"Mom, you do know I feed horses for a living right now."

"Well, if there was a way, we'd love to see you there."

"How are you getting to the airport?"

"We were just going to cab it."

"I have an idea. Leave it to me. I may even find a way to get us together this evening. Are you in a rush to go, or can you wait a minute?"

"We can wait for you," John said.

"Good, two shakes."

I ran to my trailer and found my phone. I was sure Ian said he was free today. I quickly dialed his number. It rang a couple of times, and on the third ring, he picked up.

"Hey, Ian, did you say you were free tonight?"

"Yup, I'm off at five. Want to get together?"

"Yeah. Actually, would you mind having dinner with my parents?"

"Sure."

"I have another question to ask you." I was getting braver already.

"Rain, as you are leaving in a couple of weeks, I'm pretty much at your disposal."

"Well, would you mind getting up early tomorrow to drive my parents to the airport?"

"Ha, well, I will see if I can get my shift covered. Then we could have the day together afterward, right?"

"Right!" I'd actually have to check to see if I was riding, but I assumed that I could change my lesson if I needed to.

"Then consider it a plan."

"Thanks, Ian. I really appreciate it."

"Oh, I may have a surprise to show you tonight."

"I can't wait! How about you pick me up here? We'll go get my parents afterward."

"Sounds like a plan."

I heard a knock on my trailer. "I've got to go, but I'll see you soon."

"Bye, Rain."

I put my phone on my counter and answered my door. It was my mom, who looked a little anxious.

"Come in. What's wrong?" I moved and let her in.

"I just got a call from the social worker. It seems as though Martha is pushing back. She is trying to say that what you and Ivan are saying is a lie."

My mom sat down at my little table. I poured her a glass of water and handed it to her. "Mom, it's going to be okay. We're almost out of here."

"But we are leaving tomorrow, and I am worried at what she may try to do to you." My mom took a sip of water.

"Where's John?" I inquired.

"He's giving Tanis the heads-up. We want to protect you. I honestly don't think I will be able to breathe until you are home with us."

I joined her at the table. "Mom, you've taught me about how we have to have faith. I don't care about Martha. I do, however, care about my dad. But I have to let him go. Maybe one day he'll see what he's lost. I have to trust that God has a plan in all of this."

"Listen to you. You've been a Christian for a moment, and you are right. I have to remember that."

"We get to be together. We'll get to know each other, and Ivan and I can finally have some fun together."

My mom smiled as she pictured it.

"Oh, and some more good news. Ian is going to drive you to the airport. Oh, and he's also taking us out to dinner tonight."

"That is good. I just have to trust that you'll make it home."

"Ian said he'll drive me to the airport too."

"He's such a good man."

"It really is a pity that I finally found someone I like enough to be around, and I have to leave him."

"It's true. Maybe you two will find each other later in life."

"Maybe. But Nova Scotia is far away."

"I met John in Nova Scotia. I had to move from Winnipeg to Nova Scotia to marry him."

"Well, I'm never going to live in Ontario again, no matter how much I like Ian."

"I don't blame you. I should go see where John is. We really need to get going."

"Okay. Please don't worry so much about Ivan and me. We've made it this far. We'll be okay."

"I'll try." Her smile was weak. I leaned over and gave her a hug. This new year would be good. We'd find our way back to some peace.

My mom and I met up with John and Tanis. Todd was nearby, so he got filled in on my assorted past. I looked at him. He was a strong man, the kind who could cause some trouble if needed. He did, however, possess kind brown eyes and had a large grin. I felt instantly at ease. I could see why Tanis liked him. I bet Martha would stay out of my way with him around.

There were still a lot of cars coming and going from the farm, and most of the kids waved at us and went straight to the barn. It was odd in such a busy place that I felt a sense of peace. It could just be the smell of the farm air. Whatever it was, this would be hard to leave.

My parents hugged me and thanked Tanis again for everything. I assured them that I'd be okay and that I'd see them in a bit. I still wanted to get a ride in before Ian showed up. I would probably need to clean up as well. I wanted to wash the stain of Martha's handprints off me. I looked at my arm, and the bruise was disappearing.

The other bruises would heal eventually.

Chapter 29

I managed to ride Mia, and she was fabulous! We got to ride outside in the fresh summer air. A new horse named Picasso had been added to the barn. He was a paint horse with a gentle temperament. Lindsey got to ride him after Kat. She and I moved our schedules around, so we got to ride together. She was much more advanced than I was, but the cool thing was, she helped me with my confidence. In fact, she had challenged me to canter Mia in a two-point position, something I hadn't done before.

I was nervous when I started to get up in my jumping position, but she talked me out of my nerves. Once we did it, I was hooked. We cantered like this for some time before my legs started to get shaky. I really hoped that I'd be able to keep riding when I moved. I was sure that there'd be barns there too. I wasn't sure if I could ever replicate A&T though, not to mention Mia.

Lindsey mentioned that there was going to be a beach ride late this week. I was sure I could make that happen before I left. Taking Mia on the beach would be thrilling. I had once ridden a horse named Rambo and had the privilege of taking him swimming. That feeling never left me.

Lindsey and I cooled our horses out and talked a bit more about the upcoming changes. She had become such a great friend in the short time I had known her.

I got Mia brushed and put her outside to enjoy the summer day. I didn't have a lot of time before Ian would pick me up. Seeing as I had to say goodbye to my parents today, the least I could do was not smell of horse.

I found Lindsey and thanked her for the fun day. This was such an escape from the trials of Martha. Riding had already been a way for me to cope.

I showered and made myself look presentable before I got Ian's text saying that he was on his way. I had on one if his T-shirts with my jeans. I pulled my hair back in a loose braid. It really was time for a cut.

I left my trailer and waited for Ian out in the parking area. As I waited, Cami and Murphy trotted up to me, wanting some love. I had never seen such happy dogs in all my life. Patio Kitty, the resident barn cat, joined us. I sat on the red bench and stroked her black fur as she purred and walked over my jeans. So much for not smelling like animals. Murphy started to get jealous and leaned on my legs, practically moving me with his strength.

"Okay, okay, you're important too." I petted him, and he practically smiled at me. Cami joined in, wagging her tail at me. "I love you all." I laughed at my little entourage.

I saw a red car pull into the lot, but I didn't pay much attention to it as Ian always drove his gray Impala. I was shocked to hear his voice. I looked up, and sure enough, it was him.

"Hey, I didn't see you pull in."

"That's because of the surprise I was talking about. Come on, let me show you."

I looked over to the red car that had pulled in. Sure enough, it was a flashy new Impala. "Is that yours?"

"Yup. They gave me full value for my old Impala. Wait till you sit in it!" he added excitedly.

I got off the bench, putting out all the animals, but they followed us to his car. "Nice color."

"It's called siren red."

"Nice. Of course it can't just be red." I chuckled.

"Nope. Look at all the chrome!"

He was right. There was chrome in all the right places. And I noticed that the tailpipe exhaust was now built into the car.

"I have to admit, it's gorgeous!"

"Why, thank you. Are you ready to go? And are your boots clean?"

I looked down at my boots self-consciously. They weren't great.

"It's okay. I've got extra mats."

"Ian, I don't think I've ever been in such a fancy car. My dad has always driven older cars, and Martha always had ugly station wagons."

"Then you're in for a surprise." He opened the door for me, and I got in. I was overwhelmed with the smell of the new car. The seats were charcoal gray with designer stitches, and the dashboard, black. It was so sharp. He joined me in the car. "What do you think?"

"The inside is as nice as the outside."

"Wait till you hear the motor." He pressed a button, and I couldn't tell if the car had started or not. "So quiet."

"You're right. Is it on?"

"Yup." He laughed. "This is what I was doing earlier. I'm glad I was able to get it all settled before you left. I wanted you to see it and experience it. Let's go get your parents, and then I'll take you to that new restaurant I was telling you about."

"Thanks again for taking them to the airport tomorrow too."

"As you're leaving so soon, I want to see you as much as I can before you go." He looked at me and gave me one of his crooked grins. He was in dark fitted jeans and a plaid button-down top. He really was handsome.

We pulled out of A&T and headed to my parents' hotel.

Chapter 30

The ride to see my parents was unreal. I had always loved old cars, but sitting in Ian's new one sure made me appreciate how far GM cars had come. The car was so quiet, and Ian seemed so content. I knew one day I could get my own car, but it would take me years to afford a car like Ian's.

Ivan had managed to move things around in his day so he could join us too. Good thing there was a lot of room in the new car.

When we pulled up to the hotel, my family was waiting outside. The weather had been so nice while they'd been down. It was a hot summer, but after all the snow, we earned it.

Ian got out of the car, and I joined him. I heard the gasps from my mom and John. Ian was in his glory while everyone fawned over his new ride. John had been a GM man too, but he had never driven an Impala before. They all loved the chrome as much as I did. We finally all got settled in, and Ian explained the rules of the car. No slamming the doors, no dirty shoes, etc. I laughed, but I think he was serious.

"Where are we going for dinner?" my mom asked.

"A new place that just opened a few weeks ago. It's called Oak & Thorne. It's a pub, but all ages can dine there."

"What's the menu like?" Ivan inquired.

"So good! Their loaded burger is out of this world! You've got to try it, and the deep-fried pickles are super tasty too."

"With all the horseback riding I've done today, I'm hungry," I added. I realized with all the drama over the course of the day, I had skipped lunch.

Ian held my hand intermittently during our drive. Whenever he did this, my heart would leap. I was also very conscious of my parents and my brother sitting in the back seat. They liked Ian. I mean, what wasn't to like? He was such a gentleman. I was just sad that in order to move on with my life, I'd have to leave him behind.

"How was Mia today, honey?" my mom asked.

"She was terrific! We did some new things that we hadn't done before. Actually, Mia and I are probably going to go on a beach ride together before I go. I so wish I could bring her with me to Nova Scotia."

"I think you'll miss Mia more than me." Ian turned to me and smiled.

"It's a tie." I smiled back at him. My face flushed.

"That's good enough for me."

"That's high praise coming from Rose," John added.

Ian drove us to an area that seemed to be recently developed. I recognized it, but it had been a long time since I'd been in that part of town. There were a lot of new townhouses and condos that weren't there previously. We didn't go out to eat much as a family. Ever since Ponderosa closed its doors, it had been hard to justify taking a family of seven out for dinner. Most of the meals were prepared by me. I wasn't great in the kitchen, but I did learn how to make something out of nothing. The family sure wasn't happy when I went on my healthy kick, but no one else wanted to cook.

Things had changed over the past few years, with many of the kids no longer being kids anymore. I still had my work cut out for me though. I was still responsible for cooking for the parents and younger siblings.

"Penny for your thoughts," Ian whispered.

I waited a beat before answering.

"You okay?" He glanced at me, concern resonating throughout his features.

"Yeah. I was just remembering why I never really went out for meals."

"Let me guess, that was your job too?"

"Yeah, pretty much." I looked out the window, taking in the nice summer evening.

"It's true. If Rose didn't cook, we didn't eat. That woman, Martha, couldn't cook to save her life," Ivan piped.

I was pretty sure I heard my mom chuckle.

"It's true," Ivan answered in return.

"Oh, I know," Mom added. "When we were in Winnipeg, she always had someone else cook for her. I seem to remember many times where dinner would be burned if she tried making it. When your dad and I moved into the house to help after her surgery, I quickly became the chief cook and bottle washer."

"It sure was his loss, Mom."

"Thanks, Rose."

"Well, it's a new day for all of you, and tonight's dinner is my treat."

"Ian, you don't have to do that," my mom protested.

"It's your last night here, and I received a bonus check today, so it's my pleasure. We're almost there."

I noticed Ian had moved into the turning lane, and I saw the huge sign that read Oak & Thorne. The building looked cool. The name was in neon bubble lights. I then realized I'd been there before. "Hey, didn't this used to be the old Swiss Chalet?"

Ian maneuvered his car into the busy parking lot. "Yup, this company took it over a few months ago. I was here opening weekend, as I know the manager. It was nuts!

"I heard that someone finally took the lease over. I had some friends who used to work here when it was Swiss Chalet."

"The inside has totally changed. You won't recognize it. I made reservations for us, so we won't have to wait."

At the thought of food, my stomach began its rumbling again. I hoped no one noticed.

Ian found a parking spot that he approved of. "Here we are. Get ready to be impressed!" We all got out of his beautiful car, careful not to slam the doors.

Ian led us to the pub. I was blown away with what they'd done with the place. We walked in, and the lobby was decorated with old records, some of which my older sisters used to have. After we walked through another set of doors, I noticed a huge pizza oven to my left.

I took in all the incredible smells of burgers and pizza that wafted around me. I had been hungry before, but now I was ravenous.

There was a pretty woman, probably in her midtwenties, with shoulder-length blond hair, who was at the door when we entered. I noticed Ian was shaking her hand and smiling at her. He beckoned me forward, introducing me to her.

"Dani, this is Rose, the person I told you about. And this is her family."

I took Dani's outstretched hand and shook it. She smiled warmly at me. Her blue eyes seemed to shine as she took us in.

"I've got your table already for you, Ian. Come on in, everyone." Dani lead us to a large booth by the window. "Here's the booth you wanted." There was a Reserved sign on the table for us.

I looked around and saw that the place was almost full. Good thing Ian booked us in. I was aching to get my hands on one of those burgers he'd been talking about. We all got settled, and Dani seemed to go out of her way to make sure we were looked after.

In no time, we had our orders in and drinks on the table. Neither Ivan nor I were old enough to drink, so Ian suggested a couple of virgin Caesars. He had good taste, as Ivan and I drank them down eagerly. Then the pièce de résistance. I had never had a burger like this one. Between the goat cheese and the bacon on the burger, I was hooked! I hoped they'd open one of these pubs in Nova Scotia.

The food and the company were amazing. It was incredible to think that less than a month ago, I was still living in my own slavery. If anyone had told me I'd have a boyfriend, I'd have told them they were crazy.

Ian decided that we needed dessert, so he ordered us a sticky toffee pudding to share. I was almost too full, but I had a couple of bites. All the riding from the day had garnered me quite the appetite. It was still going to be another week until my move, so I wanted to savor the time with Ian and my family.

Long-distance relationships so rarely worked, not that I had any experience. But that was what I had heard. Would we be the exception to the rule? I didn't realize that I was lost in my thoughts until Ian elbowed me.

"Hey, Rose, you okay?" He leaned close to me so the others couldn't hear him.

"I'm okay. This has been marvelous, but I was thinking how much I'll miss you." I sucked in a breath as it caught me off guard.

"We'll find a way." I just smiled weakly at Ian. He was always the optimist when it came to us. I knew it wasn't the time or the place to have the debate, so I left it.

Mom and John were telling Ivan all about the Fortress of Louisbourg that we'd have to visit. I loved history, so I was in. She was letting us know about all the sights we'd have to see. There'd be some time when we arrived before Ivan got enrolled in school, if he decided to stay. As for me, I'd find a job, then figure out my long-term plan.

Dani came back to make sure we'd had a great time. She had been gracious and taken care of part of the bill as well. Ian must be a regular here. A lot of the servers knew him. He was always friendly without being flirty, for which I was grateful. He introduced us to almost everyone in the place that he knew. I liked how proud of us he was. No one had ever treated me like that. I almost felt like royalty around him.

We finished up at the pub and headed back to drop off my parents and Ivan. Tomorrow would come fast enough. I gave my parents huge hugs good night. I was thankful that we'd have tomorrow morning together.

Ivan confided in Ian and me that he was pretty sure that he'd be staying in Nova Scotia as well. I'd get to know him again. This delighted me so much! Plus, I wouldn't be alone when I got there.

Ian drove me back to the barn. We were both pretty quiet on the drive back. I loved the feel of his new car. It was so smooth. I was actually surprised that he drove it to the barn. It was now dark out, and only the dogs and cats greeted us as we got out. Ian always came prepared with treats for the animals. He bent down and petted them and gave them their goodies. He was thanked by tails wagging and kitties meowing. I just smiled to myself and petted them all as well.

He looked at me. "I guess I'd better walk you home."

"I guess so."

He took my hand, leaving the animals behind us. We walked to my door, and before I went in, he turned me toward him. "Rain, Rose, I am going to miss you so very much." He ran his hand across my cheek. He smelled so good.

"I'm going to miss you too," I leaned into his hand. He turned my face up to meet his and kissed me softly on the lips. I kissed him back, thanking Tanis in my head for having the trailer door face away from the parking lot. I didn't need another Jayden episode.

His kiss got a bit more urgent, but before it could turn to trouble, he pulled away. "Sorry, Rose, I don't want to get carried away with you. You're not like anyone else I have ever met. I don't want to mess this up."

"It's okay. I also don't want to mess this up."

"So I'll see you bright and early."

"I can't wait." He leaned in for one more kiss, this time a lot quicker and a lot safer.

I watched him leave, all the while my heart was going a million miles an hour. Why couldn't I have met him earlier?

"Because then you wouldn't leave Ontario," I heard in my spirit.

"You're right, Jesus. Thank you."

I had spent my whole life running from God's voice. It was almost a relief to let him back in.

I got changed and made it to bed. I was so wound up from the day, but I heard God's voice saying that he gave his beloved rest, I was his beloved. I let that envelope me as I closed my eyes.

Chapter 31

My alarm went off far too early, and that was saying something as I usually get up at five thirty to feed the horses. I pressed snooze, but my phone's ringing got me up. I wasn't late, or at least not yet.

I dragged my hand through my mop of a braid. It seemed like a good idea last night. I groped in the dark for my phone. "Hello," I answered groggily.

"Hi, Rose, I wasn't sure if you'd wake up on your own. It is early."

"Thanks, Ian. Truth be told, snooze and I were getting along just fine." I lay back down.

"How about I pick you up one of those coffees you like and a muffin? Will that inspire you to wake up?"

I sat up. "Yes, that will do it. Thanks, not just for breakfast but also for doing this."

"It's like I said, I don't have a lot of time left with you. I'm going to cherish every opportunity, no matter how early it is."

I could picture his smile even through the phone. It made me smile. "Well, I appreciate it more than you know."

"My pleasure. I'll see you in half an hour."

"See you then. And it's mochas I like, easy on the whip."

"Perfect. Bye, Rose."

"Bye."

I had gotten used to Ian calling me Rain that it was almost odd to hear him call me Rose. But when he did, something welled up in my heart. He really cared for me. I had never been treated like this before.

I couldn't lie in bed and get sentimental. I had to move. I wanted to feed Mia before we left too. Luckily, I had showered the night before, but my hair was in disarray. It really was time for a change. I undid the braid and tried to detangle my blond mass. It was a wavy mess. I decided I'd put it in a ponytail and be done with it.

I chose my new A&T top that Kat had given me. It felt snug, but the fact that it said Staff on the back made me happy. I threw on my jeans and boots and didn't bother with breakfast seeing as Ian was bringing me goodies. I took my phone and keys and headed out toward the big barn.

The sun was peeking out, and it promised to be another hot day. The girls weren't there yet, so I took the liberty of taking a flake of hay to Mia. I created a ruckus, as in no time, the other horses saw what I was up to. The neighing started, followed by some of them banging on their stall doors with their hooves. Dakota, true to form, was the loudest. I quickly went down the aisle trying to pacify them, until I came to Mia's stall. There she was with her big brown eyes looking my way. It was as if she were waiting for me.

"Hi, girl, you hungry?" I opened up her stall and gave her the hay. She nudged me playfully as she bit into the flake. "You were hungry." She had come so far with her stall manners. There were times she'd still give me the cold shoulder, but they were becoming few and far between. I stroked her dark neck and wrapped my arms around her, filling my nostrils with her scent. "I'm going to miss you, girl. I so wish you could be mine." She neighed back at me, content to munch away at her breakfast.

I was so lost in the moment that I didn't hear Ian join me.

"I figured this is where you'd be."

"What? Oh, hi. Good morning."

"And here I was worried that you'd fallen back asleep."

"Did you try to call?"

"I tried your trailer. I didn't want to wake anyone else with my knocking. I figured I'd try here, and sure enough. By the way, those boots aren't supposed to come into my car."

"Hey, it's not my fault that you're now driving a luxury vehicle."

"You do score points for calling it that. But wait, I've got another surprise for you."

"Ian, you spoil me way too much!" I gave Mia another couple of strokes before leaving her.

"Come and see. It's not much. Aren't you a bit cool?"

"Now that you mention it, I probably should have brought a sweater."

"Good idea. Come on. We don't want to be late."

"You're right. Bye, Mia, I'll see you later." She lifted her head toward me, looking for treats. "When I come back, I'll bring you some carrots."

"Bye, Mia. Let's go."

I locked her stall back up and was going to leave a note for Jen when I saw her arrive. I wondered if she'd find it odd to see Ian and me here so early. If she did, she didn't show it.

"Hi, you two. You're here early, Ian." She smiled at both of us. Jen's face looked as if it had been kissed by the sun. Her brown hair had also showed some blond lights.

"Never too early to see Ro—Rain."

"It's okay, Ian. Now that the cat's out of the bag, you can call me Rose here. I didn't want to explain to everyone, so some people still call me Rain."

"It's a good nickname," Jen offered.

"Exactly. Ian's taking my parents to the airport with me, but I'll be back later to ride Mia."

"Such a good guy. How's your sister, Ian? Is she going to buy Calvin?"

"She's good. She's not sure about Calvin, but I'm sure we'll see soon enough."

"Well, you two have fun. See you later, Rain."

"Thanks, Jen."

Ian and I headed to his fancy, new car, and I remembered to wipe my boots off before getting in.

The sun had risen, and it promised to be another beautiful day. I saw Lindsey arrive, and I waved at her.

As I got settled in, Ian looked at me and smiled. "The surprise I have for you is in the back seat. And your coffee is here." He handed me my Starbucks mocha. I took in the smell of the delicious coffee.

"I do draw the line of eating in here. But I did bring you a muffin too." He gave me the brown bag.

"I can wait for food, as long as I can sip on my coffee."

He reached into the back and pulled over something wrapped in brown paper. "Your surprise."

I took the large package. "What is it?"

"Open it. I hope you like it."

I put the coffee back in the holder and held the present gingerly. I started opening up the present, then pulled away the paper. There was a box inside, which I opened. Ian had given me a beautiful light-blue sweater with a picture of a horse that looked like Mia on it. I held it up and grinned. "It's beautiful. It's Mia!"

"I saw it and thought you had to have it."

"Thank you." I unbuckled myself and reached over to give Ian a hug. I wasn't thinking if anyone was looking as it was so early. Little did I know that Jayden had picked up my shift. There she was, pointing at us and laughing. I let go of Ian and looked down.

"What happened? I was enjoying that hug."

"Jayden happened."

"Oh, she doesn't mean anything by it." Ian turned toward her and waved. She waved back. "There'll be more time for hugging later. I'm glad you like it."

I took the tags off and slipped it over my head. It was a really warm hoodie, perfect for this time of the morning. "No wonder you asked if I had brought a sweater."

Ian pulled out of the parking lot and headed toward my parents' hotel. It was all so bittersweet. I'd be seeing my parents soon. Ian, however, was another story.

It didn't take us long to arrive at the Sandman. Both Mom and John were in the lobby waiting. My mom looked like she was anxious to get going.

Both of them loved my sweater. I sipped on my coffee, looking forward to breakfast. Neither of them had slept much. They were both too worried about Ivan and me. Ivan wasn't able to come with us, but we'd be all together soon enough.

"Rose, before we leave, I want you to know that your dad tried to sway me from convincing you to come home one more time last night. That was part of the reason that we couldn't sleep. Ian, will you please help her stay away from that side of the family?"

"Of course. You have my word on it."

"Thank you, Ian."

"I won't go back, Mom."

"I know, but I like insurance, plus I can't trust him or Martha. They both play dirty."

"That I can attest to. What did he say last night?"

"He tried to guilt trip me. It was his last-ditch effort in having you stay behind. As if he didn't already have you for most of your life! He infuriates me. Rose, I will never keep you from your father, but I will say, please be careful. He will play any card he has to in order to get his way."

"Just keep your eyes open," John added.

"I promise that I will be on that plane in a week."

My mom reached over to my arm and gave it a squeeze. "I can't wait."

I smiled back at her. I was excited too, but I was still afraid of all the change.

Ian got us to the airport early. We had time for breakfast together, which was nice. But far too quickly, it was time to say goodbye. I had waited all my life to get to know my real mom, and this short period wasn't enough.

The Toronto airport was always buzzing with activity. It was the major hub for almost all flights going across Canada. I hadn't traveled much, but I had come to the airport to meet friends and family sometimes. The four of us kept to ourselves, not minding the flurry of activity around us.

We still had some time after breakfast, but John was anxious to get to their gate on time. I gulped my emotions down. We'd be reunited soon. As we walked toward the gate, my mom held on to my hand. We stood near the line that was going through the main area.

Ian decided to make the first move and shook both of my parents' hands, but they embraced him. John patted him on the back, telling him to take care of himself and me. My mom hugged him again and thanked him for everything he had done for me. Ian drew back, giving us some privacy to say our goodbyes. I couldn't help it. The tears started to come.

"It's okay, Rose. We'll see you in a week." But her eyes betrayed her. Her light-blue eyes, that matched my brother's, were turning red. "It's really okay." She tried to catch herself. I hugged her tightly, not wanting to let go.

"It's not fair. We've only just begun." I sniffed.

"But it's the start. We can wait a week." She took a deep breath, trying to compose herself.

John wrapped his strong arms around us. "It'll be okay, you two. We will have an incredible reunion in a week."

"It's true, but it feels too long to wait."

"I've waited so many years for this. I can wait one more week." I laughed, and she joined me.

John took a step back and found Ian. "We're a bit of a mess."

"It's okay. I've had to say goodbye to my parents when I was in the military. It doesn't get easier."

"That's true. Come on, you two, we need to get to our gate." John patted our arms, and I released my mom. I gave John another hug, then embraced my mom one more time.

"Call me when you arrive, okay?"

"Of course, dear. See you in a week."

Ian stepped forward and waved to both of them. He took my hand, giving me the strength I needed to let them go.

"Bye." I waved them through the line. "See you soon."

Both John and Mom took one more look at us and waved. I saw my mom's cheeks were wet with tears.

"It'll be okay." Ian drew me in beside him.

I buried my head in his firm chest. I looked up into his beautiful chocolate-colored eyes. "No, because next week, I have to say goodbye to you."

He squeezed tighter. "Don't worry about that now. One thing at a time. You ready to go?" I nodded. He continued to hold on to my hand as we made our way through the throngs of people in the airport. Ian was almost stoic in the way he led me out. "I have to confess, I'm not a fan of crowds. I can handle strangers in small doses."

"I understand. I'm kind of an extroverted introvert."

Ian chuckled at that. "Okay, Dr. Cooper."

"Well, I am."

"You've diagnosed yourself?"

"Yup."

"Good, good. And what am I?"

"You're an introvert with some extrovert tendencies."

"You're so official."

"Yup. I like to read."

"That's a good trait to have. I like to read, but then I usually fall asleep and forget where I was in my book. Then I have to start all over again. It makes it hard to finish a book."

"I guess. Maybe you need a better book."

"Maybe. Here's the exit."

We both kept a steady pace getting to the car. The day was proving to be a hot one. I was anxious to get a ride on Mia before it was too hot out. I hoped Ian would be okay with that. I'd have to split my time between Mia and Ian in the week I had left.

Ian got my door.

"You're such a gentleman."

"I'm just trying to make it difficult for you to date when you move to Nova Scotia." He winked at me.

He had a point. I was ruined.

Chapter 32

After my parents left, my time seemed to fly by. I had been Martha-free for almost a week, which was lovely. My dad had also been silent, which wasn't unusual. What was odd was that no one else from my family, or what was my family, had tried to contact me. I had grown up with six siblings. Only Jenna and Ivan had reached out to me since I had left.

However, Jenna hadn't even called me. I hadn't actually heard from her since our tearful goodbye. No wonder that hit me hard on that day. I'd be spending a lot of time with Ivan in the near future as we'd be flying out together, so I wasn't worried about him. Jenna, on the other hand, I missed sorely.

My most recent welts had healed from my last meeting with Martha. I also hadn't had the need to slap anyone since then. I still didn't know what John had said to her, but my mom mentioned that they threatened a restraining order on her. That would be enough to keep her away. She was so big on her persona but gave no thought to her actual personality. There was no growth there.

Out of my six siblings, Ivan was my only full brother. We had all supposed that Jenna was our half sister, but it was never proven. The blue eyes and blond hair was a dead giveaway to me. The rest of Martha's children all had dark hair and brown eyes and didn't need glasses. Plus, Jenna was so much like me.

The others—Annette, Nancy, Robert, and Maggie—all had their own things going on. I was closest to Maggie after Jenna, but she and I had become so different in our teen years. She was popular in her high school, and I was usually on the fringe of everything. In fact, once, she had a party at our place, and when I showed up, people wondered why I was there.

It was still weird that here I was about to travel halfway across Canada and not a peep. I had always been a lone wolf. Most Christmases, I ended up in our garage loft crying because I was so lonely. It got worse when Ivan got kicked out of the house. I was still able to form a small group of friends. I spent most of high school sneaking out at night so I could hang out with them. They were a fiercely loyal group, and I hoped that we'd stay in touch.

I was in my last week at A&T, which was why I was feeling a bit sorry for myself. Tanis said that I didn't have to work this week, as she figured that I had lots to do before I left. The truth was, without work, I felt pretty depressed. I had begged her for shifts, and she gave me a couple. I was going to be able to ride Mia today. They had built a new outdoor riding area close to the cross-county field, and I was anxious to ride out in it. I had gotten to help with some of it, and we were all excited. This was the first week that it was ready to be used.

I checked my clock; it was only 4:00 a.m. I didn't need to get up for over an hour. I thought of texting Ian, but I couldn't text him whenever I was blue. I actually was trying to distance myself from him. I figured, why go to Nova Scotia heartsick? He figured out pretty quick what I was doing. I did that a lot in life. If you got too close, I'd make sure to reject you before you could reject me. At the end of it, I realized I had wasted too much time not seeing him.

Yasmin had come up again, and I was pretty sure she'd be buying Calvin this week. So many changes were coming my way. I felt like I needed to do something drastic. I had a thought. I wondered if one of my friends could give me a ride to see my hairdresser before I left. All of a sudden, I wanted to cut off my long hair. I didn't just want a trim, but something drastic. I felt a rush of adrenaline as I contemplated this. I felt my mass of hair that surrounded my shoulders. I would do it! I would surprise Ian. I hoped he'd like it. I could also talk to Kat or Tanis and see if they could help me with my plan.

The rush of the thought of change must have calmed my soul, as next thing I knew, my alarm was going off. It was time for work! Finally! I did realize that I'd need to go back home one more time to get my stuff. Since I was trying to spend as much time with Ian as possible, I'd ask him to take me. I quickly grabbed a pen and jotted down the things I had to do before I left.

As I got up, I found my plane ticket and held it close to my chest. "Thank you, Jesus," I whispered. "I'm going to my forever home."

I felt peace again. It would be good. I could grow and learn. This time, I did text Ian. I confirmed that we could meet at four. I also figured I'd have to call the house and let them know I was coming. I still had a key to get in, so even if no one was there, I'd be okay.

I made haste and put my ticket back for safekeeping. I smiled and remembered my plan of cutting my hair. Today would be a good day!

I met the usual crew, and we all got to work. They told me not to make plans for Friday as we were all going out. In no time, I'd be on that plane! This was also the last week of camp. It was the one that Jenna never missed. I wondered if I'd see her. I so hoped that I would. Or maybe she'd be home when I went there later on.

Because we all had worked together so much this summer, in no time, we were almost finished our chores in the big barn. Camp was due to start soon. I was off by ten, so I'd have lots of time to spend with Mia. My lesson wasn't till the afternoon, but she loved getting to go out for grass and such.

Then the barn started to fill up with the camp kids. I scanned the heads for a certain blond youngster. I didn't see Jenna, so I figured I was out of luck. I put the blower away and got to saddling up some of the ponies.

I was shocked to hear my name. I was still going by Rain, as it was too weird explaining to everyone why I changed my name. Truth be told, I preferred Rain anyway. But this time, I heard Rose, and it wasn't just by one person but several. I turned around, and there were Sandra and my other close friends from school.

"What are all of you doing here?" I exclaimed.

"Surprising you!" They all laughed. I hugged each of them.

"You stink," Sandra said.

"You've ridden. You know how it is."

"We hear you're leaving us," Angelica, one of my best friends, piped up.

"I am."

"It's about time," Daryl added.

"Thanks."

"And what did it?" he asked me.

"Let's just say that at eighteen, it was one slap too many."

"We're proud of you, Rose," Sandra chimed in.

"So can we steal you away for a bit?" the three of them asked in unison.

"I'll check. I actually begged to work."

"That sounds like you," Angelica said.

"Yeah. I'm a little nuts like that. Give me two shakes." I looked at my small group of friends. "I never would have guessed you'd all end up at a barn with me." I grinned widely at them.

"It was Sandy," Daryl added. "She told us what was going on. We figured it was the least we could do."

"Well, I appreciate it."

"And we all just happened to be here this week, so we could make it happen."

"Thanks, Sandra. I am so glad that I ran into you when I first arrived. I have lots to fill you in on. Oh, and is there any way one of you would be able to take me to my hairdresser?"

"Whenever you cut your hair, Rose, you can't even tell," Angelica said.

"Not this time."

"What? Is it time?" Sandra asked.

"Finally, it's time."

"Then consider it done. I'll figure out a way. Now go get off work, will you?"

I hugged each one of them again. I knew today would be good, but I didn't realize how good it would be.

I practically skipped toward Jen who was beaming at me. Seeing as since she'd known me I have been either afraid or nervous.

"Rain, what's up? You look like the cat that swallowed the canary."

"Well, it turns out that the news is out that I'm leaving, and my best friends decided to come up here and surprise me. Would it be okay if I finished early?" I asked quietly.

"Of course! Tanis said that you had begged her to work today. It looks like she knew better. Or maybe someone called her to tell her."

"Really? That's so nice of them. So you're really okay?"

"We'll be fine. We've got some extra hands with camp on today anyways." Jen grabbed the pitchfork and went back to mucking Kiran's stall.

"Thank you so very much!"

"You're welcome. Now go and have fun!"

I turned around and went back to my friends. Only Sandra was really comfortable with horses. The rest of them just stood awkwardly by Mia's stall.

"I see you've found my dream horse." I came up and stroked Mia's face. I had fed her today, so she was all lovey with me."

"I've never seen her be like that with anyone else," Sandra offered.

"Really? Well, we've been working together a lot. The truth is, if I were staying, I'd find a way to own her. But it's important that I actually get to know my mom and John."

"Horse or no horse, I'm glad you finally get a proper family." Daryl was always protective of me, and now was no different.

"Remember when we were over and she set the timer for us? She let us come in but only for fifteen minutes. She's nuts!"

"Yes, Sandra. Unfortunately, that wasn't enough to get me to go."

"We're all glad it's finally happening."

"Thanks, Angelica!"

"Now go grab your stuff and let's kidnap you for the day," Sandra added.

"You can kidnap me until my riding lesson."

"Sure, of course. I'm glad you found your passion, Rose."

"Me too, Daryl. Okay, want to see my place?"

They all nodded. I took them out of the big barn, introducing them to the main horses. I couldn't help it; the horses had become my family.

As I was coming to Calvin's stall, I saw the blond hair that I had been looking for. She was here! But was Martha?

I asked my friends to wait for me out of the barn. Jenna had caught my eye. Was she trying to hide from me? She looked almost afraid. I walked slowly toward her. She shook her head at me. I looked at her questioningly, but she just kept shaking her head. I wouldn't enjoy my day out if this was how we'd leave things.

I was in luck. The other campers were signing in, and she was almost alone. I motioned for her to come over to me. She looked around her and followed me. I went into the feed room, which I knew was empty. The room was full of the fragrance of grain. I breathed it in before I began. I turned, faced her, but my confusion was piqued as I noticed her eyes were welling up with tears. I came to her and put my arms around her. "Jenna, what is it? What's wrong?" She heaved sobs into my chest. "Jenna, it's okay." She held me tightly, not willing to let me go.

"It's too hard, Rose. It's too much to ask of me."

"What is?" I loosened her grip on me and looked into her light-blue eyes.

"I knew I had to come to camp this week. I knew it was the last time I'd see you. But I promised that I wouldn't try to find you and talk to you. I lied, of course, because I was going to make sure I talked to you. My mom is banned from here, so Dad dropped me off. I had to make sure that he left before I talked to you. It's such a mess!" She was about to start sobbing again.

"Jenna, it's okay. We will talk obviously. And I'm so glad that they let you come."

"I called Kat and implored her to let me come. She knew how important it was for me. Besides, I used the excuse of the event coming up. Beanie and I still need more practice."

"Good for you. Now, Jenna, I just remembered Sandra and a couple of my friends came up to take me out today. I'll be back later for my lesson. Wipe your tears now."

I heard the campers coming back into the barn. Most of them were headed to the lounge, but I didn't want Jenna to be embarrassed. She took a deep breath about the same time that Jen came looking for her.

"Jenna, have you already signed in?"

Jenna pulled herself together. "Yup, I'm all good."

"Okay, I'll see you upstairs in five."

"I'll be there."

Jen left us to finish our conversation.

"Jenna, go have fun, and we'll get to see each other as much as we can this week."

"I don't like lying, but it's worth it to see you."

"You shouldn't have to lie about talking to your sister. It's all so wrong." I saw her face about to fall again. "It's okay." I gave her another hug. "Love you, sis."

"Love you too. I'm proud of you, Rose. At least you're going to get to know your mom."

We pulled away from each other.

"That means the world to me."

Jenna left in better spirits than when she found me. I went and met my friends, ready for my adventure for the day.

Chapter 33

I was back in my trailer and in front of my bathroom mirror. I had done it! I had chopped my hair off! I couldn't believe it. I went from one extreme to another today. I had come into Angie's salon with long locks and without a style and left with a cute chin-length bob. I almost went shorter but decided there was time for that later.

I hadn't told Ian what I was doing, but I was sure he'd like it. I wasn't going to tell my parents. They could see it when I landed in Nova Scotia. So far, I had only seen Tanis, and she loved it! I just felt free. I twirled around in front of the mirror. I grabbed my brush and combed through my hair again. I just wanted to see how it felt. I walked away from the mirror, feeling much more like my real age. I had a lesson with Kat that I had to get ready for and then one of my last dates with Ian. I took one more look and smiled at myself again. This would be a good week. It would be hard, but good.

I nearly skipped to the barn, forgetting that Jenna was at camp today. I saw her with her group of friends. I let her be, as she looked happy with her group of friends. She deserved happiness after the few months she'd had.

Jen saw me as I came into the barn and stopped in her tracks. "Whoa, Rain, you look amazing!"

"Thanks, Jen. I love it!"

"Did you tell your parents you were doing it?"

"Nope. I'll surprise them when I land."

"You may want to warn them, or there'll be looking for a girl with long blond hair."

"You may have a point. I've got to get Mia ready. But I'll see you afterward."

"Have a good lesson."

"Thanks, Jen."

I moved past the other campers. Quite a few of them didn't recognize me. I should have cut my hair when I first left home. I could have hidden a lot longer.

I grabbed Mia's tack and went to her stall. "Hey, Mia, are you ready for a ride?" She peeked her head out at me and put her ears forward. "I take that as a yes."

I brushed her and tacked her up. I would miss this mare so very much. Maybe one day I'd be rich, and I could come back here and buy her.

I put my helmet on. It was so easy to put my hair back under my helmet now. I went back into Mia's stall and put her bridle on. I was in my happy place, until I heard a familiar voice that stopped me in my tracks. I turned hesitantly and saw my dad. I should have ignored him. He probably wouldn't have even recognized me. What was he doing here? But there he was outside of Mia's stall.

"Rose, I was hoping I would run into you." His light-blue eyes pleaded at me. I had to make a move; I had a lesson to get ready for. He looked slightly pathetic, but my heart did go out to him.

"Dad, I need to go." I did up Mia's throat latch, trying to hang on to my calm.

"Can we talk? At least one more time before you go? Please, Rose, it isn't too much to ask for, is it?" He moved his face closer to me.

I gulped and held back my tears. I looked back at him. "Fine. We can talk. But, Dad, I am not going to change my mind about leaving. As long as that's not your sole purpose in talking to me, then we can talk. I need to come by the house and pick up my stuff. We can talk then, as long as Martha isn't there. I don't want to see her before I go." My voice was shaking, but I stayed resolute.

"Okay. When are you coming?"

"Ian was going to bring me by tonight, if that's okay. You know I'm leaving at the end of the week, so I don't have a lot of time." I hadn't actually nailed down a time, but the sooner I got things cleared away, the better.

"That should work. I'll need to check with Martha as she may need to be home tonight."

"Dad, you do know that both Ivan and I could press charges with all the things that Martha has done to us. Just the other day, she tried to hurt me again. I honestly don't know how you can stay with her. But it's your conscience, not mine."

He started to tear up, which just unnerved me. I heard Kat come in from outside and call over to me. She hated people being late, and here I was about to get one of my last lessons ruined by my dad!

"I'll be right there, Kat."

She looked down the aisle at me and spotted my dad. I was talking to my dad. She didn't hesitate to come to my rescue. "Rain, you okay?" She looked over at my dad. "She needs to get on Mia. I think it's time for you to go." Kat might not be very old, but she was used to bossing around horses, and my dad was no match for her.

"I'll call you about tonight, Rose." He shrugged. He looked like a man who had lost everything. I had pity, but not enough to stay.

I just nodded at him; I had no words for him. I didn't wish him harm, but I did wish him truth.

"Come on, Rain, let's go have some fun!" Kat took Mia's reins from my hands and went to Mia and finished the job. I put my gloves on and tightened up my helmet. At least I had riding today.

Kat surprised me with taking Mia and me out back to the cross-county area. She told me that we needed a fun ride after what I was going through. But as usual, she didn't pussyfoot around. She had the uncanny ability to combine fun with a challenging lesson.

Before long, she had us cantering around the field. It was such a release! Mia seemed to sense that I needed a calm ride. She and I were in such sync that it was hard to believe we hadn't been together for years.

As we slowed down to a trot, Kat remarked how she wished that Mia could come with me. "You know, she's for sale," Kat said as we started to walk. Kat joined us.

"Really? But I can't take her across the country."

"You could. I'm not saying it would be cheap, but it's possible."

"Hmm. I can dream. There's just something about her."

"It's like you two belong together."

Mia kept her stride, and I gave her head. She stretched down, snorting happily.

"I feel that way too. I really will miss this place. I only wish I had found it earlier. I had gone to camp with Jenna at the other farms, but not here. Probably because she came here for advanced camp."

"You two are equally good riders." Kat stroked Mia as we walked.

"Really? You think so?" I looked down at her, my heart skipping a beat.

"Yup. It's probably why Martha wouldn't let you come. I get the feeling that she wants Jenna to be the best."

"That's the truth. I once did better than Jenna in a horse show, and I got in trouble. We weren't even in the same classes! It was so ridiculous! And Jenna was so happy for me."

"How did Jenna turn out so nice?"

"I raised her."

"That explains it. She was good at camp today. I could tell she was slightly distracted, but she handled Beanie much better than she has in the past. And she did really well jumping today."

"That makes me so happy. Kat, when she comes up here, can you keep an eye out for her?" I stopped Mia.

"I'll do my best. And I promise not to ban her from here, only Martha."

"Thanks. I appreciate it."

I stroked Mia's long neck and let her graze on some grass. The sun was out, but in the back, under the trees, it was comfortable. I looked up and saw Jayden coming for her lesson.

"I guess it's that time again," I said sadly.

"Yes, I guess so. Keep riding Mia until you leave. Just make sure that you have someone watching you. She really doesn't like being a lesson horse, and she's happy with you. It's nice seeing her not being such a mare." We both laughed at that. Mares were a different breed, that's for sure.

"Thanks for everything, Kat."

I swung off Mia, and my feet found the ground. It had been an exhilarating ride. The worries of the past hour had melted off me. Mia nudged me with her long nose. She could almost knock me over with her head, but I thanked her for being such a good mare.

I led her away from Jayden and Kat. Jayden waved at me, smiling her wide grin. I was sure she was still thinking of Ian and me kissing in the back. I returned her smile. It was fine. Everyone now knew about us anyway.

I took in the smell of the summer, mingled with the scent of Mia. I wanted to bottle both and take them with me. What would the smell of the sea be like?

"Mia, I am off to a new adventure. Want to come with me?" She nudged me playfully. "Thought so."

I led her around the farm, cooling us both out. It was a time for prayer and for reflection. I was so grateful for this new journey I was on. All the pain from the scars that Martha had given me, both internally and externally, would finally heal. I had been told that I was stupid and fat and would amount to nothing for the majority of my life, but for once, I didn't believe her. I was strong. I could ride. I had muscles that I never knew I had. I could haul a wheelbarrow and throw hay bales. I now had calluses, which I was proud of.

In all the darkness I had lived through, I felt a ray of sunshine peek through. I finally had dreams again. It had been a long time since I had dared to dream, but now I felt my heart opening to the possibilities. "Thank you, Jesus," I whispered.

Mia again nudged at my back. I turned around and held her head in my arms. "Love you, girl." I breathed more of her in, closed my eyes, and wept.

Chapter 34

After putting Mia away, I came back to my trailer and got ready for Ian. After washing my hair, I was still pleased with my new look.

My dad had called and said that I could come by and pick up my stuff. He had tried to invite me for dinner, but I wasn't going to stay. My heart was aflutter just thinking about entering that house of horrors again. I had talked to Ivan, and he had tried to convince me to leave everything and not go back. It was different for him though. He'd been gone for a long time. I had journals, books, and clothing that I wanted to take with me. It would be so nice to wear more than three outfits again. If it wasn't for Ian, I'd have no clothes.

I heard my phone vibrate. It was Ian texting me, saying he was five minutes away. I pulled on my jeans and laced up my faithful boots. After returning home, I'd have sandals to wear! As much as I loved my boots, it would be nice to have options.

I took a deep breath and picked up the suitcase that Tanis had loaned me. She had actually given it to me. I did have some money now, but I needed some for the flight, and I didn't want to be without money when I first got to Nova Scotia.

I looked out my window and saw the familiar Impala. I grabbed my phone and left my safety net to see Ian. He had exited his car and was standing beside it. He looked very James Dean in his skinny beige khakis, burgundy top, and aviator shades. There went my heart for a very different reason.

"Hey, Rain, wow! Don't you kook amazing!" I forgot I hadn't told him about my hair. I blushed as I came toward him. "I love it! You look so sophisticated."

"Thank you. I'm glad you like it."

"The question is, Do you like it?"

"I love it!"

He looked around and didn't see anyone, so he gave me a quick kiss. I had been such a fool to try to keep him away.

"Are you ready to pack?" I pointed to the suitcase that I had brought with me. "Looks good to me." He went around and opened the passenger side for me. "My lady."

"Why, thank you." I got in and took in the smell of the new car. He really had done well on this.

He pulled out of the barn. I had given him directions to my old home. I was silent, as I contemplated what lay ahead. I felt assured with Ian by my side. Without him, my resolve to leave could waver.

"You okay?" Ian broke through my dark thoughts.

"Just…" I swallowed hard. I didn't live far from the barn, so I knew it wouldn't take long.

He placed his hand on my arm for support. We were stopped at a red light, so he took the opportunity to face me. "I'm right here. If you decide you don't want to do this, we can turn around."

"I need to face this. I can't just run and not look back. I feel they've won if I don't."

"You have already won. You chose to reconnect with your family. You're leaving them."

The light changed green, and Ian focused his attention back to the road. Even in the car, Martha used to be a bully. I remember her pinching me to make me stay awake. She drove terribly. I was certain I'd die driving with her. She got in an accident almost yearly. I wasn't surprised, and it was almost always at Christmas. I always wondered how that happened.

Ian passed one of the local schools, and my heart rate doubled. I knew we'd be there soon. My mind was listening to all the lies that Martha had raised me on, and I was quickly becoming the victim I used to be.

"Rain, Rain, we're almost there."

I didn't respond. I hadn't realized that Ian was trying to get my attention until he pulled over and stopped the car.

"Rain, are you sure about this?" His kind eyes were making their way through my thoughts.

"I think so."

"You're not trapped anymore. You have a way out."

"I have to believe that. I just know that there will be a trap set for me. Please watch out for that for me."

"I know Martha hurt you. I don't know all of it, but one day if you'd like, I'm here to listen."

"Thank you. One day I'll fill you in."

"Let's get this over with so I can take you on our date." He smiled at me.

I answered his smile. "Okay, I'm ready." And I was.

Ian got us back on the road, and not five minutes later, we were passing the Dundas driving park. One more turn and we'd be there.

"Your dad is expecting you, right?"

I nodded. "I asked him to have Martha out, but I doubt that will happen."

"If she is anything like you've told me, she'll be there."

I saw my neighbours' homes. The other homes on the street were so much nicer than ours. Ours reminded me of a horror movie. I hadn't been away for long, but it appeared that they'd done some upgrades. Maybe they were trying to mask the evil in the house now that the cat was out of the bag.

"Is this it?"

"Yes. Just park on the street. I want to know we've got a getaway." Ian obliged. I took in one more deep breath.

Ian put the car into park. He turned to me and said, "You're strong and beautiful. You can do this. I will be right by your side."

"I am with you also," I heard God whisper to me. It was time.

"Let's go." I got the suitcase out from the back, and we walked together hand in hand to the door.

I forgot the key, so I knocked. The door opened. It was Martha. Of course, it was her.

"Oh, Rose, it's so good to see you!" She threw her arms around me. I didn't respond. I could sense Ian seething beside me. She finally let go. "Dad told me you didn't want me here, but I thought I could help you see reason. You know, he won't say it, but he's been so upset ever since you ran away. Our family hasn't been whole since you left."

My resolve was shaking. "I don't believe that. I'm sure you're all fine. Jenna's kept me up to date."

"Don't even get me started about Jenna. She hasn't stopped crying. You know, you're her whole world."

Ian interrupted her falsehoods. "Martha, I know that Rose needs to be back at the barn in an hour, so we'd better get a move on." Ian walked boldly up the two stairs at the doorway. God bless Ian!

"Is this true? You won't even have dinner with us? I made your favorite chicken dish." Her British accent seemed extra strong tonight.

"You cooked? You never cook."

"Without you here, I've had to learn," she said dramatically.

"Well, I'm sure it's good for all of you. Where's Dad?"

"Oh, he couldn't be here right now. He was too upset to see you pack."

"What? He's not here?" I was going to be sick. I felt the sting of rejection so deep. I wanted to crawl into a ball right there and then.

"Rose, let's move," Ian broke through my thoughts. He had my case.

I nodded. "Martha, I'll see you before I go."

"Martha? Since when did I become Martha? I've always been your mother. You know I raised you since you were five, and your mother abandoned you."

"If you mean you stole me and Ivan and abandoned my mother and you had us be your slaves, yes, thank you!" I stormed away from her. "Come on, Ian, let's get packed!"

I stomped through the living room with Ian following behind. My sister's cat, Cuddles, that had become mine was whining after me. "I'm sorry, Cuddles. I have to go." I bent down and stroked her gray tabby head. She purred at me. There were bound to be a lot of changes without me around.

Up the stairs we went to the second floor. I passed Jenna's room and saw the light on. I peered in. "Jenna," I called out. I heard tears. I entered. I asked Ian to wait a minute. "Jenna, are you okay?"

She was in the corner of her purple bedroom, huddled with her arms around her small frame.

I knelt down beside her. "It'll be okay," I assured her.

She grabbed me close and hugged me. "I'm going to miss you so much, Rose." She sobbed.

"Oh, honey, I'm going to miss you too." The tears came freely now. "I can't stay for long. Martha will think I've changed my mind."

"Have you?" She looked up at me.

"No. I have to go. I'm sorry that I'm leaving you. You're my biggest reason to second-guess my decision, but it's time I do this for me. I want to get to know my mom and John. I've missed Ivan too. You can come visit me, okay?" I tried to dry her tears, and I pushed back her blond hair off her face. It was only then that she actually looked at me.

"Rose, you cut your hair!" She laughed through her tears. "You actually did it!"

"Yes, I did." I smiled back at her.

"I like it. You're so brave. I hope that when I grow up, I can be like you." She was trying so hard.

"You already are. Who raised you?" I helped her up.

"You did."

"Then you know you're going to turn out a lot more like me than your mom." I put my arm around her slender shoulders. "Want to help me pack?"

"Okay. I can tell you, my mom won't be happy with me. She was sure that you'd change your mind today."

"Did she ask you to help with that?"

Jenna looked guiltily at me. "She asked me to be honest with how I felt and to not hold back." She couldn't look at me.

"It's okay. I can't blame you. It's not your fault your mom is a little, how shall we say, controlling."

Poor Ian, he had been waiting patiently by Jenna's room. "Ready?" he asked.

"Yup. And Jenna's going to help."

We walked toward the next flight of steps that lead to the third floor and my previous bedroom. We passed by the small room that I had spent many years in.

"Ian, this was my old room." I pointed to the little room painted orange.

"Terrible color," he quipped.

"There aren't a lot of good memories in there. I was pretty happy when they said I could move to the third floor. But I did like that Jenna and I were close together. We used to sneak into each other's room after bedtime and read together."

"It was more like Rose would tell me stories of all her secret boyfriends."

"Oh, really," Ian added.

"No, not really."

"I thought you had only ever dated me." He winked at me.

"Yes. And I'm your first girlfriend, am I not?"

"You're definitely the first horse girl I've ever dated. Oh, and the only girl with two different names."

"See, I'm original. I'll show you my recent digs."

The three of us climbed the winding staircase. The walls on the way up had still not been painted since we'd lived there, and we'd been there a long time. They had redone my sisters' room, but never mine. I never minded, as it meant I could hang as many posters as I liked on the walls.

My room was closed; it was almost as if no one had gone in since I left. I pushed open the door, and Ian muttered something under his breath. It wasn't neat as I had left in a rush. There was still clothing left on my bed. I had a large doll collection that would have to stay behind for now. Jenna pushed past us and sat on my bed. Ian put the suitcase beside her.

"Put me to work, Rose. Where do you want to start?" I hadn't taken a large suitcase, so I'd have to be a bit choosy. "You've got quite the room here. Very interesting." I was feeling more vulnerable than I expected.

My room had slanted walls on either side. It was like living in the attic, but I didn't mind. There was a huge window in the middle where I had put my bed. I could see the stars and dream about being free from the life I had lived there. You could really only stand up in the middle of the room as the sides were only about four feet tall.

I moved to my closet and pulled out a couple pairs of pants. I went to work and pulled out shoes and other clothes that I'd need. I also decided to bring my teddy bear that I'd had all my short life. Ian and Jenna helped with the folding of my clothing. I also found a couple of my old journals.

"Jenna, I need you to promise me that you'll hide these or pack them and send them to me."

"I can do that for you. I guess we'll have to pack up your dolls too."

"If you could, that would be great."

I was happy that Martha had left us alone, but I was sure we hadn't heard the last of her. I was so disappointed that my dad hadn't even made an appearance. I made a promise to myself that whoever I'd marry would have a backbone. He hadn't followed any of my suggestions for tonight.

"Is that it?" Ian asked.

"That suitcase looks full."

"It is. You may need to bring another bag for your bear and toiletries."

"I have one." I went back to my closet and pulled out an old carry-on case. I think I had actually received it from my mom years ago.

"Rose, you'll write to me, right?" Jenna jumped off my bed; her eyes were watering up again.

"Yes. Of course I will. And when you're a bit older, you can come visit me."

"I hope so."

"Let's go." I had my carry-on, and Ian had the bigger case. They both left the room before me. I took one last moment to survey my room. "Bye, room. I won't see you later." I got a bit choked up. It wasn't as if I were leaving a bunch of happy memories behind, but I was about to face a new chapter. The unknown, Nova Scotia, would it be easy? It couldn't be as hard as the last eighteen years.

I remembered sneaking out of my room at night in order to make a life of my own. I had my first kiss on one of those nights. I had only been caught twice, and to think I had snuck out hundreds of times, that wasn't bad. I made the mistake of telling Jenna one night. She tried to get me into trouble, but it had backfired on her. She had felt awful later, but it kind of proved that I was highly trusted.

I looked into the corner where some of my dolls lay. I saw the one that I had been given as a baby. I had named her Anne, after my grandmother. She was in a bad way. I scooped the poor doll up gently. I had to take this one with me. I had bandaged her up when I couldn't heal myself. I cradled her gently, and I felt my spirit tighten. "It'll be okay," I whispered to my doll. I sure hoped it would be.

Ian came back into my room and walked in quietly. He touched me on my shoulder. "You okay?" He put his strong arm around me, and I melted into him. I broke only for a moment, but the tears of the past came tumbling down. "It'll be all right. Your mom and John will be able to take care of you."

I nodded. I knew he was right, but I needed a moment. I had bottled up all my pain for so many years, and now I was in a safe spot to let it go.

"I told Jenna to wait for you. I thought you might need a moment." He hugged me close.

I felt like such a little child. I couldn't go downstairs a mess; I had to show Martha that I was strong. I sniffed and wiped my tears. "I can do this. I only have to walk downstairs and outside. Did you see if my dad was back?"

Ian loosened his grip on me. "I didn't see him. I know I shouldn't be surprised, but I did hope for your sake that he'd return."

"It's typical. It's why I left in the first place. I was his firstborn, but it was as if I were adopted. I have a sneaking suspicion that I'll feel like I belong a lot more when I go home to Mom and John."

"I'm excited for you. I'm going to miss you like crazy, but I'm happy for you."

"I'm going to miss you too."

Ian turned me around and kissed me, then he kissed my remaining tears away. "We'll see what the future holds for us. But for now, let's go face your past and get ready for your future."

"That I can agree with." I gave him a peck on the cheek, took my doll, and we closed my old bedroom door behind us.

Chapter 35

The scene before me was shocking! If I hadn't been under Martha's control forever, I would have been more surprised. There in front of me was my dad with tears in his eyes. It seemed that Martha allowed him to say goodbye to me. That, or it was her last-ditch effort to get me to stay.

She also had assembled a couple of my sisters. Jenna had made sure that she stayed strong. I was so appreciative of that. Ian tensed beside me. He whispered "You can do this" in my ear.

"Thank you, all, for coming to say goodbye to me. Dad, I see Martha found you." There was an edge to my voice. He had me for the past eighteen years. If he'd taken care of me, we wouldn't be here today. None of them really cared, besides Jenna.

My dad took a step before me. "Rose, we will all miss you so much," he said through his sobs.

It didn't move me. In fact, it had the opposite effect. "I'll miss you all, but it's time to go." I looked at Ian and smiled. He returned the smile, and I could see that he was proud of me.

I embraced my dad, but I didn't cry. My T-shirt was wet with his tears. He'd get over it. I loved him, but at this moment, I had no respect for his emotions. I was sure my heart would soften in time, but not today.

"I love you too, Dad, but it's time to get to know my mother. You've had me almost all my life, but you didn't take care of my heart," I said quietly to him.

He pulled away and looked into my matching blue eyes. "I'm so sorry."

"It's too late. I'm not saying that I don't forgive you, but I'm saying today is a result of the past fifteen years. You can't erase it with an apology."

"I know. But I am truly sorry." He gave me one more hug. It was the most he had hugged me since I was five years old.

I heard Martha clear her throat. I had to go. She could have my father. She already did.

Nancy and Maggie both came forward and wished me well. They both encouraged me in their own way to keep doing what I was doing. I had found new respect in their eyes. I wasn't going to hug Martha, but she leaned over to me. I stayed straight as a board. She gripped me harder than necessary. "You will regret this," she said so that only I'd hear her. More bruises on my arms, but she could no longer touch my soul.

I didn't comment. I looked at Jenna. "Want to walk us out?" She nodded.

Ian carried my suitcase and said bye. The three of us walked out to his car. We had done it! As soon as we left the house, my shield started to crack. I'd cry later, but not in front of Jenna.

Ian put my luggage into his trunk. I turned to Jenna. "Be good, sister. Don't forget all of the lessons you've learned from me. I also want to tell you that Jesus loves you, like really loves you. When you feel all alone, he'll comfort you better than I ever could. And we'll talk on the phone, and maybe you can come visit when you get a bit older. Don't forget to listen to Kat, and trust your horses. Oh, and please give Mia so much love. I'm going to miss her so much!"

"More than me?" she asked coyly.

"Never! You I will miss the most, Ian next, then Mia."

"As long as I get top billing."

"Always!" I grabbed her into one more bear hug. "Love you, sister. Friends forever."

"Friends forever." She held it together.

I let go of her and got into Ian's car. Jenna's bottom lip was quivering. One more minute and I could fall apart.

"Ready?" Ian asked.

"Ready." I smiled at him.

I waved at Jenna one last time as Ian pulled out. As soon as we turned down Cayley Street, I let the waterworks come. I bawled like a baby. I'd be strong later. I had done it. I was leaving Dundas on my own terms. They had tried to make me into nothing; I would show them that they would not have the last word.

Ian stayed quiet as I bawled. He put his hand on my leg in support and handed me some tissues. My spirit was breaking a bit, but I knew it could now actually heal. I heard that voice again, "I will never leave you or forsake you." It wrapped around my soul. I wouldn't let go of him. He would help me.

My tears started to slow. Ian turned to me and said, "I'm really proud of you. You could have fallen apart in front of them, but you didn't. They don't know what just happened. I promise you that if you ever come and visit me here, I will make sure that they never hurt you again." In his eyes, there was a strength that I hoped I would one day achieve.

"Thank you, Ian. Because of you and my real parents, I am able to be where I am now. I have wanted to leave for the past five years. Jenna wasn't old enough. I couldn't have her be raised by Martha."

"But you were just a child yourself when she was born."

"It didn't matter. I wanted to make sure she was okay. Even now, it's so hard to leave."

Ian looked to be heading back to A&T. I felt bad as here we were in our last days together, and I was such a mess.

"Hey, Ian, you don't have to go back to the barn. You wanted to take me out tonight, didn't you?"

"I didn't think you were up to it." We were at a stop light, and he turned to look at me. I was sure I seemed a mess. He looked back to the road.

"I'm sure if I can wash my face, I'll be fine."

"I don't want to make things more stressful for you."

I smiled at him. "I'm sure glad I didn't date much in high school."

"Why do you say that?"

"Because you have now set a new standard for me." I saw him smile. Good. He deserved to smile.

"Okay. Then I'm taking you to one of my new favorite spots. Do you want me to take your stuff to the trailer first?"

"No. I want to start living." Another smile. Was this what life could be? I was feeling freer by the minute.

Ian took a sharp turn, which caused me to laugh out loud.

"What are you doing?"

"I've got a surprise for you."

I pulled down the mirror and tried to fix myself up. At least my hair still looked good.

"I do love your hair."

"Me too!"

I sat in Ian's car and soaked in my new freedom. I had been Cinderella since I was five. I was finally free!

Chapter 36

It was late when Ian dropped me back to my trailer. We had to open up the gates and explain to Tanis why we'd gotten back so late. But it was worth it! Ian took me to a supercute, new, trendy Italian restaurant. The food was divine! But the company was even better. I was going to miss him so much.

I lay in my small bed reliving our evening. I wasn't really working now, as I was leaving soon. Tanis knew I would do what I could to help out. I didn't have to get up at the crack of dawn tomorrow, but I didn't want to take advantage of her kindness.

Ian promised me that he'd come visit me when I moved home. I hoped he would. Before we pulled into the farm, he had given me a kiss that I couldn't forget. I traced the lines of my lips, remembering how it felt. No guy had ever kissed me like that. I smiled. I could easily fall in love with that man. If only… But moving would be good and necessary.

I heard a noise. I got off my bed and went to my window. I only saw the cats in the main parking area. I couldn't sleep, but I didn't want to wake anyone else. I decided to find one of my journals and write a few lines. I pulled my suitcase over to me and unzipped the front. Sure enough, I found my journal. I got a pen and sat down at my small table. I opened the journal, and a letter fell out. It was folded, which piqued my curiosity. As I opened it, my stomach dropped. It was from Martha. I gulped.

"God, give me strength," I whispered.

It read:

Rose,

You may not believe it, but your leaving is tearing the family apart. I can't believe you are leaving Jenna, whom you say you love. We have provided you with a home and a family all these years, and you decide to leave.

    Your mother wasn't there to pick up the pieces when their marriage fell apart. It was Mike and I who worked every day to make sure you had food to eat. You are ungrateful, just like your mother.

    Good luck. You may not know this, but she is mentally unstable. I know you will come back when you see what you left behind.

                                    Martha

    I let out a breath. She was awful! I wanted to rip up the letter but thought better of it. I'd show Ian or my mom. There went my beautiful evening. But no, I wouldn't let her take my joy!

    I took the letter and tore it into little pieces. "You have no say over me, Martha! I am free!" I would have set the letter on fire if I could have.

    I put the pieces into the garbage and stretched my legs. I looked at the clock; it was only 1:00 a.m. It was too early to call my mom and too early to go see Mia. I wished I had a book. I'd try to sleep and hope to get up early to help feed the horses. I closed the journal and went back to my bed.

    I shut my eyes and asked Jesus for peace. Just before I fell asleep, I heard my phone buzz. I picked it up. It was a text from Ian. He said, "Rain, thank you for the wonderful evening. I can't wait to see you tomorrow. You are finally free! Xoxo, Ian." I smiled and texted him back. I would be okay.

I woke with the sunrise. I actually had a good night's rest despite the interruption of my peace. I stretched out and took in my surroundings. I had come to love this small trailer. It would be odd to occupy a whole home again.

I was excited for the day, as I knew I'd see Ian again and Mia too. I wouldn't see my brother until the day we left. He'd already moved out, so he was a lot further ahead than I was. I wondered if my dad or Martha would try to make one more ditch effort to cause me to stay. I think if I could get through last night, I could get through anything.

My cell rang. I looked, and it was my mom calling. I sat up and answered. She wanted to know all about my move-out day and if I needed any support. I assured her that I had made it. It hadn't been easy, but I did it. I also told her about the letter that was left for me to find. She wasn't surprised and told me to stay strong. That was my plan. I knew with Martha's track record. It wouldn't be easy.

I remembered the day I finally got to go to school full-time. Martha had always told me to leave the house and hide until my dad left for work. Then when his car would pull out, I would make my way back to the house. I did this up till grade 10. One day I got sick of it. I went to school, and boy, did I get in trouble for it. But it was the first time that I had stood up for myself and won. I declared that I was henceforth going to school. So in grade 10, for the first time, I was a full-time student. It was a miracle that I graduated with honors and could now choose the college that I wanted to go to.

It had taken me my whole life to stand up for myself, but once I started, it was hard to stop. I was still verbally abused by her until I ran away. But not having to hide physical scars was easier than the mental ones.

Many people who met me thought I had life easy because of my sunny disposition. But over the years, I recognized that I had a will of steel. I actually had a friend who used to call me Rebar, because I didn't bend. I wasn't sure about that, but to me, it meant that I had fight in me.

It wouldn't be easy leaving all the painful memories behind me. I was sure that those might take years to disappear, but at least I was moving to a loving environment that could help in that.

I heard a knock at my trailer door. Odd, who would be knocking at this time in the morning? I gulped, and fear swept over me. Would Martha actually have the nerve to come here today?

There was another knock.

I can do this, I thought. I got up from my bed and went to the door and opened it.

Relief coursed through me as I saw Tanis in front of me. "Morning," she said brightly.

I laughed and let her in.

"What's so funny?" Her blue eyes were sparkling.

"I'm so relieved that you're not Martha."

"That would make two of us." She laughed back. "Were you expecting her?"

"Truthfully, I'm not sure. They let me leave last night, but I don't trust her. She left a note in one of my journals. Talk about intrusive."

Tanis sat at the little table with me. "Well, I come with much better news. Oh, and I do love your haircut. It looks so fresh on you."

"Thank you. I love it too! Kind of like new me."

"Don't try to change all the great things about you, like how generous you are and helpful and kind. Those are all wonderful traits. You know, I don't hire just anyone here."

"Thank you." I blushed at the compliment. It would take time to get used to compliments.

"I speak the truth. I know your mom will make sure you stay on the right path. We will miss you here, and I know Mia will too. I wish I could send her with you."

"I wish you could too, but I have no idea what life will be like in the maritimes. I hope I get to ride though."

"I'm sure you will. We'll keep you updated on Mia too," she smiled kindly at me. "Now the reason for my early knock at your trailer."

"Your trailer."

"Well, it's still yours for now. Ian stopped by yesterday and asked for my help with something."

"He did?" I was intrigued.

"Seeing as this is your last week, he wanted to make sure it was a memorable one. So he asked me to give you this." She handed me a card that looked like an invitation. I took it and held it gingerly. "Go ahead and open it. I'm supposed to give him your answer."

I tore the envelope open and pulled out the teal-colored card. It read:

> Rain,
>
> Will you do me the honor of spending the day with me tomorrow? The whole day is about you. You need to be ready to go at 8:00 a.m., and we will be back late. Please give Tanis your answer.
>
> Xoxo,
> Ian :)

"He's so crazy!" I smiled.

"Is that a yes?"

"Of course! I wanted to spend as much time here as possible before I leave, but I have a feeling this will be fun."

"Excellent. I'll let him know. And I'll be right back."

She got up from the table and went outside for a minute. I truly had never been treated the way Ian treated me. I was sure I'd never be again. He raised the standards way too high for anyone else.

Before I knew it, Tanis was back holding a large gift bag. She handed it to me. "This is because you said yes."

"He doesn't need to do all this."

"He knows that, but as you're special and you've lived most of your life not knowing that, I'm not going to dissuade him."

"Thanks. I wonder what's in here." I peered inside and grinned.

"You enjoy. I'm going to check on the schedule for today's camp group. I'm sure I'll see you later."

"Actually, I was going to help out. I have my stuff from home, and I don't really want a lot of downtime."

"You are more than welcome to, and is Kat fitting you into a lesson today?"

"I think so."

"Have fun! See you soon."

"Bye."

Tanis left my trailer, and I took Ian's bag into my bedroom. Before I opened it, I sent him a text, thanking him. He texted me back, saying he was delighted that I said yes. Like I wouldn't have. I knew he'd have to work the whole day today in order to get tomorrow off, but I kind of missed him.

I opened up the bag, and there was another card in it. I unsealed it. It read:

> Rain,
>
> Here is a little outfit that Tanis helped me pick out for our date tomorrow.

Inside was a yellow, black, and white floral-print summer dress. It was so pretty. There was also a pair of cute black flats. As if that weren't enough, he'd popped in a smart white jean jacket.

There was another note:

> Rain,
>
> This is for the second half of our date. Dress in jeans and a casual top for the beginning of the day. Bring this for later. I can't wait to spoil you.
>
> Xoxo,
> Ian

I wondered what tomorrow would bring. I was giddy with excitement! I bounded off the bed. It would be hard to come down from my cloud of joy, but for today, I'd throw on my breeches and help the staff get the day going. Of course, I'd need to give Mia some love. I wasn't sure if Jenna would be at camp this week or if Martha would let her. I wanted to see her one more time, but not if it meant running into the rest of them.

Camp didn't start for a while, so either way, I was in the clear. In a few short days, I wouldn't have to worry about either Martha or my dad coming across my path. I wondered if my dad would actually make the effort to come and see me. I doubted it. Martha would never allow him out of her sight. She had to have control at all times. I really hoped that when I grew up that I wouldn't control my husband that way. I knew whomever I'd marry would have to have strong will that I couldn't bend. I think that was why I was so drawn to Ian. Not only was he charming but I also felt that I couldn't push him around.

I knew in high school I had used my skills at manipulating to get out of a sticky situation or two. It wasn't something I was proud of. I had also lied my way out of getting caught sneaking out of the house on occasion. When you aren't allowed a life, you make one. I sure had some fun with Daryl and Sandra. They were always the ones who stood up for me. I had a feeling that we'd stay in touch even with the distance.

I heard some cars pulling into A&T, so if I was going to be helpful, I'd have to get a move on. I threw my hair into a much shorter ponytail. I loved my new look. It was so easy. I finished getting my barn clothes on and grabbed an apple from my tiny fridge.

First stop, Mia. Second, being helpful.

Chapter 37

Mia was happy to see me. She came right up to me and nuzzled me. I petted her bay coat while whispering sweet nothings to her. She soon found the apple I was trying to hide from her.

"Yes, this is for you." She took it greedily. She was so messy with her apples. Before too long, I had her slobber on my shoulder. "Really, Mia, next time, you get carrots." She was full of kisses now. "I'm going to miss you so much." I felt a lump in my throat, but I held back my tears. I couldn't start today, not when I still had the week to go. If I lost it now, I might not get on that plane. And I had already promised my mom that I was coming. Plus, I felt in my gut that it was the right place for me.

Mia had gone back to her hay after demolishing my apple. "Enjoy your breakfast." I smiled at her, feeling more content than I had in years. I was sure I couldn't stay there all day, but it was tempting. At least I had a lesson today. Kat promised me that I'd get to jump too!

I was so caught up in my thoughts that I didn't hear my name. I was known by Rain at the barn, so I wasn't expecting anyone to call me Rose, let alone her. I gulped. "Jesus, I need your help," I whispered with my spirit. I took a breath before I faced my nemesis.

"Martha, I'm surprised to see you up here. I thought Tanis had banned you."

"I come in peace, Rose," she said softly.

"I don't think we have anything more to say to each other."

"Can't you hear me out?" Her light-blue eyes pleaded at me, but I didn't fall for it. She was dressed in one of my dad's striped shirts and her usual older lady shorts. She never looked tidy. In fact, she and my mom were such opposites in every way possible. It was hard to see how one man could fall for both of them.

"I'll give you five minutes." I turned to Mia. "Bye, Mia, I'll see you in a bit." She answered me with a snort, which made me smile in spite of myself.

"She's really taken with you."

I nodded. I didn't want Martha to interfere with my relationship with Mia. It was as if I thought she'd taint it. I closed her stall and led Martha to the back of the barn. The camp kids were making their way into the barn, and the noise was starting to rise.

"Is Jenna here today?" I asked.

"That's why I'm here." Again, she was pretending to be nice. Typical.

"I see." At least I'd get to see her today.

I didn't want to go far. I hadn't forgotten our altercation earlier this week. In fact, I still wore the bruises. I assumed that today was one last-ditch effort to sway me to stay. We walked to the spacious outdoor riding area. I leaned back on one of the poles. I needed something to keep me grounded. Besides, there were horses all around me outside.

"Okay. What is so important that you're disregarding Tanis's wishes?"

"It's about Mia." My ears perked up.

"Yes, what about her?"

"Did you know she was for sale?"

"Kat had mentioned something, but taking her to Nova Scotia is out of the question."

"I know that. I was thinking of buying her for you. If you stay, I promise that things will change. Jenna and your father will be heartbroken if you leave. They need you." She paused for dramatic effect. "I need you. Things haven't been the same with you gone." Her voice was starting to quiver.

Oh boy, she was good. What a carrot to dangle in front of me. I knew in my heart that the answer was no, but part of me wanted to say maybe. I wanted Mia so badly, but I knew I couldn't stay here. I knew things wouldn't change. She had never changed even after all the promises. The only reason they did was because, I decided to fight. I decided to go to school. I decided to flee.

"Rose, or Rain, if you prefer, will you at least consider it?" She lowered her gaze in an effort to show humility. But I knew. I knew better. I knew those blue eyes were full of steel. I knew how crushing her rough hands had hurt me when they squeezed my arm. I knew how hard her hand was when it spanked me for ten years. I saw her lifting the wood and placing it on my rear. I saw the knife that she used to cut me when I was twelve. I saw the pain in Ivan's eyes as he was banished from our home. I saw how she manipulated my dad so he had no fight left in him. I saw it all.

At that moment, I knew that I had to leave. The whole week was almost too long. I wanted to run from her, but I steeled myself. I remembered that I had heard Jesus's voice telling me not to be afraid, and at that moment, I felt him like never before. I was ready to speak.

"Martha, I will not change my mind. I will not stay. It is time for me to get to know my real mother. It is time for me to have a life where I am no longer a slave, but am free. To a home where I am loved not for what I do but for who I am. I thank you for feeding me and clothing me and for introducing me to riding. But it's my mother's time now. My father had his chance, and quite frankly, he blew it."

That did it. I had opened up a storm! I saw Martha's face go red before she turned. She leaned into my face and almost shouted, "Why, you ungrateful brat! I offered so much to you, and you slap me in the face like this."

The ruse was over. I knew she wanted to grab me, but there were too many people around. Out of the corner of my eye, I spotted Jenna. I smiled to myself. This exchange would be over. She must have noticed something too, as Martha started to cry, saying that I didn't know all they'd done to keep me safe. She was right. I didn't, as I was never safe! She backed away from me. She could never keep up the facade in front of me for long. I was a trigger for her. And today it worked out to solidify my resolve. I was ready to go.

She backed away as Jenna approached us. She was leading her horse with her, looking at me with concern lining her young eyes.

I smiled at her. "It's okay, Jenna. Martha was checking to see how my move was coming. But she's leaving now, aren't you, Martha?"

Martha knew her goose was cooked. "Hi, dear. Yes, I wanted to make sure that Rose had taken everything she needed from the house. Your dad is so upset, Rose. Jenna, try to talk some sense into your sister."

"Mom, I think she wants to go and get to know her mom. Besides, things have never been fair for her at home, so I understand. We'll be okay. It won't be easy, but we'll get through it."

Her horse nickered slightly. It was as if he were in on it. Bless Jenna. She was too mature for her young years.

"See you at home, Jenna. Rose, that was my last offer for you. Have a safe flight." She turned and left us. Good thing too, as Tanis had spotted her from the house.

I watched her leave, and my heart resumed its regular pattern. I hugged Jenna. "You are awesome! I am going to miss you so much." I started to cry. Jenna had been the glue that had held me together.

"I'm going to miss you too." She joined me in tears. As we pulled away, her blue eyes glistened. She smiled through her tears. "Rose, I saw the exchange. I was worried she was going to grab you right here, in front of people!"

"She was going to, there was no doubt. You stopped her by seeing her. I'm sorry I can't take you with me."

"I don't think that would work now, would it?"

"Probably not." Her horse started to nudge her. "You'd better get back to your group. I don't want you setting a bad example."

"You're right. I hope to work here next summer."

"I'm sure you will." I squeezed her hand. "I'll see you before I go."

"Promise?"

"Pinky swear."

She laughed at that and went back toward her group. I took a moment of solitude. I walked in the pathway that led to the cross-country field. I wanted to be alone and take in the moment of victory I had felt. I knew the strength I showed was otherworldly. I felt so grateful that Jesus was on my side.

I would enjoy my last bit of time here in Ontario, but my heart was ready to embrace Cape Breton.

Chapter 38

I had been able to have an incredible day at the barn even with the Martha situation. Mia had behaved so well. My lesson was amazing. Jenna took her lunch with me too, so we could talk about our future plans to meet up with each other. I wasn't sure if it was realistic, but I wasn't going to dissuade her. I told her to stay away from boys for as long as possible. Having a horse sure helped in that department. I knew we'd stay close even if our relationship was about to change. She'd be forced to grow up without me at home. I also shared my faith with her. I wanted her to know she wasn't alone. She had hope. She couldn't help who her parents were. I felt sorry for her a bit. At least I had a mother to get to know. Jenna knew her mother, and she wasn't nice. How Jenna turned out so well, I'd never know. Jenna said it was because of me. I wasn't sure I could take the credit for that.

I started putting some of my things into the suitcases that Tanis had loaned me. I found some of my old journals where I had kept a lot of the poetry that I'd written. I didn't want to take all my past with me, but I did cherish the poems. A thought hit me. I really wanted to find a way to put some of my poems into a book and get it published one day. I knew it was a big dream, but after getting to know Ian over the summer, I was learning to dream again. True to form, I heard my phone go off. I reached around and saw that I had a message from him about our date tomorrow. My heart started to do the butterfly thing again. I would miss him and Mia so much. Maybe one day I'd see them both again. However, I was pretty sure that I'd never live in Ontario again.

I kept up with my organizing until exhaustion took over. I was counting down the nights. I had hoped that today would mark the last encounter with Martha.

Chapter 39

I woke with a start. Today was the day! It would be my last full day with Ian. I readied myself quickly, remembering to pack the dress and jacket for later in the day. I had on my light jeans and one of the cute T-shirts that Ian had picked out for me. I had washed my hair the night before, but it still needed a bit of love. With having shorter hair, I couldn't get away with what I could with my long tresses.

I wanted to say good morning to Mia before Ian arrived. I'd try not to smell too horsey. I knew he'd appreciate not covering his car with all things horse. I ate a small breakfast and picked out Mia's treats.

I was practically skipping through my morning. A text from Ian told me he was on track. I texted him back that I'd be ready for him. I felt a little like Cinderella getting ready for the ball.

I kept my phone in my back pocket and left my trailer.

I saw that the morning staff was already finished in the small barn. I waved to Jen and Lindsey. They had become good friends in a short time.

Brussels and Cleo, two of the barn cats, were following me into the big barn. I stopped a minute to pet them. Maybe I'd be able to convince my mom to get a cat when I got home. I smiled to myself at the thought. Home, I was going home.

"Okay, you two, I have to go see Mia. I'll be back." I stretched up and continued into the big barn. It was pretty quiet, which I found odd. I kept going though, stroking the horses as I passed them by.

Mia must have heard me coming as I saw her head pop out of her stall. I grinned at her. "Hi, girl, how are you?" I heard her knicker at me. I was in front of her stall when my heart almost stopped. There was a sign on her stall. It read, "Congratulations, Rain and Mia!" I stopped dead in my tracks, my mouth gaping open! What did this mean? It was then that I found out why the barn was so quiet. All of a sudden, a flurry of activity came rushing toward me, including my mom! I was still stunned.

"Rose, do you know what this means?" my mom asked me. I shook my head in disbelief. "She's yours!" My mom threw her arms around me, and I started to shake. I couldn't believe it. I didn't have to leave Mia behind.

That did it. I started bawling. My mom joined me. Before I knew it, Tanis, Kat, Jen, Alicia, and Lindsey all had us in a group hug. I then noticed Jenna. She was here too. They'd all been in on it. And Ian, he was off to the side smiling. Mia wasn't sure what all the commotion was about. I heard her snort. I started laughing. We pulled away, and my mom held me at arm's length. Her eyes were red from crying, matching my own.

"We did it! She'll have to travel separately, but she's coming home. I even found you a stable to keep her at, thanks to Tanis."

"I can't believe it! She's mine?" I looked over at her.

"You're the only one she likes," Kat chimed in. "We couldn't separate you two."

I moved over to Mia. "Did you hear that, girl? You're coming to Cape Breton!" I kissed her on her nose and offered her the apple I had for her.

I was in a dream, and I didn't want to wake up. I had so many questions, but first, there were a lot of people I had to thank. I turned to the small group that had become so dear to me. "Thank you, each and every one of you. I think it's time for this girl to dream." I choked up. I wouldn't be able to keep it together for long.

Each one of them came and gave me a hug. Jenna had a hard time letting go of me, but I saw in her eyes that she was happy for me. Lastly, Ian moved in. He smiled at me. His brown eyes were wet with tears.

"Rain, I am so pleased for you. You deserve the world." I wanted to kiss him, but with the crowd around us, we thought better of it. But he did give me a kiss on my cheek. I'd get my kisses later.

It then hit me. "You knew about this?"

"I may have known a little about this." He winked at me. I wonder how much he was involved in this surprise.

There was too much to process, but I opened up Mia's stall and gave her a huge hug. I took in her scent, wishing I could bottle it. "You're mine, girl, all mine." It was as if she'd known all along.

I heard Kat and the girls start to delegate some things that needed attending to, but they each came to congratulate me before they left. Then it hit me. My mom was back here. What did that mean? She and Ian came closer to Mia's stall.

"Mom, you came back!"

"I couldn't miss this. I had to be here for your first horse."

"I'm so glad!" I stroked Mia's neck. She stayed by my side. "Does this mean we get to go home together?"

"Yes, Rose, it does."

"Really? We get to travel together! How exciting!"

"There's only one caveat."

"And that is?" I felt a lump forming in my throat.

"I had to change some things around to make it all not cost a fortune. So we are all leaving tomorrow."

"Tomorrow?" The lump was so big I could hardly speak.

"I know, honey. I know it won't be easy. But just think, at least Mia will be following you."

I nodded. It was all I could do. I looked at Ian, and the tears fell again. I buried my head in Mia's neck. At least she'd be there.

My mom entered the stall. "It'll be okay. We'll be together. And when you're ready, you can come back and visit. Just promise me you won't stay too long."

"I promise," I said between sobs.

My mom rubbed my back as Ian looked on. "Ian tells me you have a fun day planned." I nodded again. "Take your time. I'm going to go to the house with Tanis and go over transport information for Mia. Come and say bye before you leave, okay?"

"Okay."

She rubbed my arm and leaned into me. Then she stroked Mia's long neck. "Take care of my girl, Mia." Mia almost looked like she understood. As my mom left the stall, she spoke to Ian, "You take care of my girl today too, I finally have her back in my life."

"She's VIP to me too." He saluted her as a sign of respect.

Ian entered Mia's stall. "It'll be good. I'm so happy you get your dream horse."

"If only there was a way you could come too."

"I know. But you're young, and I'm your first real boyfriend. Hopefully, I've set a standard for your future suitors." He chuckled, but I wondered if I'd ever meet anyone like him again.

"Was this part of your plan for today?"

"Partially. I'd been talking to your mom and Tanis. We all got together and found a way."

"It's all pretty wonderful. Did you know that Martha was here yesterday trying to bribe me with Mia? And now look! She's mine! How incredible! I am sorry that this is our last day though."

"We'll make the most of it. Want to go and explore with me?"

I dried my eyes and hugged Mia one more time. "Let's go!"

The barn was filling up with another day of camp activities. I looked at the sign on our door and stood back in satisfaction. This was more than I would have ever asked for. It was all too much.

Ian and I left the big barn as the noise filled the space around us. It was all too much to process. As I had a long journey tomorrow, I'd take the time then. For today, I'd enjoy Ian's company and the hope of the future.

I was going to be home with my brother Ivan and two parents who actually loved me. I was going to have my own horse to care for and ride. I would have a new standard for dating that I never had before.

Then it hit me. I remembered seeing a Bible verse on someone's wall that said, "'For I know the plans I have for you,' declares the Lord, 'plans to prosper you and not to harm you, plans to give you hope and a future.'"

I finally had hope and a future.

About the Author

Rebeckah Hassam has always loved the freedom that comes with writing. It was journaling through her childhood that filled her with hope. Rebeckah is the author of the Victoria series, a vampire trilogy based in Langley, British Columbia. However, poetry is definitely her heartbeat; her first book was a small book of poems that she wrote growing up.

If you follow her on social media, you will find her writing about her dog, cat, and horses. She takes the everyday mundane and turns it into charm. Creativity has always come easily for Rebeckah, but while having dysgraphia, she knows firsthand of the challenges that come with writing. Her hope is that she can inspire others who struggle to find their voice in journaling.

While not tackling one of her many projects, you can find her working as the programs director at A&T Equestrian in Surrey, British Columbia—a job that allows many ideas to come to life in her writing. She lives with her husband in Langley and enjoys all the inspiration that their home and surroundings bring.

CPSIA information can be obtained
at www.ICGtesting.com
Printed in the USA
BVHW031703030223
657499BV00004B/2